ELIZABETH I:
—— THE ——
PEOPLE'S QUEEN?

Liz Woodhouse

Matador
9 Priory Business Park,
Wistow Road, Kibworth Beauchamp,
Leicestershire. LE8 0RX
Tel: (+44) 116 279 2299
Fax: (+44) 116 279 2277
Email: books@troubador.co.uk
Web: www.troubador.co.uk/matador

ISBN 978-1780883-076

British Library Cataloguing in Publication Data.
A catalogue record for this book is available from the British Library.

Cover image of Elizabeth I by Nicholas Hilliard (c.1547-1619)
Private collection UK, courtesy of Bonhams

Typeset by Troubador Publishing Ltd, Leicester, UK
Printed and bound in the UK by TJ International, Padstow, Cornwall

Matador is an imprint of Troubador Publishing Ltd

To Richard

CONTENTS

Tudor family tree

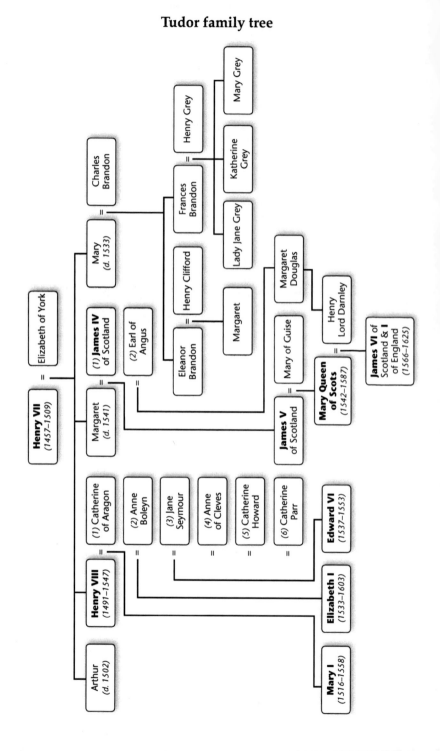

PART 1

Lady Margaret Bryan

My name is Lady Margaret Bryan. It may be familiar to you? I am the widow of Sir Thomas Bryan, and I held the important position of Lady Mistress to the late King Henry's three children. That is to say that I had the great responsibility of looking after Lady Mary, Lady Elizabeth and, finally, Prince Edward from their births until they were old enough to have tutors or governesses.

I am writing this in the Year of Our Lord 1547. Two or three years ago I was asked to set down my memories of the royal children, as they could be useful for historians one day. I have devoted a lot of time to this, with several rough drafts, but I have finally finished a fair copy in my best hand-writing.--

I decided to write a separate memoir for each child: each memoir would be complete in itself, although it would entail some necessary repetition. I naturally started with Prince Edward as the only boy. Of course, he has recently become King Edward at the tender age of nine! I pray for God's blessing upon him for a long and peaceful reign, as he follows in great King Henry's footsteps. May he have many fine sons of his own in God's good time.

My second memoir concerned Lady Mary, daughter of Queen Catherine – that is the *Spanish* Queen Catherine. She is now thirty-one years old, so my memory had to reach back a long way to her nursery days.

And, finally, I'm embarking on the story of Lady Elizabeth, now thirteen and the least important in the line of succession. As this is my third memoir, I think I can say that (in spite of my sex) I have become a competent historian.

Firstly, I must tell you a little about myself and –

particularly important in Elizabeth's case – the background. I came to Court as Margaret Bourchier at the age of twenty in 1490, when I married Sir Thomas. The Bryan family were long-standing courtiers. I am proud to say that Sir Thomas was a Knight of the Body to both King Henry VIII and his father, Henry VII. Courtiers have many privileges, but they must know the rules. We saw others rise and fall but (with one exception) we held our places there, through troubling times too, I may tell you. Sir Thomas and I were blessed with three surviving children, and they all became prominent at Court. My son, Francis, was appointed a gentleman-in-attendance to King Henry VIII, and kept His Majesty's favour throughout his service. My two daughters made excellent marriages: one to Lord Henry Guildford, the Comptroller of the Queen's Household; and the other to Sir Nicholas Carew, the King's Master of Horse, who both became Knights of the Garter – a rare honour. Sadly, my daughter, Lady Margaret Guildford, died young in childbirth.

I first became Lady Mistress to the baby Princess Mary when she was born in 1516. My husband, Sir Thomas, had recently died. His last position at Court was Vice-Chamberlain to Queen Catherine, and Her Majesty in her kind way appointed me as Lady Mistress to comfort me in my bereavement. I remember Queen Catherine questioning me, and setting out her wishes for the proper care and upbringing of the royal children. Poor Queen Catherine! She had six babies – including several boys. Some of them were stillborn, some lived a few weeks, but only Princess Mary survived. Such hopes (such important hopes) and such disappointments! So many children have to meet death young. It's always been so, hasn't it? God and his Blessed Mother have a special place for them in Heaven. Queen Catherine told me that, and she was very religious.

Well, the Succession was the problem. There were no

suitable male heirs then, you see. King Henry had no living brothers, and his only nephew was the King of Scotland, which was not friendly towards England. As time went on, we were all worried, not just the King. The Tudors were fairly new to the throne, and my mother and her generation well remembered the terrible civil wars before that. They are known as the Wars of the Roses because of the emblems of the rival armies: my own father died in one of the battles when I was only a baby. Civil wars are the ruin of prosperity. And, of course, successful Courtiers need continuity not change. Since King Henry's father, by the grace of God, became King, peace and security had brought prosperity back to England. But if the King had no heir, the future looked dangerously uncertain again. By 1528 the King was thirty-seven and Queen Catherine was forty-two, well into middle age. It was then that, as I see it now, God Himself began to ordain changes. Heaven knows we went through nine years of turbulence and tension! But in the end God granted our prayers.

What happened first was that Anne Boleyn, Sir Thomas Boleyn's daughter, won the King's heart. She was a witty, bold and outspoken lady. At that time, God was revealing to the King that his marriage to Queen Catherine had been forbidden by The Bible because she had first been the wife of his late brother, Arthur. So after long debate, and even separation from the Church of Rome, the King overcame all hindrances, divorced his wife and married Anne Boleyn in 1533. Queen Catherine was banished to Ampthill Castle in Bedfordshire, and my dear Princess Mary was declared illegitimate. I wanted to write and comfort her, but the King would not have approved. In fact I know many people were sorry for good Queen Catherine. But by the divorce she was forty-six, and the King forty-one. He was a strong man then. There was still time for a prince to grow up, but only just.

So, in spite of deep sympathy for the old Queen, many of

us at Court felt relieved that a new, younger Queen had arrived. In any case, it must have been God's will.

It's fourteen years ago now, I suppose, but I clearly remember being led into Queen Anne's apartments in Richmond Palace on a summer's day in 1533. She had been crowned in Westminster Abbey a few weeks before, and was expecting her first child in September. She was laughing at cards with two ladies and her brother, Lord Rochford, when I was announced. I remember her then, sitting straight-backed with her dark hair over her shoulders, and her green satin dress gleaming in the sun.

"Who?" she asked loudly to the top of my head as I curtseyed low.

"Lady Bryan, Your Majesty," prompted my lady-in-waiting. "You wanted to see her about the nursery."

"Oh yes," said the Queen. "I did. I do. But not this minute. Have her wait in the antechamber until I'm ready."

I backed out of the door and waited with several others for the Queen to give me a little of her time. I had often met King Henry, of course, when I was Lady Mistress to Princess Mary, and I knew he approved of me. But Queen Anne had a mind of her own and wanted to assess me for herself. And, in those crucial few months, she had great influence: if she had taken against me then, the King would not have overruled her.

After some time I was called back into the Queen's presence, and she then gave me her full attention. I always felt at ease with Queen Catherine, but, with Queen Anne I was unusually nervous, under her direct gaze and quick tongue. (In fact, I came from a higher lineage than her. The Boleyns had not been nobility for long, although I grant that Lady Boleyn was a daughter of the Duke of Norfolk.)

That afternoon I answered Queen Anne's many questions about me and my experience, and it must have satisfied her, for she finally said, "It is an enormous honour for you, Lady

Bryan, to be entrusted with the care of the heir to the throne."

"I will spare no effort, Your Majesty," I replied.

She was silent a moment, and then burst out laughing. "He's kicking me now! The kicks are so strong. It can only be a Prince, can't it? All the doctors say so. What do you say, Lady Bryan, with your experience?"

"In my experience, the mother usually knows best, Madam."

"Yes," she said, laughing again. "I'm usually right – I'm usually right."

I was busy after that, hiring nursemaids, finding a wet-nurse, and seeing to the cleaning of the nursery at Greenwich Palace. The nursery rooms hadn't been used for a long time and needed some new furniture and hangings. And I remember asking for three cats to get rid of the mice! And then there were the baby clothes and caps to be assembled. Lady Boleyn, the Queen's mother, helped me supervise all these preparations. She was very close to her daughter and, before the King and Queen had married, Lady Boleyn had her own rooms near her daughter in Whitehall Palace. She wanted to ensure that everything possible was done for the baby's health – and for the Queen's. My own daughter often came to call as well. She was quite amused to find me taking charge again of a nursery in my sixties!

I've mentioned the Succession anxieties, so you can imagine the nervous anticipation surrounding this royal birth. Prayers were said in the churches; the summer weeks passed; and on 7th September 1533 Queen Anne gave birth.

But of course the baby turned out to be a princess, not the longed-for prince. The news flew round the country: "Another girl!" said some. "She'll have to do better than that!" said others. What a terrible disappointment that day was! It must have been a body blow to King Henry. All the divisive upheavals of church and state he had braved to give

England an heir! It was bitter news indeed to have another daughter. I don't know who dared break the news to him but I do know it wasn't the doctors or astrologers: they had all foretold a son.

I kept to the nursery rooms and chivied the nursemaids about their duties, which had suddenly begun. I know the Queen and her family were deeply downcast after their hopes and prayers for a son hadn't been answered. The Boleyns had risen fast, and were resented by some. My daughter came up to see me and whispered that there was a sombre atmosphere in the Palace and people just didn't know what to say to the King.

He was silent – shocked they said – and brooding. Tournaments and bonfires had been planned for the expected Prince of Wales, but they were now cancelled.

So that was Elizabeth's reception into this world! The Princess was at least given a grand christening when she was three days old, and Archbishop Cranmer was her godfather.

The Queen had had a long and arduous labour, but she got up from her bed after only two weeks. I think she wanted to show herself fit and powerful again. She was always brave: she must have resolved quickly not to give her detractors time to run her down. She knew a queen needed sons. She must face childbirth again to give our noble King a boy.

However, this unwanted Princess was a strong baby with a loud voice, and she sucked well from the wet-nurse, Marjorie Johnson. So, thanks be to God, she grew well, and the nursery at least became a happy place.

Now, when I first met Queen Anne, she hadn't struck me as a motherly lady. Nor did she need to be, because it wasn't a queen's job. But to my surprise she adored her daughter. When she visited the nursery, she would hold her close and sing lullabies. She was thrilled when the baby began to smile, and called everyone over to see. "Look!" she cried with delight.

"She knows her mother. Don't you, my sweet? Such a happy Princess!"

We were also honoured by three visits from the King himself those first three months. The Lord-in-Waiting would tell us that the King intended to come to the nursery, and we should dress the Princess in her finest robes. Then we would wait (sometimes for hours) for His Majesty to be announced. He was proud of his healthy baby, in spite of her sex, and would lift her from the cradle and search her face for a likeness.

"Yes, you're a fine Tudor," he would say. "My colouring! And my mother's eyes. Well, Lady Bryan, this augurs well for the future. You're off to Hatfield soon and we must see that you're kept busy for several years. There won't be much time for that tapestry of yours now!"

I curtseyed low and said, "May God be with you, Your Majesty."

"God and the Queen, Lady Bryan," he replied. "God and the Queen!"

His grin had the courtiers laughing, and we all relaxed. We knew what a setback the Princess had been for him. But by then he had learned to display it as a passing delay, soon to be remedied.

He was right about one thing: my entire royal nursery establishment was going to Hatfield House. We left Greenwich in early December when the Princess was about three months and judged strong enough to make the journey. Perhaps you don't know that royal children don't live at the big palaces in London? They may visit Whitehall or Greenwich or Hampton Court at Christmas and other special occasions, but for most of the time they live in smaller royal manors two or three days from London. The air is healthier in the country, and there's far less risk of the plague or the wasting sickness.

What's more, the royal nursery moves between the manors every few months so that the rooms can be thoroughly aired and cleaned and food supplies re-stocked. So we lived in a sequence of houses such as Hatfield, Hunsdon, Ashridge, Eltham and Hertford. Some were more to my liking than others: Hunsdon was particularly old and dark, and Hertford Castle had no chimneys and was very smokey. I sometimes longed for my own hall in Chelsea by the Thames.

I was very well looked after in the royal manors, but they weren't my home. And so many moves – although I had very little say in any of them.

Princess Elizabeth's household was put in charge of the Queen's aunt and her husband, Sir John and Lady Shelton. I, of course, was in direct charge of the baby herself and the nursery servants. But the Sheltons supervised the whole household and its expenses. There was always a company of guardsmen to protect us, as well as many indoor and outdoor servants, just as any other important house would have.

The Sheltons were courtiers and the only members of the household with the same status as me, so I sat with them at the high table in the hall at dinner. I tried to make it my business to get on with them, and anyway our respective provinces were usually clear cut and in accord. I can only remember one occasion when I quarrelled outright with Sir John but I'll come to that later.

So, as I was saying, the infant Princess Elizabeth and her household, which numbered about forty people, set off that December from Greenwich to Hatfield. Queen Anne saw us off, and shed tears at the parting. She had instructed me to write to her every week about the Princess's progress. She arranged for the Princess to travel right through the City of London for her first public appearance. The Queen's uncle, the Duke of Norfolk, led the procession, and escorted us all the way to Hatfield in two days.

When we arrived, the Duke announced to me and the Sheltons that the King had instructed him to bring Lady Mary to join her new half-sister's household. He set off the next morning for Essex with some guardsmen and returned three days later with a reluctant and miserable Mary. Of course I had looked after her for many years when she was little, always, always hoping that brothers would follow. Now she was seventeen and long out of my care. The King's Grace had recently declared her to be illegitimate, and had refused to allow her and her mother to meet. I went out of my way at Hatfield to show her kindness and affection but she felt bitter and refused to call the baby 'Princess'. She unwisely claimed that she was the only true Princess of the Realm and angered the Duke of Norfolk terribly by telling him she had no message of submission to relay to the King. She also showed displeasure at being in the care of the Sheltons because Lady Shelton was Queen Anne's aunt.

I know that time was a hard trial for Mary. But at seventeen she was a grown woman and should have behaved more prudently. The first rule is to obey the ruler. She wept and prayed a lot in those first weeks at Hatfield. But I should tell you that like her mother (and me too) she was very good at sewing and she eventually began to come to my chamber or the nursery to sit with me while we worked on new bedspreads. This kept her busy and gave her some enjoyment and she gradually became calmer. We chatted about the happy days of her childhood, and I even made her smile sometimes, but naturally I could not be drawn into any criticism of His Majesty or Queen Anne. She gradually realised that my lips were sealed on that matter and she soon stopped pouring out her grievances.

By now you will have realised that I did not have an easy task trying to run Princess Elizabeth's household. It wasn't only Lady Mary's sudden and unwilling arrival that taxed my fortitude. It was also about having all the new nursery servants to train. At Greenwich Palace I'd had some help from Lady

Boleyn and my daughter, and the new servants were excited to be at Court with the King and Queen and other great people in fine clothes. Hearing all the below-stairs gossip too, no doubt, and making friends with the other servants at Court.

But when we were moved to Hatfield House, there were some long faces. Usually behind my back, mind you. "So quiet!" "Nothing happening." "Missing my friends." Then they would get used to country life, and begin to make friends among the local servants. Soon afterwards we'd decamp to Ashridge or Hunsdon, so it was a disruptive period in their lives. But if I heard any grumbles, I would remind them to count their blessings. After all, they were well housed and fed, and, God willing, were likely to have work in the nursery for years to come. They were also gaining useful experience in the best nursery with its trained nursemaids, laundresses and grooms of the chamber, who would never want for work. I had the power of dismissal, of course, but very rarely had to use it. We became a happy company that banded together for about ten years, as it turned out. I'd like to think they have fond memories of me, as I do of them.

As for me, I couldn't have undertaken the position if I had still been married. What husband would follow his wife in and out of the royal manors? But I was a free agent and well suited for my important role. Widows (the wealthy ones, at least) enjoy a freedom and authority unique among women.

Even though we were living in the country, we did receive visitors sometimes. The King himself came for a day in January while on a hunting trip. I remember being surprised that the Queen wasn't with him, as she was an excellent horsewoman.

"I hope Her Majesty is well, sir?" I said.

"Couldn't be better, Lady Bryan," he replied with a smile, "But she shouldn't be out on these rough roads in winter."

He admired Elizabeth and exclaimed how much she had grown. But he wouldn't see her sister, which deeply disappointed poor Mary as she was hoping for a sign of reconciliation.

The Queen regularly sent beautiful new clothes and caps for her daughter. And I sent my weekly bulletin about the baby's health and suckling. Then at the end of March we left Hatfield and moved to Eltham Palace. The King had spent much of his own childhood there, and it was conveniently close to Greenwich. So for the next few months we had plenty of company.

The Queen was thrilled to see her daughter again, now seven months old and very responsive to any attention. She cuddled her a lot, and sometimes brought musicians along to play for the baby. I remember she said, "We must see to it that she is musical like her father. In a few years I'll find a lute teacher for her and the King will be delighted!"

The Queen's parents were frequent visitors too, as was her brother, Lord Rochford. The Queen's sister, Mary, and her two children, Catherine and Henry Carey, aged ten and eight also came. Catherine Carey was a delightful, warm-hearted little girl, and Henry was energetic and lively. Throughout my time with Elizabeth her Carey cousins were regular visitors, and Elizabeth was always thrilled to see them. She grew to admire Catherine greatly and look up to her, as younger children tend to do. They were very affectionate with each other, and Elizabeth tried to copy all that Catherine did. Elizabeth, being of such high rank, hardly ever had other children to play with so she particularly enjoyed it when she did meet children. Personally, I think it is good even for royal children, especially young princesses, to learn to take turns and share their toys. After all, princesses have to obey their husbands when they get married, which is not easy for them if they've always had their own way. But forgive me; I'm getting ahead of myself. We must get back to Eltham Palace in the happy Spring of 1534 when Elizabeth was just a baby.

The news then was the best news of all: the Queen was pregnant again! What a relief for us all, and, of course, hope of a boy! Our hopes were dashed later that Summer when I heard from my Court connections that the baby was born too early and stillborn. By then we had removed to Hertford Castle, so our household was fortunately distanced from this second great disappointment. Many people thought it was a sign of God's displeasure at the King's second marriage. The King himself was certainly displeased. My daughter told me that his love for Queen Anne had already cooled and that he was not spending much time with her. From then on there was tension in the atmosphere at Court and the Queen became increasingly anxious as her influence began to ebb away. As she began to lose the King's love, she also lost the attention paid to her by all the courtiers and ambassadors. It's their job to know which way the wind is blowing. They take their cue from the King.

Meanwhile, as the months passed, Princess Elizabeth's household moved on from manor to manor. At its centre the baby grew, crawled, walked and talked. She was a very advanced child, especially when it came to talking. When she was two I sent a formal request to Mr. Secretary Cromwell for the King's permission to wean her. The King assented so it was time for our wet-nurse, dear Marjorie Johnson, a warm-hearted woman, to leave the household. She was the person Elizabeth had often turned to for comfort when she was upset and of course Marjorie was very fond of the child. But she had her own family to get back to now. Elizabeth missed Marjorie a lot and kept looking and calling for her: "Nursey, Nursey! Where are you?"

I tried to calm her down, "Now then, Madam Princess, you're a big girl now. You don't need a nurse anymore, dear. Marjorie has gone back to her own home."

"I want to go to her own home," she sobbed.

14

"That's not possible, sweetheart. You're a royal princess. You've got much better homes than Nursey."

"But I want Nursey."

There was no satisfying her, of course. It's often a wrench for a child when the wet-nurse leaves. I told the nurse-maids, "Least said, soonest mended." We tried not to mention Marjorie again and I was proved right: the child soon forgot her.

In preparation for Christmas 1535 at Court, I ordered portraits of the King and Queen to hang low on the wall in the nursery. I pointed them out to their daughter every morning, and we made a practice of curtseying to the images and saying "God save you, Your Majesty" to each before breakfast. The other nursery staff joined in and it soon became a ritual for us all.

That Christmas at Greenwich the King and Queen made much of Elizabeth and were delighted at her prattle. Once, she was even dressed in cloth of gold and paraded in front of the whole Court. By now the Queen was thin and looked tense and apprehensive. I heard that she had miscarried again that summer. But her daughter's company delighted her and she spent a lot of time in the nursery. It was during that stay at Court that we heard that the Princess Dowager Catherine (who had been Queen) had died. I was truly sorry for the sad end of her life but knew her soul would be well received in Heaven – as I told Lady Mary later when we returned from Court to Hunsdon. The King and Queen rejoiced at the news. They gave a party where the King, in good humour, carried Elizabeth around while the Queen led the clapping. She hardly knew her father and I was fearful she might cry and reach out for me, but she was a brave child and my training bore fruit in the spirited way that she smiled and waved round the hall. The King was well pleased, and he singled me out and graciously nodded as I curtseyed.

Soon afterwards we moved back to Hunsdon. I remember Elizabeth repeatedly asking to see the Queen. I'm sure she had known she was loved. I kept up my weekly reports to the Queen and she kept sending clothes and little presents. Now that she was old enough to remember, I tried to keep the Princess in mind of her parents. I wished later that I hadn't made such a point of it, but I kept reminding her of the Court and what great people her parents were. I told her that all her clothes and presents came from the Queen and, of course, we still curtseyed to their Majesties' portraits every day.

We went back to Greenwich for Easter. It was early that year being at the end of March. It was not a happy visit. My daughter told me that the Queen had had a miscarriage in January. We all knew (herself above all) about the cloud that was darkening over her. In the past people used to cluster around her, laughing at her jokes, trying to curry favour. Now they didn't bother. And she made no jokes. She still came to the nursery with her ladies (queens are always accompanied). The ladies praised and petted the bright little girl but Queen Anne's nursery was too empty. Where was our prince? The King was now forty-five and the Succession was not secured.

I've never enjoyed Court less than that time. There was a lot of gossip relayed to me by the nursemaids about Queen Anne having let down the King and the country and in so doing had lost his love. And there were rumours about Lady Jane Seymour receiving the King's attention quite openly. There was even speculation about another divorce and the Queen being banished from Court like her predecessor! I told the nursemaids in no uncertain terms that for their own good they should mind their own business and not deal in rumours. I know that the King never visited the nursery that time.

I saw the King only once that Easter. It was one morning when I was with the Queen and two ladies. We were taking Elizabeth for a walk through the main courtyard, when the

Queen suddenly scooped up her daughter and held her towards an upper window. I followed her gaze and saw His Majesty there, looking (I have to say) full of resentment. I sank into a curtsey, but when I dared raise my eyes again, he had gone. The Queen turned away hugging Elizabeth close to her. No-one said a word.

In the nursery we hardly had any visitors except the Queen's family. Archbishop Cranmer did come once but her other godfather, the Duke of Norfolk, never came, even though he was the Queen's uncle. I noticed that Lady Boleyn was always worried. I remember she asked me a strange question one day, and it has stuck in my mind.

"Lady Bryan," she said. "This is between you and me. Has anyone been asking you questions about the Queen and her friends?"

"Who do you have in mind, my lady?"

"I don't know. Anyone at all. Maybe a courtier, maybe one of your own household. Just think a moment."

"No, my lady. I don't suppose anyone would ask me. They'd ask the Queen herself, wouldn't they? People speak to me about the Princess all the time of course, but that's because I'm the best person to ask."

The other thing that stuck in my mind happened near the end of our visit, when the ladies-in-waiting were diverted by Elizabeth's prattle. Queen Anne leaned over to me and said in a low voice: "I'm thankful that Elizabeth is in such good hands as yours, Lady Bryan. Remember, please, that I hope you'll stay with her for many years."

The Queen, of course, never said 'please' to me, and I think that's why I've remembered her words so clearly. Also Matthew Parker, Queen Anne's chaplain, visited us. When I expressed surprise, he told me that Queen Anne had recently begged him to look after Elizabeth's welfare in future. He said no more and neither did I, but I think we understood each other.

You'll understand my relief at leaving the ominous atmosphere of Court and returning to Hunsdon. But the peace of that place could not shut out the turmoil that soon followed. Looking back now, the first shot across our bows was near the end of April. A rider arrived from London with an urgent letter for Lady Shelton. She was summoned to London by Mr. Secretary Cromwell 'to undertake a special commission for the King'. We were dining in the hall when the message came. Lady Shelton was taken aback and went quite pale. She and Sir John tried to find out more, but the messenger apparently knew no details. I helped her that evening with her packing.

"What can it be, Lady Bryan? What can be the matter?" she kept repeating.

She had to set forth the next morning escorted by some of our guardsmen.

A few days later the shocking news reached us that the Queen had been arrested and was a prisoner in the Tower! Lady Shelton in fact had been summoned with two other ladies in preparation to be in attendance on the Queen. The next news, only a week later, was that the Queen had been tried and found guilty of plotting to kill the King's Grace and of adultery with no less than four men, including her own brother! She was sentenced to death. Two days later she was beheaded on Tower Green. It all happened so fast – only seventeen days between arrest and death. I found my heart beating too quickly. I wished I could talk with my son and daughter to find out what was happening at Court. In fact I was very frightened for the safety of my son and son-in-law, because, like them, two of the executed men (Sir Henry Norris and William Brereton) were Gentlemen of the King's privy chamber. The servants kept whispering in corners as we waited for any news. I tried to concentrate on keeping the days normal for Elizabeth, and to stop mentioning her parents.

No. I didn't tell the child. How could I? She was only two

years and eight months old. I couldn't face all the questions that she would have asked. I was in a state of shock myself, and, try as I would, my mind kept being drawn back to Queen Anne in the Tower. It was not for me to judge her crimes but I did know she had loved Elizabeth very much, and she always responded immediately to my letters and requests.

Lady Mary was with us, of course. She was still mourning her own mother, and spent more time than ever in prayer. She was not openly triumphant at Queen Anne's death, but it seemed to confirm her deep faith in the old religion. She would quote the Bible: 'Vengeance is mine,' saith the Lord, 'I will repay.' We heard that King Henry had issued a proclamation that Elizabeth was now illegitimate and no longer royal: in fact she was to have the same status as her sister. Mary, by then nineteen, who had never been unkind to her small sister, now became almost motherly towards her. She visited the nursery much more often, and sometimes even invited Elizabeth to her own chamber. It was a comfort to me at that dreadful time to see my two motherless charges becoming closer.

The very day after Queen Anne was executed, King Henry announced his betrothal to Lady Jane Seymour. And the following week they were married. As I say, "It all happened so fast."

Back at Hunsdon, Lady Shelton returned very silent. After a few days she asked me to come to her chamber. As I entered, she sent her maid out. She told me she wanted to unburden herself of the terrible scenes she had witnessed.

"I know you will listen kindly, Lady Bryan," she said. "Sir John says these are ladies' matters, and he doesn't want my confidences."

She then told me how she had been escorted to see Master Cromwell, with two other ladies, Lady James Boleyn (her sister-in-law) and Mrs Cosyn.

"He informed us that the Queen was about to be arrested

for adultery and conspiring to kill His Grace, the King," she continued. "She was to be imprisoned in the Tower to await trial. We three had been chosen to attend her there, 'For no longer than two or three weeks', Cromwell had added meaningfully. You can hardly imagine the shock we felt. After a moment, Master Cromwell went on with an intent gaze. 'I must impress on you that it is your duty to the King to listen carefully to everything Queen Anne says, and report back to the Constable of the Tower, Sir William Kingston, anything that supports the terrible charges against this shameless lady. Rewards will be given for useful evidence'."

"He then rang the bell on his table and his steward and two guards came and escorted us to a chamber (with a barred door!) where we spent a wakeful night. The next morning, Lady Bryan, we were rowed to the Tower. There we were met by Lady Kingston, Sir William's wife, who was to join us in attending the Queen. I remember she was calmer than the rest of us. She at least was familiar with the Tower and its functions. Then we waited in suspense."

"At about two o'clock the Queen arrived with Sir William and a body of Yeomen. She, poor soul, was looking around her in fear and disbelief. 'But will I have justice?' she cried to Sir William. 'Even the poorest subject of the King has justice,' he replied. The Queen then began laughing distractedly. We four ladies curtsied to her, and she then noticed us with dismay: 'I want my own ladies with me, those I'm fondest of,' she cried. Sir William said, 'These are good and honest ladies.' She knew us all but we were of an older generation and had not been close to her. She then said, 'It is unkind of the King not to send my own ladies.'"

"I can't tell you everything, Lady Bryan. We had a dreadful seventeen days. The Queen often wept when thinking about her mother, my sister-in-law Elizabeth. 'Oh my poor mother!' she would sob. 'You will die of grief!'

"I felt quite sick and once asked Sir William if I could be replaced as I was unwell. He said quite gently, 'Do you really want me to tell Master Cromwell that you wish to renounce the important charge he has laid upon you? I would not advise it, Lady Shelton.'"

"As for the injunction Master Cromwell had given us, we truly had nothing useful to report. Queen Anne in all her despairing talk made no shadow of an admission. In fact she constantly proclaimed her innocence. And, Lady Bryan, did you hear that Archbishop Cranmer himself came to the Tower on the eve of her execution to hear her last confession in this world? Queen Anne insisted that we four ladies and Sir William were also present to hear her swear on the Holy Bible that she was going to her death innocent of the terrible accusations. The Archbishop seemed much moved, and could hardly speak. Because she had been found guilty at the trial, he could not give her absolution. But he prayed that God would have mercy on her soul, and we all said 'Amen.'"

"I must tell you, Lady Bryan, that the Queen often asked me about little Elizabeth – how she passed her days and how she was talking. She charged me to pass on her gratitude to you, and beg you to stay with the Princess as long as you could. She also thanked me and Sir John for running the household. Sir William wrote copious reports to Master Cromwell on what the Queen was saying and doing, but his job was not concerned with her as a mother. In fact, between you and me, I think he may have refrained from including references to Elizabeth in case it annoyed the King."

"Don't ask me about the execution. It was horrible. But at the end of her short speech on the scaffold, the Queen said, 'If anyone looks into my case, may they judge the best of me.' Afterwards – after we ladies had lifted the Queen's warm, bleeding body and head into a wooden box – we went back to the Queen's rooms to collect our belongings. Sir William formally discharged us from our 'Duties of State' as he put it. He then read us a short final report he had written for Master Cromwell: 'The Queen died bravely. May God take her to His Mercy.'"

Lady Shelton, weeping a bit, paused and then added in a lower voice, "Do you know, Lady Bryan, that street-ballads are circulating in London claiming that Queen Anne was not guilty, and that the King's remarriage eleven days later was too hasty?"

At that point I put my arm firmly around Lady Shelton's trembling shoulders to comfort her, and also to cut short any further speculation. My mind was spinning and wandering into dangerous territory. "Now, now, my dear," I soothed. "We mustn't listen to dissenting voices. I can see you and your tender heart have endured a terrible experience. But, believe me, it's our duty to bear in mind that the King's Grace must have his reasons. He is our noble sovereign and we are his faithful subjects. 'Le roi le veult: the King wills it.' That's enough for you and me."

I haven't told any outsider before about Lady Shelton's story. But I'm growing old, and I'm not as well as I was. Those troubling times are far off now, and I think it's right to chronicle what I heard from an eyewitness.

Not long after Queen Anne's execution Master Cromwell sent out orders to the royal palaces and state buildings that all pictures of the late Queen were to be taken down and destroyed. Even her initials in stonework, as at Hampton Court, were to be obliterated and replaced with Queen Jane's initials. The first I knew of this was when two guardsmen entered the nursery one morning intending to remove our portrait of Queen Anne.

I stood up and said, "Knock, if you please. This is my domain. What do you want here?"

"Pardon, Lady Bryan," said the captain, "but Sir John told me to remove the painting of the late Queen at once."

"Well, wait outside please. It is not the right time while Princess Elizabeth is in the room. Don't worry. I shall go and see Sir John this minute."

That was Sir John for you. He never deigned to consult me or warn me about changes he was making. I hurried down to the parlour and found him looking over the household accounts.

"Good morning, Sir John."

"Yes, Lady Bryan?" (never a 'good morning' from him!) "What is it *now*?"

"I've come about the Queen's portrait," I said.

"The *late* Queen," he corrected me impatiently. "It's no use protesting to me. Master Cromwell has instructed me to remove it."

I paused a moment before continuing, "But, sir, we must consider the child's feelings. Could it not be taken down this evening when she's asleep?"

"This evening does not constitute 'forthwith' as Cromwell has ordered. Anyway, a child that young will not notice the removal of one picture."

"But she is a very forward child, Sir John, and she is very fond of that painting. I only ask for a little time."

He frowned as I stood my ground. Just then the farm manager came in on estate business, which was much more to Sir John's liking. So, to cut short my importuning, Sir John said ungraciously, "You have half an hour, Madam. Make of it what you will. And I will hear no more on this nursery matter." With that, he turned his back on me and greeted the farm manager.

I hurried back upstairs, and told the officer to come back in half an hour. I chivied the nurse-maids to dress Elizabeth in her coat and take her out to play in the garden for an hour. And so the portrait was removed and, I believe, burnt with the rubbish. In the nursery the lone portrait of the King immediately drew Elizabeth's attention to the fact that the other was missing. But by then I was ready with my explanation that the Queen's picture had gone to be cleaned.

That evening I decided to call the nursery servants together. I took it upon myself to instruct them not to speak to the Princess about her mother, or mention the late Queen again. In that way I hoped any memories would fade sooner. And in time I believe they did. But at first the child did sometimes mention Queen Anne because she had been accustomed to receiving regular parcels of new clothes from London.

One day she asked, "Where is my new dress from the Queen?"

The nurse-maids all turned to look at me, so I took a deep breath and started to broach the sad subject. "My dear," I said, "I will try to find out. But I'm afraid I've heard that the Queen, that is Queen *Anne*, er, your mother, is very ill in London. I'm afraid she's too ill to send a new dress now."

"She'll be better soon," pronounced Elizabeth.

"Well, we can only wait and see, my dear. We must pray to the Lord Jesus that he will look after her."

I used the Queen's 'illness' as an excuse several more times but references to her dwindled, as I'd hoped.

It must have been around this time that we had a new addition to Elizabeth's establishment. I remember it was only about two months after Queen Anne's death (may God rest her soul) that Katherine Champernowne joined us as a 'gentlewoman-in-waiting' to Lady Elizabeth.

This came about through my dear son, Francis's, great prestige at Court. Naturally I wrote frequent letters to my son and daughter while I was away from Court. In that dreadful, unprecedented time after Queen Anne's execution I poured out my troubles to them. I remember I even hinted that now I was sixty-five the responsibilities of my office should be devolved onto someone else. I soon had an answer from my daughter, Lady Carew, advising me to remain at my post, and saying she was urging Francis to obtain some help for me. Francis, the dear boy, put himself to the trouble of searching out a most suitable helper for me in Katherine Champernowne. He had to go through the usual channels and apply for Master Cromwell's permission, but even Master Cromwell could hardly refuse an application from one of the King's Gentlemen of the privy chamber! Francis (because of his demanding work) only rarely responded to my letters. But this time I received a letter from him urging me at all costs not to resign from my post but to expect to receive a young gentlewoman to help me within a few weeks. I still have his letter with me as I write this.

Soon afterwards I had a note from Master Cromwell trusting I would be happy to accept the services of Mistress Katherine Champernowne in two weeks' time. Anyway, Kat, as we all came to call her, proved to be a very welcome addition. She came from faraway Devonshire, and was of gentle birth and an excellent education. She was aged twenty-four and a most friendly, cheerful and unassuming lady. She had a spontaneous and demonstrative temperament and was full of affection for Lady Elizabeth. She soon became a favourite with our whole establishment. She had a lively sense of humour, and very much helped to lift our spirits at that worrying time. I think her appointment reassured us that our household was not going to be disbanded because of the change of queen; most of my servants were suffering such fears then. Kat was always most deferential to me, and I need not have feared that my authority might be undermined by the newcomer.

So that was Katherine Champernowne in July 1536: a newcomer to royal life, and a breath of fresh air to Lady Elizabeth's household.

It was Kat who expressed her surprise at how worn and small some of Elizabeth's clothes were becoming. I had relied of course on the lavish supply from Queen Anne. I sounded out Lady Shelton about this difficulty, but she doubted whether

Sir John would take the matter up for me. I doubted it too, but I nevertheless consulted him, only to be repulsed with, "This, of course, is purely a nursery matter, Lady Bryan. We know our respective duties, I hope, by this time."

Well, we certainly did, but sometimes the dividing-line was an issue. For instance, Sir John now took to insisting that the Princess (or 'Madam Elizabeth' as he now called her) should have her dinner in the great hall at the high table. I think his motive was to save expense and labour, because it did take time and trouble for the kitchen servants to bring our food up to the nursery apartments.

"The child finished suckling ten months ago," he declared. "It's high time she and her personal attendants joined the rest of the household for dinner. Starting from tomorrow."

Sir John would never run his suggestions past me to gain the benefit of my experience. Oh no! He would simply make pronouncements. Between you and me, I suspect that he didn't want to take the advice of a woman. He certainly didn't listen to Lady Shelton whenever she made one of her rare suggestions. But then she was his wife and owed him obedience. I was in a position of some authority, and he couldn't get used to such an unusual situation.

In the nursery, Elizabeth ate the simple dishes that we put in front of her with no trouble at all. But on the high table she would have seen an array of unsuitable meats, bread, sweetmeats and fruits spread out in front of her; naturally the little child would have called and shouted and pointed at what she fancied. Then she would have cried when it was denied to her. She was a high-spirited child (like her parents, I may say!) and when thwarted at that age, she could throw a real tantrum. She knew what she wanted, and would not be easily diverted from it. She was always tenacious. As she grew up, of course, she had to learn self-restraint, but under the surface she remained focused on what she wanted.

Anyway, while we were dining I had warned Sir John that I feared an appalling hubbub at the high table if Elizabeth were to sit there. Sir John was shocked, and sought to blame me!

He said in a deliberately loud voice, "Your anxieties do not say much for the upbringing this child is receiving, Lady Bryan."

"I only warn you, sir, that Elizabeth is far too young to dine in the hall."

"She has obviously been over-indulged. I had no idea she had not been trained in manners and decorum; I have sometimes wondered what you do all day, Lady Bryan. You have certainly been found wanting in this instance."

I was bursting with indignation, but my courtier's training came to the fore, and I said in a low voice, "Sir John, you and I must not be seen by all and sundry in this hall to be in dispute. Let us withdraw to the parlour now, and try to settle this matter."

He looked round and saw that the household on the lower tables had stopped their chatter and were staring up at us.

"Dinner is over," he announced loudly. "Clear the tables." And with bad grace he led me away to the parlour.

Well, you won't be surprised to hear that we had a disagreeable dialogue in the parlour.

"I must insist, Sir John, that Madam Elizabeth is far too young to be corrected much, let alone sit in state at the high table."

Sir John, however, was in no mood to give ground. Especially to a woman.

"No child is too young to be disciplined! Your attitude shows that Madam Elizabeth's education has grave shortcomings. I maintain that she should be old enough to behave suitably at table, if properly instructed. It is your duty to so instruct and discipline the child. I insist that she comes to the high table, and I will expect her manners to be appropriate."

At that intransigence I made up my mind to stand firm. "It's just not good for the child. And for that reason I shall write to Master Cromwell this afternoon and ask his permission to keep Elizabeth in the nursery for meals. He is the King's Secretary and has the authority to settle this matter since you and I cannot agree."

I had hoped he might have backed down then, but not Sir John!

"He will not want to be bothered with trivial nursery matters, Lady Bryan. He's a busy man. I warn you that you will get small thanks for your impertinent interference."

"Nevertheless, sir, I must do as I think right for the Princess. And until I hear Master Cromwell's decision, I will keep her in the nursery for meals."

"I see you want to defy me, Madam.Well, expect no sympathy from me when you get a put-down from your 'Master' Cromwell."

"What do you mean by that?"

"You *are* behind the times, Lady Bryan! Didn't you know that His Majesty knighted Cromwell last month? For services rendered. He is now *Sir* Thomas. There I go, helping you to address your ridiculous letter correctly."

I didn't forget my manners. "Thank you for letting me know, Sir John. Good afternoon."

I felt quite flustered by all the unpleasantness, and first I went straight up to the nursery. I needed comfort, and Kat and my kind nursemaids knew it. They hovered round my chair to calm me down.

Someone fanned my face, and Kat brought a cup of cold milk. There were murmurings of "What a shame!", "It's not right", "Well done, my Lady", and "It's not my place to say it, but Sir John gets above himself." I said nothing. I shut my eyes for a couple of minutes and rested my head on the chair-back. When I opened them, I saw Elizabeth had come up to my chair and was staring at me.

28

She clutched my knees and laid her head on my lap. I stroked her hair, and said she was a good girl. I had felt extra protective of her since her mother had died, and I was determined to shield her from Sir John's unrealistic expectations.

I soon took myself to my room to write my letter. As I took stock of my position, I realised that there was more than one problem I needed help with now. Since Queen Anne had died so suddenly, no-one at Court seemed to remember her daughter. I'd received no new instructions about Elizabeth's changed status. I knew no precedent for it, and I needed guidance from higher authority. Elizabeth seemed alone in the world at that point: His Grace the King was absorbed with Queen Jane, and did not want to be reminded of her recent predecessor. The Boleyns were in mourning and had retreated to Kent. Elizabeth needed a champion, and it would have to be me, her Lady Mistress.

So that day in August 1536 I wrote to Sir Thomas Cromwell, the King's first minister, with a cry from the heart, a 'cri de coeur'. Firstly, I pointed out that since Elizabeth had been demoted from being a princess, I didn't know what her status was, nor whether we should change the way we behaved to her. Then I told Cromwell how Elizabeth had grown out of most of her clothes, and needed a whole new wardrobe – not just outer garments but underclothes, nightdresses and even handkerchiefs. I remember writing, "I've made do for as long as I can, and I can't put it off any longer." I was at my wit's end about the clothes, I can tell you!

Then I explained my differences with Sir John about Elizabeth dining publicly in the great hall. I warned Cromwell that if she ate the rich food she saw on the high table, I would not be able to safeguard Elizabeth's good health. I finished by saying that she was the most advanced and delightful child I had ever known, and that I was sure the King's Grace would be proud of her. My words just tumbled onto the page.

When I had sealed my letter, I took it downstairs myself. I gave instructions to Joseph, our London rider, that it was important business and should be conveyed as soon as possible.

He read the name on the envelope and nodded. "I'll start at sunrise, my lady."

I daresay news got round the whole household that evening that I'd written to Cromwell; they'd know what it would be about.

Sir John had told me that he was the master of the house, and he looked down on me. But he didn't know everything. He didn't know how well I stood with the King. Cromwell, on the other hand, did know, because not much escaped his eye. It was crucial for him to know who was in favour. I had a reply only three days later, while Sir John received a separate letter. Both were to my liking. What's more, Sir John never crossed me again on any point.

I was instructed to treat Elizabeth as His Majesty's acknowledged daughter. And I could order her wardrobe as I pleased through the services of my own daughter at Court. Moreover, Elizabeth was to eat in her own nursery!

It was all most satisfactory, and I wrote and told Cromwell so. However, there was a lingering atmosphere at Hunsdon between me and the Sheltons; I hardly ever quarrel, and it was not comfortable in such a small establishment. So I decided to take the bull by the horns, as is my way, and try to ease the situation. While at my embroidery with Lady Shelton and Lady Mary, I broached the subject of young children's manners. I remember making the point that when Lady Mary was two-and-three-quarters she too had suffered from the occasional infantile outburst, and she had not been expected to sit at the high table until she was five years old, and even then not every day. "And now see what perfect manners Lady Mary has!" I concluded.

Lady Shelton, at whom this had been aimed, made no comment. But Lady Mary looked up from her sewing and, with a rare smile, said,

"Dear Lady Bryan, I do indeed acknowledge that you should take some credit for my upbringing. But I'll never forget (and I'm sure you won't either) that my beloved and saintly mother set me a wonderful example. As you know, she had the exquisite manners of a true queen. The royal blood of Spain flowed in her veins, as it does in mine. It's my other heritage. I pray, you know, for her dear sake that one day England will be in alliance with Spain again."

Lady Shelton and I were rather taken aback by this emotional speech, but I naturally confirmed that Queen Catherine had always displayed great courtesy. After that I didn't know how to return the conversation to childish tantrums. So we just bent over our tapestry again in silence.

In fact, by that time Lady Mary was no longer living with us so much, and was no longer just an appendage to her little sister's household. No, she had finally, and wisely, capitulated to the constant pressure on her to acknowledge King Henry as the head of the Church of England, and also to acknowledge that her parents' marriage had been invalid. Mary had many tearful qualms of conscience about yielding on these great principles. She had held out for so long. But her change of heart bore great fruit for her, as I had known it would.

In July she was summoned from Hunsdon to meet the King's Grace, whom she hadn't seen for five years! She was back in favour at last, and Queen Jane showed Mary great attention and respect. From then on when she was at Court she took precedence over every other lady except the Queen. In fact it was rumoured that the King's Grace might restore Mary to her title of Princess, and to her place in the Succession. But that didn't happen. Mary was twenty years old by this time, and should have been married long since. But she had been under

31

a cloud of her own making (as I told you). King Henry was not the man to plan a great marriage for a daughter who had dared oppose his will. Now that she was back in royal favour, I hoped a suitable husband might be found. But, I suppose because she was still officially illegitimate, foreign princes or noblemen were not falling over themselves to ask for her hand. And, sadly, she's remained single to this day, and the years pass her by.

Where was I? Yes, going back to 1536, Mary's star was definitely rising: she was much happier, accorded high status at Court, and was once again honoured as the King's daughter. This gave me grounds for hope that her little sister might one day follow the same auspicious path.

One more bolt from the blue came in that terrible year: in October, we at Ashridge were shocked to hear of a rebellion in the North. A lot of misguided people there still clung to the old religion. It's difficult to imagine that now, isn't it? They were easily roused to revolt by some disaffected (or ambitious) nobles up there. I was told they were angry that the great abbeys and monasteries were being shut down, and it was whispered that they even questioned the King's right to be Head of the Church! They also demanded that the King should restore Lady Mary to the Succession. They had the nerve to call their heretical revolt *The Pilgrimage of Grace*! And they took over the great city of York. Rumours multiplied that the rebels planned to march South soon, and memories of the civil wars were stirred.

I'm not one to panic but I must say I was relieved when an urgent message came from Cromwell summoning the King's daughters to the safety of Court. It was always a tiring upheaval to get our establishment on the road, and I had to organise this move in a great hurry. The urgency of the preparations made the servants fearful, and the fear seemed to feed on itself. Some of the permanent Ashridge Manor servants tried to join the exodus, but of course our guardsmen soon put a stop to such hopes. I remember warning the nursemaids to keep calm and unworried in Lady Elizabeth's presence, as a child of three must be sheltered from outside anxieties. Lady Mary, of course, listened to all the news avidly, but, whatever her sympathies were, she wisely remained tight-lipped.

Ashridge was a three-day journey to London for our slow convoy, which included a litter for the child and me. Word had spread that the King's daughters were on the road to London, and there were plenty of townsfolk and villagers cheering, staring, bowing and waving as we passed. Mary on horseback was very gratified, and occasionally acknowledged the crowds. Sometimes I drew back the litter curtains for Elizabeth to be seen, and I told her to wave too, which she did cheerfully in her pretty way. It was six months since we had been on the long journey to London: this was the first time she became aware of the attention of the people, and she was very excited by it. The more responsive she was to the crowds, the more they cheered, and she loved it!

We arrived at Whitehall Palace where a small nursery wing had been prepared. We didn't often stay in London itself, but that October we had to be in the city for our safety. My daughter at Court was such a help to me then, in arranging at short notice for suitable accommodation to be ready. Our rooms were rather dark and pokey, and not ideal for children. But my daughter had done her best. I did miss my family, and I so enjoyed their company when I came to Court. My two grand-daughters were growing up fast – the eldest, Mary Carew, was eighteen, and her sister, Anne, sixteen. I wrote lots of letters to them while I was at the royal manors but I wish I had seen them more!

It was Kat Champernowne's first visit to Court and, in the flurry of our unexpected journeying there, I hadn't had much time to train her in all the protocol and niceties of precedence and manners. I decided to keep her with me as much as possible, so that I could alert and advise her on the spot. Also, now that we had been conveyed to the Court so unexpectedly, I had a worry I wanted her help with. In a nutshell, I didn't know what memories of the Court Elizabeth might still have: would Court life stir images of her mother? The child talked so well. And she had an excellent memory. During our long journey to London my thoughts kept straying to dangerous questions Elizabeth might ask of the King himself or the new Queen.

I confided my worries to Kat on our first evening in the vast Whitehall Palace. Kat was someone who faced up to problems, and was constructive. She didn't try to brush my fears under the carpet with soothing words.

"I'm almost hoping, Kat, that the King's Grace won't even want to see Elizabeth, let alone talk to her!" I said.

"That would be sad but safest, milady," she replied. "But it's out of our power to arrange."

"I dread seeing the King's face darken, Kat. He hasn't had much to do with young children, you know. I'm sure I would be expected to have stopped the child's mouth long ago on the subject of her mother."

"Well, she's only twice mentioned her mother to me since I've been with you these last three months. But I suppose if she saw His Majesty, she just *might* expect the late Queen too."

"That's it, Kat," I said. "I was sure we wouldn't meet the King till Christmas, if then. But now this wretched rebellion has brought us here too soon!"

"Let's have a plan then, milady, just in case," Kat said. "We need to think ahead. Let's choose a couple of topics to raise with Elizabeth if we need to divert the conversation. Then at least we'll be prepared."

"You're right, I must be positive. This worry has been hanging over me the last few days. And I'm so tired with all the packing and travelling as well. Not like me!"

"No, indeed, milady," Kat said. "You deserve a good rest. Can I suggest Elizabeth's riding lessons as a talking-point?"

"She loves those," I agreed, "and that would certainly catch her interest. And perhaps one more topic in reserve? What about the apples she helped pick the other day?"

Kat smiled. "She's been chatting a lot about that morning in the orchard. So there we are! It may not work. But you're sure to be with Elizabeth, Lady Bryan, if she does meet His Majesty. So keep riding and apples on the tip of your tongue."

"Thank you, Kat," I said. "I feel better for talking to you. Such a delicate matter. And there's no precedent for it! Everything is so irregular! I'll still be nervous, mind you, but I'll keep your plan in my mind. And I'll say my prayers too; I know the Blessed Virgin will understand."

Kat smiled and curtseyed to say goodnight, before she slipped away to the nursery. I had my own small chamber, and went to bed quite worn out that night, but I slept well.

My little establishment gradually settled in at Whitehall. It had shortcomings for a child: it was a vast, modern palace, but it was in a big city and didn't have the gardens or fields of our country manors. However, I made enquiries of the Lord Chamberlain, and was permitted to take Elizabeth to a quiet courtyard to run about every day. I was well aware that at Court my establishment was a subsidiary one. I had no authority over Court officials and had to remember my place!

The King's Grace was very busy arranging to protect his people from the wicked northern rebellion. It was, of course, the talk of the Court. Messengers from all over the country sped back and forth to His Majesty as he summoned contingents for the army. There was tension in the air again. The old religion, which had been dormant for several years, was trying to re-assert itself, with help, it seemed, from our enemies abroad. However, thanks be to God, by November better news began to come through. The King in his great mercy negotiated a settlement with the rebels, and the relief at Court was enormous.

One morning soon afterwards he suddenly summoned Lady Elizabeth to his privy chamber. The King's gentleman usher came to our quarters to deliver the royal summons. I was to take the child to His Majesty in one hour's time and the usher would wait to escort us there. I chose a fine dress and shoes for Elizabeth and left the nursemaids to see to her. I also told Kat to explain to the child that she was going to meet her father. She needed to help her practise her curtsey and remind her to say 'Your Majesty'. Then I hurried to my chamber. My maid helped me change into my black satin with a gabled headdress. In my anxiety my heart was beating alarmingly fast. When I returned to the nursery, everyone was excited, especially Elizabeth who loved dressing up.

"My dress is brighter than yours!" she said as she skipped around the room in her lively way with a big smile. I can see her now, so charming in the yellow dress with her auburn curls, pale skin and dark sparkling eyes. She was never shy, was Elizabeth – how could she have been with such bold parents? – and she rose to big occasions with delight. Kat steadied her and laid a kind hand on my arm too. I held out my hand to the child and she grasped it.

"Now, Lady Elizabeth," I said, "I expect Kat has been telling you that His Majesty the King has graciously invited you to visit him. Your very best manners are needed, and a beautiful curtsey when we enter his presence. We'll follow this Gentleman of the Court."

The usher, tapping his way with his Staff of Office, led us downstairs, along corridors and finally up a grand, wide staircase. I remember we passed courtiers and servants who stopped and stared, nudged each other and murmured. To my surprise a couple even bowed. The usher knocked on a vast door and we were admitted to an antechamber.

The King's chief gentleman-in-waiting, Sir John Dudley, came forward and greeted me before briefly bowing to Elizabeth. "I will inform His Majesty that you are here."

The other gentlemen in the antechamber looked at us speculatively, and raised eyebrows at each other, but they didn't speak. Unusually, Elizabeth at that point must have felt overawed by the silent room filled with unsmiling male strangers, for she gripped my hand more tightly and I responded with gentle pressure.

After a few minutes, Sir John reappeared at the far doors. "Come forward, Lady Bryan, with your charge. The King's Grace will give you an audience now."

We walked ahead into the privy chamber and Sir John followed, closing the doors behind him. I dropped my deepest curtsey, and Elizabeth did the same.

"Well," boomed the King, "It's my old friend Lady Bryan. Rise, rise."

We stood and raised our eyes to King Henry, whose eyes were not on me but fixed on Elizabeth. She gave a smile of recognition and piped up: "It's the King!"

The King grinned and nodded at her announcement. He was wearing a morning robe and had three gentlemen in attendance. "And how are you, Elizabeth?"

"I'm very well, Your Majesty," she replied.

"And what do you do all day with Lady Bryan?"

"Lady Bryan isn't with me all day, you know," she said, turning to me. "I say my prayers with you, don't I, Lady Bryan? And I do dancing with Mistress Watson, and I play in the garden with Kat and Sally. But Sally's got a cold now."

The King seemed tickled by her babbling. He sat on a chair to be at her level and continued to prompt her to chatter. "And I hear you know your sister Mary."

Elizabeth nodded. "I like Mary but she doesn't live with us much now, because she's grown-up. I miss her, but she gave me a kitten to catch the mice, because Lady Bryan is frightened of them. Lady Bryan told Sir John that his cats were no good at catching mice, didn't you?"

I nodded. "Yes, my lady."

"And how old are you, sweetheart?" the King asked.

"I'm three," she replied, not at all overawed by him. "I had my birthday soon and I got this beautiful dress. And another one, too."

The atmosphere was so friendly that I was brave enough to enter the conversation. "Please tell His Majesty about your new pony."

"He's brown," she said.

"Your Majesty," I reminded her.

"Your Majesty," she echoed.

"And what's his name?" asked the King.

"His name's Tudor," she said.

"Tudor!" the King exclaimed as he turned to his gentlemen. "An excellent name from Wales!"

We all laughed with the King.

Then he turned to me and said, "So, Madam Elizabeth Tudor is learning to ride? How is she finding it?"

"She's most brave, Sir, considering her age."

"Good," he said as he reached out a hand and patted the child gently on the head. Then, turning to his gentlemen he pronounced, "This little daughter of mine is very good company already, and we shall entertain her at Christmas at Greenwich. We shall expect you there, Lady Bryan."

As Sir John moved forward, I knew our audience was at an end. I made another deep curtsey, and was glad to see Elizabeth copy me.

"Goodbye, sweetheart," said the King, still amused as we left the chamber.

Sir John was all smiles as we made our way back through the antechamber. I saw that the courtiers there noticed it. They smiled and bowed before us this time. Elizabeth quickly became aware of this attention and made another of her best curtseys, which amused them all. Sir John beckoned an usher to escort us back to our nursery quarters, and then turned his attention to the waiting (and unsmiling) Spanish ambassadors.

In the nursery Kat and the nursemaids welcomed us back with great anticipation, all agog to know how the King's Grace had received us. I sank into my chair still holding Elizabeth's hand, suddenly feeling tired after the tension of the morning.

"Lady Elizabeth did us all proud," I said. "She showed both spirit and good manners. The King displayed great affection for her in front of his gentlemen. So word will quickly travel through the Court that the child is not to be disowned or shunned. And he specifically invited us to Greenwich for Christmas!"

As Sally and Martha (both beaming) took Elizabeth off to the dressing-room to change out of her grand dress, Kat asked me quietly whether Queen Jane too had welcomed Elizabeth.

I shook my head. "Queen Jane was not there."

"That's a shame. Do you think she disapproves of our Elizabeth?"

"You need to learn that Queens don't really matter, Kat. The King is the one with the power, and the one we must strive to please at all times."

"Did Elizabeth say anything amiss?"

"No, God be praised! Although I did head her off the subject of her dresses. Her mother used to send her regular presents of clothes, you know. Anyway, I bravely butted in with mention of the pony, and no chasm opened!"

"Well done!"

"The Blessed Virgin must have heard my prayers," I said. "I shall thank her on my knees in my chamber in a moment." And so I most fervently did.

We moved to Eltham Palace near Greenwich soon

afterwards. I was glad to get to proper and more spacious nursery quarters. There was room for the child to play outside and practise her riding again. Nor did I have to worry about another sudden summons from the King!

I remember taking the opportunity then to give Kat important advice about living at Court. I had to warn her to guard her eager tongue and laughter. The caution one had to practise at Court did not come naturally to Kat and I feared for her sometimes. She had not been trained in Court etiquette and pitfalls as I had. She was an artless lady, very open and trusting. I had to impress on her to keep her opinions to herself, and never to discuss the King or anyone near the throne. She had an enquiring mind, and was most interested in the 'new' religion; I strongly advised her not to debate that topic either. Times can change, and it's not prudent to reveal strong opinions at Court.

We enjoyed the Christmas festivities at Greenwich, and Elizabeth did then meet Queen Jane. The King was proud of the child and her forwardness, and often went out of his way to greet her and have a chat. If the Queen was with him, she would smile at Elizabeth, and I would prompt the little girl to make a curtsey. On the feast days, the King expected Elizabeth to dine in the Great Hall as a member of the Royal Family. She didn't sit at the high table with Lady Mary, but she sat between me and Kat. By her presence His Majesty was thus displaying to his Court the status he bestowed on this three-year-old daughter. I couldn't help wondering – along with the rest of the Court – whether the Queen was pregnant. The word from her ladies was that she was not. She had been married for seven months, and the ever-present Succession question still hung in the air.

In that New Year of 1537 we moved back to Hatfield and settled down to our normal routine again. One change, though, was that the Sheltons had left. A gentleman called

William Cholmondeley was appointed as the new steward of our establishment. He had been steward to Lady Mary ten years earlier, and I wondered whether Mary had initiated this change. She had never got on with the Sheltons, especially as Lady Shelton was Queen Anne's aunt. Now that Mary was in high favour again, she had more say in the people who served her. Mary still spent about half her time with Elizabeth in the country manors, but she was often at Court too. In fact I remember Queen Jane often used to summon her there, saying that she had no other companions of suitably high status.

Elizabeth continued her dancing and riding lessons, and we learnt some songs too. It was a settled time for her. Sometimes her Carey cousins Catherine and Henry, (aged thirteen and eleven by then) would pay a visit, and she was always delighted when they played with her. There was a great lack then of children of high enough status for Elizabeth to play with. On the King's side the three Grey girls had not yet been born, and their mother, Lady Frances Brandon, the king's niece was the same age as Lady Mary. I knew it would have been good for Elizabeth to learn to share toys, take turns in childish games and make friends. I remember the lady housekeeper at Hatfield had a daughter of the same age, and Elizabeth would watch her intently playing in the courtyard with her siblings. Then there was the estate manager's little girl at Ashridge, and other servants' children, of course, at the other manors. But naturally the King's Grace would not have allowed his daughter to associate with such low-ranking playmates. When she asked to join the children she saw, it was my job to deny her. I explained that she, the King's daughter, was too important and grand to play with such children. I had to impress that rule on Kat too; because of her inexperience of royal life, she actually queried whether there was any harm in Elizabeth playing with her social inferiors.

"There would be harm for you and me, Kat," I told her, "if it ever reached the King's ears!"

Anyway, with our establishment's constant journeyings it would have been hard for any local friendships to be maintained.

And, although Elizabeth did not experience the give-and-take of children's games, she lacked nothing when it came to showing good manners in front of adults. From the time she first began to talk, I knew it was my responsibility to instil in her the courtesies of royal society. At the start it was just 'please' and 'thank you', not to the servants, of course, but to me, Kat, Lady Mary, and Sir John and Lady Shelton. Then I added 'good morning' and 'God be with you', and 'sir' and 'madam'. The King and Queen were always 'Your Majesty'. Once I knew that Elizabeth was not disowned but in fact cherished by the King, I knew she would have to be properly trained in Court manners, as if she were a princess again. For princes and princesses are expected to have perfect manners, almost from infancy! At the age of three she couldn't be expected to distinguish precisely whom to address as sir or madam, but as she grew up, she would have to become acutely aware both of her own status and of other people's.

For example, she would always have to show respect to ambassadors as the representatives of foreign kings. But naturally she would no longer have to defer to me or the Sheltons. For the moment it was enough for her to recognise the difference between those of higher and lower rank within her establishment. It is important to teach a princess – or at least a king's daughter – how to show deference to others. For she is bound to get married, and will of course have to obey and respect her husband, just as all women must do. In fact she will probably marry a foreign prince or king (as King Henry's sisters did) and will then have to learn the courtly traditions of her new country as well. But at least that was not my responsibility!

As our life continued in the round of royal manors, news reached me from my family that Queen Jane was pregnant! How relieved and delighted we all were: full of hope and prayers for a prince. After the disappointment of the first two Queens, I had to keep in mind the old country saying 'Don't count your chickens till they're hatched'. But soon we heard that the baby had quickened in the womb, and the dangerous early months were passed. I couldn't help wondering then how a new royal baby, of whatever sex, would affect me. Would I be thought too old to be in charge of a new nursery? Would Queen Jane have other ideas? I knew in any case that my own wishes would not be considered.

Then came a day in July when I was summoned to Hampton Court to meet Queen Jane. My audience was a short one.

"The King desires me to appoint you as Lady Mistress of our baby's nursery," she announced in her soft but serious voice. "The baby will be born here and I shall await the birth from the middle of September. You will be here from that time, Lady Bryan. You will have the nursery in readiness with servants and wet-nurse."

"Thank you, Your Majesty," I said as I curtseyed. "May the Blessed Virgin protect and keep you."

I went to find my daughter, and told her the expected news. I enlisted her help in starting to prepare the nursery quarters for a baby again, in finding a wet-nurse, and in the purchasing of supplies of clothes. Luckily I had given the matter some thought before my summons, and had decided that I would have to leave Elizabeth in Kat's hands. I now planned that instead of moving on at the end of July from Hatfield to Ashridge, we would move to Richmond Palace. That was very near Hampton Court, and I would be able to see Elizabeth sometimes and check that her upbringing was going smoothly. It was thanks to Divine Providence that by then Kat had had a year under my wing, although she still had a lot to learn about the Court.

So I travelled back to Hatfield and explained the new situation to all Elizabeth's servants. Our establishment would be changing. Elizabeth was growing up, and did not need so many nursemaids. I would leave Sally and Meg under Kat's authority, plus of course the laundresses and men-servants. The other three would come with me to Hampton Court to look after Queen Jane's baby. I had trained all the nursemaids, and excellent they were. They would help to train the new ones I was recruiting at Hampton Court.

I explained my plans to William Cholmondeley, our new steward, and he sent word to Ashridge and Richmond about the forthcoming moves. It was all hustle and bustle. Finally, in the middle of August we moved to Richmond. I wanted to see the household well settled in before I had to stay with Queen Jane. From there I paid several visits to Hampton Court to supervise the nursery furnishings and choose more staff. It was Kat who suggested that I should hand over the reins to her at Richmond, not suddenly but gradually. Then she persuaded me into trying to prepare Elizabeth for my departure. We only had a few weeks, but it was probably a good idea: after all, I had been with her all her life.

So one morning I asked Kat to bring Elizabeth to my chamber. I didn't want all the nursery servants listening and watching the child's distress. I told the little girl that Queen Jane was soon going to have a baby.

"The King and Queen have asked me to look after the baby," I explained. "This is because I've looked after both His Majesty's daughters, Lady Mary and yourself."

Elizabeth stood by my chair and stared up at me in silence, seeming to sense that more was coming.

"The baby will be born at Hampton Court Palace," I went on, "so I will leave Richmond and go there to wait for the baby."

"But we've only just come to Richmond," she said.

"I know, my dear. But don't worry. You can stay here with Kat and most of the nursemaids. I'm the one who will be leaving."

"When are you coming back?"

"I can't come back, dear, because I'll have a new job to do. The King and Queen have claimed me, and I must go."

"But I don't want you to leave me."

"I won't be very far away. I'm sure you'll be allowed to come and visit."

"But I don't want you to go."

"This, my dear, is one of the times when we can't have what we want. Remember we must always do what the King's Grace tells us."

"I can help you look after the baby.".

"No, my dear. That's not what the King has commanded." I had to speak firmly, and she burst into tears. I drew her to me, and found I had a lump in my throat and couldn't speak.

Kat came forward, and knelt by the little girl. "We'll all miss Lady Bryan, sweetheart. And she'll miss you very much too. But she's right. We mustn't forget that the King knows what's best. And I'll be needing lots of help from you here. I'll be trying hard to do Lady Bryan's job. Can you help me please?"

But Elizabeth wasn't to be pacified. She held my skirts tight, put her head on my lap and sobbed. Kat motioned to me to let her be for a time.

Eventually I said, "Now, Madam Elizabeth, you are the daughter of our King – and such a great King – so you have to show yourself very brave indeed. You are almost four now, and we're really proud of how well you're growing up, aren't we, Kat?"

"Of course we are. We know how brave you are learning to ride Tudor, even when you fall off! And now you have to learn to be brave in another way. Let's dry those tears and show that you can be as brave as His Majesty, your father. Then we can start thinking about your birthday next week. There'll be some presents to look forward to." The child slowly turned her head on my lap and was listening. She stopped crying, but didn't speak.

"There's my brave girl," I said, stroking her hair. "Yes, I've got a lovely present for your birthday, and I know there'll be some more."

After a pause she stood up: "When is my birthday?"

"It's next Wednesday, 7th September."

"How many sleeps is that?"

"It will be five more sleeps."

"Will you come?"

"I most certainly will, my dear."

I was left feeling doubtful about the whole idea of warning Elizabeth in advance that I would be leaving her establishment. I felt Kat had persuaded me against my better judgement. Children of her age have little idea of time, and it's best not to worry them in advance. 'Least said, soonest mended' was my usual instinct. I did tell Kat later that I wished we had left well alone.

She, however, was full of admiration for my handling of the situation. "You've prepared the child so well now, milady. When you actually leave us, she'll still be very upset, but it won't come as a complete shock. She will come to terms with it much better. She won't lose her trust in us. I'm so grateful to you, milady, for breaking the news to her now."

My little girl had a very happy birthday. She was most excited by her presents. I gave her a cap I had embroidered, and Kat gave her a picture book. The nursemaids had clubbed together to buy her a doll. Lady Mary came from Hampton Court in the morning with a winter muff. She, however, left early when we were honoured with a visit from Archbishop Cranmer, Elizabeth's godfather. He spoke kindly to the child, and said some prayers and gave her a blessing while we all knelt. With the archbishop was Matthew Parker, who had been Queen Anne's chaplain. He told me how relieved he was that the child was respected at Court, and was so well and happy. I introduced him to Kat, and explained that Kat would be in charge of Elizabeth from now on as her Lady Governess.

Elizabeth was thrilled when her Carey cousins arrived for the celebration. They went outside and played hide and seek in the sunny garden. I remember Elizabeth was quite helpless with laughter at one point! Later we all gathered in the hall to sing nursery rhymes and folk songs before bedtime. That night I thanked the Blessed Virgin that the Lady Elizabeth under my care had survived the early, perilous years of infancy, and reached her fourth birthday so healthy and lively.

One of the more delicate aspects of my job was deciding who should be allowed to visit Elizabeth. The birthday party had reminded me to impart that to Kat before I left. Relatives were normally, of course, given every opportunity. But in this case it went without saying that the King's Grace would not have approved any visits from Lord and Lady Boleyn. They obviously understood that, as they never applied to me to visit their grand-daughter. Nor did Queen Anne's sister, Mary Carey, ever apply for herself. However, she did ask that her children, Catherine and Henry, could keep up their friendship with their little cousin. She probably hoped that a royal connection would advance their future careers. That request put me in a quandary, and in fact I referred my doubts to Cromwell at the time, giving my view that it was good for Elizabeth to have children to play with occasionally. Rather to my surprise Cromwell had nodded this through, writing that he had confidence in my judgement in nursery matters. I did, however, take the precaution of laying down to Mary Carey the house rules: her children must never speak to Elizabeth about her mother or, indeed, about their own. And she obviously briefed them thoroughly on that condition.

Another matter I confided to Kat was that Queen Anne had begged both me and Matthew Parker, her chaplain, to watch over Elizabeth as long as we could. "I now have to pass that request of a dying mother on to you, Kat. Thanks be to God, it does seem now that Elizabeth is not under a cloud, and her future is secure. But don't forget, Kat, that (unlike Lady Mary) she has no powerful relations on her mother's side. So it will fall to you to protect her if need be. I can see you've come to love her, so you'll find it natural to stand up for her, won't you?"

"Of course I will. You're a hard act to follow, milady, but I'll do my very best."

"Of course, if you need anything for Elizabeth – perhaps more servants, tutors, or furnishings – don't hesitate to write to Lord Cromwell, will you?" I said. "Especially if you have any doubts about her status, and what she should or shouldn't do. I've always found him most sympathetic, and he responds immediately. He will be your contact at Court. I think of him as the mouthpiece of the King for me."

How providential that I'd trained Kat well enough to hand Elizabeth over to! I won't pretend I didn't feel a little jealous of her. After all, my life had revolved around Elizabeth for four years. I had almost brought her up as my own grand-daughter. She was such a rewarding child: affectionate and quick to learn. When the day came to leave Richmond I did shed some tears, even in front of the servants. The nursemaids did the same, and we understood each other. Elizabeth cried too, of course, but I'd given her a new handkerchief of my own work, and shown her how to wave it. I hugged her close and then stepped down into the boat. As the boat pulled away with the tide, my little girl stood in front of Kat waving the handkerchief continually. I waved back for a bit. Then I made myself turn away, and I faced downriver towards Hampton Court.

The great modern palace was built of red brick by Cardinal Wolsey, and he later thoughtfully presented it to King Henry. Unlike the country manors and castles it had large windows and built-in chimneys, so it had every comfort of light and warmth, plus plenty of garderobes. As the Court was in residence, it was thronged with people and conveyances that day. The guards at the gates knew me by now, and we swept through and straight up to the nursery quarters. I was greeted by the new servants I had hired, and the crucial wet-nurse, who of course had her own infant still at the breast at that point. I introduced the three nursemaids I had brought with me from Richmond and appointed Martha, the oldest, to be in charge of the others. I remember I noticed that the screens I had ordered to keep draughts from the cradle had still not arrived, so I sat down and wrote a peremptory letter to the supplier. I headed the letter 'Hampton Court Palace', and they arrived three days later!

I had a good-sized private chamber there, and when my maid had unpacked, I changed into a smart Court gown. Then I summoned an usher and sent a formal note to Queen Jane announcing my arrival at her service. My daughter came to see me that evening, which greatly raised my spirits, as I was missing my old establishment. The older I got, the less I liked change and being uprooted. When I went to bed, I said prayers for those I had left behind, and for my new establishment, and, God willing, its success.

I spent the next two days assigning duties to each nursemaid and groomsman, and setting high standards of cleanliness and diligence to the new ones. On the third day, Queen Jane formally 'took to her chamber', as the saying goes, to await the birth. Her chamber for this purpose was near the nursery quarters, and it was expected that the baby would arrive in about three weeks. Her Majesty came to view the nursery, and I showed her the cradle, the baby-clothes and the warm fire. She expressed herself satisfied with my preparations, and asked us to pray for her safe delivery. She was a dignified, composed lady and said nothing personal to me. I did not like to ask whether Elizabeth could visit me. I hoped that the baby would make a bond between us, and that I would get to know her better in future during her early years of motherhood. We would be seeing a lot of each other then.

And so the waiting began. As it had done before Elizabeth's birth four years earlier. There was tension, anticipation and our prayers for a boy. But this time the situation was even more urgent, simply because the King was four years older. Our country still had no heir: a sure recipe for future civil war.

I passed some of the time renewing contacts with old friends and family at Court. I also worked a lot with my needle, and instructed the nursemaids in sewing skills. Doctor Butts, the King's own physician, called in one day to inspect the nursery, and he approved it. He looked more anxious than most, feeling a great weight of responsibility for the precious royal infant to come. The Queen kept to her apartments with her ladies. Four midwives were staying with her now, and they visited the nursery sometimes to pass the time. They too seemed anxious despite all their experience (though of course the days were long gone when the midwife was thought to be able to influence the sex of a baby). The trouble was that the growing expectancy in the Court and the midwives' anxiety started to affect me too. I hadn't given it a thought up to now, but I suddenly realised that, if the baby was the longed-for prince, my own position would require even more responsibility. The whole country's future would be at stake, and dependent on my care! In those few weeks of waiting I hadn't got enough to occupy my time, and I suppose that's why I began to worry. Nor did I have Kat to confide in. I did tell my fears to my own children, but Francis said, laughing, "Come on now, mother! Here's everyone longing for a prince, and you're the only person hoping for another girl! For heaven's sake don't spread that about!"

So I kept quiet and tried to display a calm confidence. Kat wrote often, and I enjoyed her tales of life at Richmond with the people I knew so well. Elizabeth mentioned me a lot, but seemed to understand that there was nobody else who could look after the coming baby! I must admit I was missing her bright face and cheerful chatter. I just hoped that she would be invited to come and visit the new baby.

During those few but long weeks of waiting, I sometimes walked in the magnificent gardens, where the trees were beginning to turn yellow, and the first leaves were falling. I was there with my daughter, Elizabeth Carew, on the day when the Queen's labour began. My chief nursemaid, Martha, sent an usher out to find me. Martha herself, of course, did not have the rank to enter the garden. My daughter and I hurried excitedly back to the nursery, and we could see that the Court grapevine was already humming with the news.

My daughter kept repeating, "Sweet Jesus, let it be a prince!"

I found that my heart was pounding, and I believe I was quite sharp with the servants when we got back. I chivied the nursemaids into putting out the baby clothes, and warming the blankets and shawls. I told Mrs Baker, the wet-nurse, to call her sister in at once to be ready to take away her own baby when the moment came. I hurried the groomsmen into building up our fires and bringing up plenty of dry logs. I was all in a fidget.

But even then we were to have a long wait. It was more than two days before the baby was born, and they were tense days and nights indeed. We took turns to sleep. The chapel was busy with services praying for Queen Jane's successful

51

delivery. And what a success it turned out to be! The Prince at last! Prince Edward, a healthy boy to save the Succession! The Court and the country went wild with relief and joy. Church bells rang out, bonfires blazed and a salute of cannons sounded from the Tower. King Henry actually wept in his happiness, and gave thanks to God who had thus given a sign that this third marriage was lawful and blessed.

Sir Thomas Cromwell's preparations for a grand christening swung into action at the marvellous news. The Prince was born on 12th October and on 15th the ceremony took place in the Hampton Court chapel. The Prince's half-sisters were both given important roles to play: Lady Mary was chosen to be a godmother, and Lady Elizabeth to carry the christening gown. In fact Elizabeth herself was carried by Sir Edward Seymour, Queen Jane's brother, on the way into the chapel. On the way out she held Mary's hand and walked with her. I was there myself of course as the Prince's Lady Mistress, and I felt full of happiness that his sisters were accorded such honours. Afterwards we filed out of the chapel and paid our respects to the Queen who was sitting in the anteroom under warm coverings, quietly enjoying her triumph. I noticed how she took Mary's hands in her own, and inclined her head at Elizabeth's curtsey. When my turn came, I curtseyed deeply and murmured my congratulations and gratitude, and Her Majesty graciously nodded. Kat was there in charge of Elizabeth, and I was able to snatch a few heartfelt greetings with them. Elizabeth rushed up to me with delight and started telling me lots of news.

But then I felt a tap on my shoulder, and a lady-in-waiting recalled me to my duties: "Her Majesty is expecting you to lead the Prince's retinue back to the nursery now."

So I had to leave immediately.

Prince Edward's nursery was a happy, warm place. The baby was strong and suckled well. Doctor Butts called in to check on him twice a day, and was satisfied with my regime. Twice a day too I had to carry the baby to the Queen's lying-in chamber so that she could take pride in her achievement, as she recovered from her prolonged childbirth. Her brothers, Edward and Thomas Seymour, were sometimes there, and thrilled with their nephew, the heir to the throne.

"Look after him for us, Lady Bryan," Sir Thomas commanded. "And when he's older, we'll take over his protection, eh Ned?"

The Queen remonstrated, "Tom, Tom, you do run away with yourself! The King's Grace and I will protect our Prince of Wales."

Sir Thomas dropped to one knee in mock deference: "Of course you will, my dear little sister, but a couple of strong uncles never do a lad any harm!"

The King himself came every day to the nursery to rejoice over his longed-for son. He called the baby 'England's Treasure', and said to me once, "This is the day you and I have been waiting for these many years, Lady Bryan. I have never lost faith, and at long last my boy is here. Praise be to God!" Turning to his attendants he declared, "Make no mistake, gentlemen, by this sign God is confirming me as His Supreme Head of the Church in England, and giving the lie to those abominable heretics in the north."

And then the Queen fell sick with a fever. Doctor Butts came in and told me not to take the Prince to her chamber for a day or two. After he'd left, a silence fell in the nursery: we all knew about the omens of childbed fever. The Court hushed its celebrations. Once again we waited. This time with foreboding. Doctor Butts rushed back and forth with medicines, muttering against the midwives, and taking some reassurance from the good progress of the little Prince. But poor Queen Jane could not be saved. She died on October 24th 1537, when her son was just twelve days old.

It was a tragic shock to the Court after all the rejoicings. But we had our heir. That was the consolation on everyone's lips, even as we mourned. Poor Lady Mary was particularly grieved. The Queen had shown Mary kindness and respect, drawing her back into Court life after her isolated years. She took the official role of chief mourner at Queen Jane's funeral at Windsor. The King's Grace naturally mourned greatly, but Court protocol is that the sovereign does not attend funerals.

Prince Edward's establishment had to remain at Hampton Court for the next three months, until he was old enough to travel. He continued to thrive, thanks be to God. I sometimes felt my nursery was the focal point of the whole Court if not the whole country. I was well aware of my responsibility, especially in those early months, and I limited the number of visitors. I often thought of Elizabeth, and I must admit that the death of Queen Jane made me feel it would now be acceptable for her to visit me. I hadn't known this Queen long, but my courtier's sixth sense had warned me that she somehow resented Elizabeth. I had inferred that it would be wise not to refer to the little girl, let alone request a visit. However, overnight Lady Mary had become the First Lady at Court, and I had no hesitation in consulting her. She quickly agreed to Elizabeth coming over, and said that her little sister would help to cheer her spirits in her sad loss. I did not forget to consult Lord Cromwell too, of course, and he quickly acceded to my request, as I had come to expect.

So began a weekly visit by Kat and Elizabeth, which enlivened the nursery and brought me great pleasure for the love I bore the little girl. Kat enjoyed those days too, as she was stimulated by the hustle and bustle of the great Court, and always enjoyed conversing with new people. Kat had explained to Elizabeth before they came that the new baby was most important, and that sadly his mother, Queen Jane, had died in bringing him into the world.

On her first visit, Elizabeth peeped in at the Prince swaddled in his beautiful cradle. "He's very small," she said.

"His Royal Highness is only three weeks old, my dear," I explained.

"Why is he so important then?"

"Because his father is the King's Grace," I replied.

"But *my* father is the King's Grace, isn't he?"

"Quite right, my dear, and of course that makes you important too; but you are only a girl, and Prince Edward is a boy." (I did not add: "And he's royal and you're not.")

"But how do you know he's a boy?"

The nursemaids suppressed giggles at this, but I'm one for plain speaking to children on country matters. How else will they learn? "I know he's a boy because he has the crest of a fighting cock, where girls have a cleft. Come to the cradle, and I'll show you." And I unwrapped the prince's swaddling bands and let her look at his all-important masculinity.

"He looks like baby Jesus in my picture," she said.

"That's right, my dear. How clever of you! Now, in this world of ours boys are more important than girls. And this baby boy is His Majesty's son. So one far-off day, in God's good time, when he has grown to be a man, he will be our King. That's why he's so important."

"Oh."

"That's why we must all show him great respect, and always curtsey when we come into his presence or leave him."

"Me too?"

"Most certainly, dear, because now this little baby is the second most important person in England. Only King Henry himself is more important. And you remember what deep respect we have to show to the King, don't you?"

"I give the King my best curtsey. And I mustn't shout or jump about when I meet him."

From that day on I always insisted that Elizabeth curtseyed

when she visited and left Edward's nursery. Kat reinforced this lesson in status by reminding her beforehand, until it became automatic. In fact the arrival of a younger brother came at a very opportune time for Elizabeth. At four years she was beginning to question rules and customs, and it was vital to instil in her then the fundamental fact that sons (even baby sons) are far more valuable than daughters. Some truths are unshakeable, and must not be questioned.

It wasn't till her second visit to the new nursery that Elizabeth asked me about Queen Jane's death. Kat, I believe, had been explaining to her at Richmond that the Queen had gone to heaven. It came about because Lord Edward Seymour (the new Viscount Beauchamp) had called in at the nursery, and was bemoaning the fact that the Queen had died.

"And after the long pains of childbirth she eventually sacrificed her life for the sake of this glorious Prince," he said. "Did you hear how she suffered, Lady Bryan? It was terrible. My wife was with her much of the time and has told me what a frightening ordeal it was. And so much blood lost! Doctor Butts feared losing the baby too, but this little lad, thank God, proved too strong. Dear Jane! I had hoped for further sons to follow too."

Well, Lord Edward is now Lord Protector for his nephew after good King Henry's death. But nevertheless I must say that he was very thoughtless in describing his sister's death while little Lady Elizabeth was in the room, listening wide-eyed. I was quite annoyed by it, but could not possibly intervene when the Prince of Wales's uncle was addressing me.

When his brief visit was over, Elizabeth (of course) asked, "What happened to Queen Jane?"

"Very sadly for us all she died and went to heaven to live with God and his angels."

"But why was there so much blood?"

"Well, that is what happens when ladies give birth."

"Does it hurt?"

"I'm afraid it does. But don't you worry about that, my sweet. The fact is it is God's will. Do you remember the story I used to tell you of when God was angry with Adam and Eve for disobeying Him? He said to Eve (and thus to all womankind), 'In great sorrow will you give birth'. So God has ordained this trial of childbirth, and we must accept His punishment, even when sometimes the mother dies. But remember that Queen Jane is happy now in heaven."

Elizabeth was silent then, but was soon diverted by dear Martha showing her the baby's clothes. I raised my eyebrows to Kat, and she came across to me. I quietly advised her to prepare herself for more such questioning from the little girl. It was not a big step from Prince Edward's mother to her own mother. "It's likely to be you, Kat, who has to handle it. But she's too young to be told the whole story. Please let it be gradual and gentle."

In January 1538 the Prince's establishment left the Court and moved up to Hatfield with a great escort. Elizabeth's smaller establishment came to join us there, and over the next few years it was often convenient for the two children to be housed together. Lady Mary sometimes came to stay as well, to keep in touch with her sister and brother. She was very fond of them. I remember thinking rather sadly that she should have had children of her own by then. I was kept occupied managing the household of Prince Edward, but of course I often saw Lady Elizabeth and Kat, and was able to advise Kat about the child's education.

I was sometimes on hand when Elizabeth asked difficult, family questions, which she was starting to do then. I can recall one about her grandmothers for instance, when I remember thinking, "I'm too old for all this!"

She began to learn needlework in 1538, and my suggestions were very helpful. She would sometimes sit with me in

Edward's nursery, while I supervised her sewing; I so enjoyed those sessions.

That autumn my own family suffered a shocking blow. Eighteen people, mainly distant relatives of the King's Grace, were sent to the Tower. They were executed in December for plotting to usurp the throne. Among them was my son-in-law, Sir Nicholas Carew, who for so long had been close to the King. The affair was called The Exeter Conspiracy, after the Marquess of Exeter. The evidence was scanty at best and there wasn't even a trial!

Some said that Lord Cromwell, fearful for his own position, had struck at high-ranking courtiers. When I heard the terrible news, I sank to my knees in my chamber and thanked God that at least my son Francis had not been swept up in this new wave of executions. I was so upset that early in the New Year I wrote to Lord Cromwell for reassurance about the safety and property of my distraught daughter. Eventually I did receive a short letter confirming that she had no cause to be alarmed.

Whatever the basis for the purge, it made for a very jittery atmosphere at Court. No one knew where the axe would fall next (literally).

Meanwhile, as my son informed me, the King's Grace had begun his search for a new wife, barely a month after Queen Jane's death. He looked to marry a foreign princess once more, so that he could benefit his country by forging an alliance. Master Holbein was sent to Brussels in the spring to paint the beautiful Princess Cristina of Denmark, Duchess of Milan, a sixteen-year-old widow. On seeing Master Holbein's portrait His Majesty decided to marry her, and sent an embassy to make his offer. My children, however, told me that the young Duchess had turned down this great honour on the grounds that our King changed queens too often! She told our ambassadors that her council suspected that Queen Catherine had been poisoned, Queen Anne had been put to death even though innocent, and Queen Jane had died from lack of care in childbirth. I must admit that King Henry had been most unfortunate in his marriages. I don't know what became of Princess Cristina, but if, God willing, she lived on, she would surely have felt some justification because our King was to make three more marriages in quick succession over the following five years!

After that disappointing setback, Cromwell persuaded the King to consider a bride from Germany. The two rival Catholic powers of France and Spain were healing their differences, and could not be played off against each other any longer. England needed a Protestant ally, and the Duchy of Cleves was selected because the Duke had two unmarried sisters. Lord Cromwell was convinced of the political advantages of the match, and he sent busy Master Holbein off to Cleves. I was told that Lord Cromwell advised the King that Lady Anne of Cleves was much praised for her beauty of face and figure. And Master Holbein's miniature portrait raised the King's expectations so much that he generously waived the need for a dowry: that dispensation overcame the Duke of Cleves's serious misgivings about his sister's future as Queen of England. Eventually Anne of Cleves arrived in England just after Christmas 1539. My old friend, Lady Browne, had been appointed chief lady of the bedchamber, so she met our future Queen soon after her arrival. She later told me that she'd feared immediately that Anne of Cleves would not suit our discriminating King.

"You wouldn't believe what un-shapely, unbecoming clothes she was wearing, Lady Bryan," she said. "And frankly her looks had no feminine allure to attract King Henry. He's quick to notice such shortcomings."

Lady Browne was soon proved right. I heard later from the same source that Lady Anne was totally ignorant of sexual matters! She was incredulous when her English ladies-in-waiting tried to enlighten her. Furthermore, she spoke only her own language, and had no knowledge of music or dancing. All in all, she was a complete mismatch with our lusty and cultured King.

The King's Grace could not send Lady Anne back to Cleves for fear of alienating the German states. He felt compelled to go through with the marriage ceremony in January, and was always polite to the lady herself. However, he could not bring himself to have sexual relations with her. He was furious at his predicament, and he directed his anger at Lord Cromwell. I was conscious of God's great mercy, in that my son, Francis, had not been involved in the Cleves marriage negotiations.

The King rapidly sought a divorce. Fortunately, an assembly of bishops of the Church of England found that the marriage was invalid, because it had not been consummated, and because the King had not undertaken it of his own free will. Queen Anne of Cleves wisely assented to the divorce in July, and lives on in England to this day as a wealthy lady with several royal manors.

On 28th July 1540, Lord Cromwell was beheaded on Tower Hill. On the same day, the King's Grace married the nineteen-year-old Katherine Howard.

I haven't mentioned Lady Elizabeth for some time, but the King's marriages were all part of the background to her life. Kat was her Lady Governess then, and it was her task to keep Elizabeth up-to-date on who the queen was, in case they were summoned to Court. I seem to remember they did attend Court that Easter to meet Queen Katherine Howard, but I didn't go as Prince Edward was only two, and His Majesty was fearful for his son's health with long journeys to the crowded Court.

According to my good contacts at Court, the King's Grace was deeply infatuated with Queen Katherine Howard. He remained so until November of the following year, 1541. Then shocking evidence of the Queen's immorality came to light and she was beheaded at the Tower in February 1542 along with others who were implicated.

Finally, after all our great King's matrimonial woes, he found a happy ending. Katherine Parr had twice been widowed, and was thirty when the king honoured her with his hand in marriage on July 12th 1543. Lady Mary and Lady Elizabeth (who was then nearly ten) were summoned to Hampton Court for the private ceremony. I'd have loved to have been there, but Prince Edward was too precious to come to Court and mingle with the crowds. In fact, although my role as his Lady Mistress was hugely important, it meant that I felt more confined and cloistered than when I had looked after his sisters. I did fret about that sometimes.

However, the following month, with His Majesty's permission, the new Queen Catherine invited all three of his children to Windsor Castle for a few weeks. This Queen was a gracious and warm-hearted lady. She was only four years older than Lady Mary, with whom she enjoyed a great friendship. She had experience as a stepmother, because she had helped to bring up her second husband's son and daughter. She really enjoyed the company of children, and they enjoyed hers. That August I was so glad to see that she made an effort to get to know Prince Edward and Lady Elizabeth. They needed family affection and she gave it to them. The Queen was also interested in learning and education, and the King's Grace respected her understanding. He consulted her about his younger children's upbringing. They were both clever children, and it was decided about that time that when Edward became six in October he would leave my care. The King declared that it was time for the Prince 'to leave the women'. Some tutors from Cambridge University were chosen for the little boy, and Master Grindal of Cambridge was chosen as Elizabeth's tutor.

I knew that it wouldn't be long before I rarely saw the royal children. I had no fears for Lady Mary – as she was now a woman of twenty-seven! – nor, of course, for England's Treasure, the Prince of Wales.

But I did take Kat aside in a quiet moment at Windsor. Until then I'd often been on hand for her to consult, but now I would be leaving the Court altogether, my role completed. The last service I could do for Lady Elizabeth was to impress on Kat the need to watch over her.

"I'm looking to the future, Kat." I said. "Lady Mary will always have her cousin, the King of Spain, to protect her interests from afar. Prince Edward, of course, is worshipped by our whole nation. And, in particular (as I should know!), he has those powerful Seymour brothers hovering round him. But our Lady Elizabeth will have no-one of importance to champion her. You've done so well by her. She's very accomplished now, I can see. She was such a forward little girl, wasn't she? Under you and me she's fulfilled that early promise. She loves and depends on you, Kat. Just try to stay with her for another six or seven years until she gets married. Then you will be able to retire like me! Come and visit me sometimes, Kat, won't you? You've been such a good friend."

So my time – many years in fact – supervising King Henry's children was coming to an end. I had loved them all, and for me it was a happy ending to see my three charges coming together as a family, united by their kind stepmother. I thanked the Blessed Virgin that She had watched over me and guarded those precious children in my care. She helped me protect their vulnerable infancy from dreadful plagues and fevers. She helped me bring them safely to this happy conclusion. I knew that they would always be a comfort and support to each other. So (at seventy-three!) I could retire sadly, thankfully and confidently – a real mixture of feelings!

Since then I have lived with my two children in turn at their country manors, so I'm still travelling round! I missed being a Lady Mistress, especially at first, when I had more energy than now. As you've heard, I was used to organising an establishment, and a royal one at that. I had plenty of ideas and experience to put to good use in my daughter's and son's households. I particularly prided myself on managing the servants, and supervising their allotted tasks. It's important to maintain standards; these days they can start to slip, unless someone with authority makes a point of keeping watch. Especially if the housekeeper is not up to her job, as was the case in my daughter's manor. And I had to dismiss my son's laundresses, whose shortcomings were all too clear.

Now, isn't it strange how a chance conversation can mean a new turning-point in life? One afternoon in 1544 my daughter, Lady Elizabeth Carew, came to admire my tapestry work. I was still an excellent needlewoman (although I had to wear glasses by then), and she appreciated the cushions I'd made.

Then she said, "By the way, Mother, I've been chatting to Francis and we've agreed that you should write down your memories of King Henry's children! You could start with Prince Edward, and then move on to Lady Mary and Lady Elizabeth. Their story is vital to our history."

"What? I've never thought of it like that," I replied. "Is there a precedent for it?"

"Maybe not, Mother. But customs are always progressing aren't they? Think how useful your experience would be to a future Lady Mistress. In fact the sooner you start the better," she concluded with a determined flourish.

"But I've never written a memoir!"

"Not yet! But we all know what a wonderful memory you've got. With such detailed observations too. And you're such a good letter-writer. I think writing comes easily to you. It will just flow!"

"Well I do enjoy writing letters. But –"

"That's just it, Mother. You would *enjoy* this project. We'd all be so proud of you. Francis has even sent you some fine quality paper to encourage you to make a start. He's sent this letter for you too."

Well, I didn't often receive letters from Francis. He had great talents, but he was not a regular correspondent. It was a brief letter, but I was most touched to read of his confidence in me as a historian.

He wrote: 'Your reminiscences, my dear Mother, will be the culmination of your long years of devoted service to the crown. They will be read in high places, and will no doubt shed further lustre on the Court careers of your children and grandchildren.'

That appeal to burnish our family's status converted me to the idea. To be honest, I was quite excited to have a new role.

My daughter then showed me to a table by the window in her small parlour. There she had set out the paper, pens and ink. "If I were you, Mother, I would make a point of coming here every morning while you are staying with me. I am sure it will be a long piece of work, and will take many months to complete. Don't feel rushed, will you? You will need to use your most careful hand-writing. And whenever you feel weary of writing, I need a large new wall-hanging for my chamber and would be so grateful for your tapestry skills."

And so I have set all these memories down. Very sadly my daughter died last year and I nearly gave up these memoirs then. But Francis told me she would have wanted me to finish them. And I think it has actually helped my grief to immerse myself in these past years. It has taken me nearly three years, and I am proud to have finished it today.

This one about Elizabeth is my last, as she is the least important. Also, I was in charge of her for less time than Mary or Edward. But, strangely, she meant the most to me. Perhaps it was because she needed me most.

Margaret Bryan
November 2nd A.D. 1547
The First Year of the Reign of King Edward VI

Post-script: I have decided to give these memoirs to my grand-daughter Anne Carew for safe-keeping. She is twenty-seven now, and is betrothed to a fine courtier and MP, Sir Nicholas Throckmorton. She has always shown great interest in my writings, and I know she will treasure them carefully. My dearly-loved son, Francis, has always been too much in demand to look at my memoirs. No doubt when he has retired he will enjoy giving them his attention.

PART 2

Katherine Ashley

They say there's a Chinese curse: 'May you live in interesting times.'

Well, as you will hear, I've certainly done that! Some of it was frightening but most of it has been a great blessing.

I was christened Katherine Champernowne, but have always been known as Kat. My claim to fame is that I've been lucky enough to serve Her Grace Queen Elizabeth for nearly all her life. When I first joined her household in July 1536, there was no question of her ever becoming Queen. She was two years and ten months old, her poor mother had just been beheaded, and she herself had been stripped of her royal status and was known simply as 'Lady Elizabeth'. She had been officially declared illegitimate, with no place in the Succession. Miraculously, twenty-two years later, she became Queen of England! I am still thankfully in her service now in this Year of Our Lord 1559, and have served her longer than almost anyone else.

So I've decided that it's for me, the person who knows her best, to tell the story of those years. Her path to the throne was hard and dangerous, and was won by Divine Providence allied with her inherent courage, acute intelligence and political awareness. Her achievements should be put on record. I believe I have a duty to bear witness to what I know, and leave it in the state archives as my testament to my beloved Queen.

I wasn't born to Court life – far from it! As far as Devonshire, in fact. My father, Sir Philip Champernowne, held a small ancestral manor there. We were not nobility; he was just a Knight of the Shires. But my parents educated me well, and I learnt Greek, Latin and French and could play the lute. I was certainly thankful for that in the years to follow. For, sadly, our fortunes did not prosper. My father, God rest him, had academic interests but was not good at managing property. And eventually it only took a couple of bad harvests and a dishonest steward to devour a large part of the estate.

I came into royal service in a roundabout way. I've explained that we Champernownes were not well off. However, my younger sister, Joan, had been contracted as a child to marry an old family friend, Anthony Denny. He had been in London for some years making a career at Court, and most successfully too. My parents (who could not provide me with much of a dowry) hoped that there might be opportunities in London for someone like me with my superior education: if not at Court, then perhaps in one of the many noble households there. We also hoped that by widening my social circle I might find a suitable husband! In June 1536, when I was twenty-five, Joan and I (with our mother too, of course) came to stay with Anthony's parents in London. The purpose of our visit was partly to discuss the wedding, but also to ask Anthony if he could exert any influence to find a position for me. Courtiers get such requests all the time, but Anthony kindly undertook to make enquiries.

Now, as it happened, Anthony had started his Court life in the service of Sir Francis Bryan, the son of Lady Margaret Bryan. She held the office of Lady Mistress to Princess Elizabeth, the daughter of King Henry and Queen Anne Boleyn. So those were the links that led me to the little Princess.

By 1536 Anthony had been appointed Keeper of Whitehall Palace, which was a most responsible job. He still often met Sir Francis there, and chanced to be with him one day in June, when Sir Francis received a worried letter from his mother at Hunsdon Manor. Lady Bryan was complaining how difficult her job had become since Queen Anne's execution the previous month. She didn't know how on earth she or the servants should treat Elizabeth now. Sir John Shelton was being uncooperative, and she had no-one suitable to confide in or share her burdens. The situation was most irregular, and frankly she didn't think that she could cope much longer.

Sir Francis (as I later realised) received far more letters from his mother than he ever replied to, but this one did stir him. He read it out to Anthony in the privacy of his room.

"Yet another problem: my poor old mother is in a state! Her position in the royal nursery brings the Bryan family added respect, you know. I wouldn't want her to give it up just because of one awkward patch. Mind you, luckily she adores that child. But I still think I'd better find her a helper. She needs educated company, not just those nursemaids."

Anthony, the dear man, immediately thought of me! As he told it, Anthony said,

"Look no further, Sir Francis! I may have the solution."

"What's that?"

"My sister-in-law to be, Katherine Champernowne, Joan's sister, could serve your purpose. She's twenty-four, excellent company and, what's more, highly educated! She loves children, has a cheerful nature and plenty of energy. She's in London now and I know she's hoping to find a position somewhere. I have to say she'd need a salary of some kind, as her father is not wealthy."

"Oh, I daresay that could be found," Sir Francis replied. "Well I'd better see the lady. She might make all the difference in helping my mother settle down again. And it would get my sister off my back too. I'm off to France with the embassy in three days. Bring her to my room tomorrow morning."

When Anthony relayed this momentous summons to us, my mother insisted on coming too, as Sir Francis had a reputation as a restless risk-taker. He was very close to the King and arranged hunting and gambling parties for him. Anthony warned us that Sir Francis had been badly shaken by the sudden execution of two of his close colleagues in the privy chamber (they were among those convicted of adultery with Queen Anne).

"Don't expect Sir Francis to give us much time tomorrow, or to express the usual courtesies," Anthony explained. "Also, Kat, for heaven's sake don't ask Sir Francis any questions! Remember we're just applicants for his patronage. You must suppress your inquisitive spirit tomorrow."

The next day Sir Francis was indeed quite short with us. He looked me up and down and fired a few questions at me and my mother. Then he said, "Your job will be to be a friend and companion to my mother as much as to care for the Princess – I mean the little girl. See to it that my mother doesn't upset herself. The King would not be happy if she left her post. And we certainly don't want to cast a shadow on his contentment with the new Queen, do we?"

I curtseyed a thank you, as I inferred that I'd been accepted.

"Of course, your appointment will have to go through Cromwell," he continued. "Anything to do with the royal children has to be approved by him. Although in the case of this child, I don't really know whether that still applies. Never mind that. I shall stick to current procedures. Cromwell trusts my judgement, just as I trust Anthony's. You may consider the matter settled, Miss Champerton. And be ready to start at Hunsdon in about two weeks, as soon as you hear from Cromwell."

"Yes, sir. Thank you, sir."

"I'll reply sympathetically to my mother and inform her that I've found someone to assist her. That should anchor her meanwhile, eh, Anthony?"

"I'm sure some kind words from you will reassure Lady Bryan, sir. I'm sorry she's distressed, but it's not surprising. After all, her world has been turned upside down by the recent events."

"I suppose it has," he said, "although she's a long way from the eye of the storm." He was silent a moment, then abruptly rang a bell and an usher came in to see us out.

When we'd left the Palace precincts, I was so excited at my prospects that I flung my arms round my dear mother and she wrapped hers around me. I would have danced a jig but we were in crowded streets. Anyway, even though I was a country girl, I did know better than to embarrass Anthony! I just seized his hand and kissed it with many a 'thank you' for being my benefactor.

When we returned to the Dennys' house, Anthony's parents and my sister were very happy for me. My mother, though, became a bit tearful at the thought of losing me. She would soon be losing Joan too, and would be far away in Devonshire 'pining for my girls' as she put it!

Anthony soon had to go back to work at the Palace, but before that he cautioned me that the establishment I was bound for was a quiet one.

"Don't expect the bustle and excitement of Court. Occasionally you may visit the Court, but the royal manors are much smaller and have a slower pace of life. Mind you, they're very comfortable, with plenty of servants to look after you, of course!"

"I expect I'll feel spoilt," I said. "London is so exciting, but I do love country life. Do you know Lady Bryan?"

He shook his head. "I've heard she's a kind lady who's very good at her job. Treat her with respect, won't you? I'm sure you'll learn a lot from her. There's no doubt it's a good opportunity for you. Lady Bryan's establishment may be a bit of a backwater, but it's a safe place to learn about royal etiquette and customs. It might be a stepping-stone to a place at Court in the future."

"Oh I'm not ambitious to climb higher!" I replied. "I'll enjoy what I've got, and try to be a credit to your faith in me!"

"Good luck, Kat. I'll let you know when I hear from Cromwell, so be ready to leave at once."

After that everything was a blur as I gathered my few possessions together and bought some new clothes. Anthony's mother kindly advised me on what would be suitable. And my mother gave me a bag of paper and pens so that I could write to her and my father, which I often did.

Cromwell approved my appointment, as Sir Francis had predicted, and in no time at all I was leaving London and heading for Hunsdon Manor. I rode with two guardsmen who had been detached from the post-rider's escort. We took two days over the journey; luckily it was an easy time of year for travelling, although it was rather dusty. I was most excited by the sudden turn my life had taken, and I was longing to meet my new companions.

I remember my arrival clearly, although it's twenty-three years ago now. Those dear manors were to become a home from home for me, and Hunsdon was one of my favourites. It looked beautiful that July afternoon. My escort took me through the gatehouse and up to the front door, where we dismounted and they handed me over to a courteous manservant.

"You're expected, Miss Champernowne," he said. "I'm to take you first to Sir John Shelton, who runs this manor. But I'll let Lady Bryan know you've arrived."

He led me to a parlour, where I waited alone for a while. Eventually Sir John came in from hunting. As I curtseyed, he said, "Yes; I've had orders from on high to include you in this establishment. How I'm expected to increase the nursery staff on my meagre budget I do not know! William!" he shouted back through the doorway. "Fetch a nursemaid down to take this lady upstairs."

"Lady Bryan has sent Martha down, Sir John," William replied.

"Whatever."

I curtseyed again and thanked him for his time.

"Are you being impertinent, madam?"

"Certainly not, Sir John," I stammered. "I meant only politeness." But he turned away and I felt abashed.

William beckoned me to follow him into the hall, and whispered, "Not much love lost between Sir John and the nursery, milady."

At the foot of the stairs stood a smiling middle-aged woman wearing the apron of a nursemaid with the royal cipher on her sleeve. She curtseyed to me and said, "Good afternoon, Miss Champernowne. Welcome to Hunsdon. My name is Martha and I am to take you up to your room. William will bring your travel bag."

"Thank you, Martha," I said with relief. "You're very kind."

Up the dark staircase we went, and then she opened a door. "You've been given your own chamber, milady. It is connected to the nursery."

It was very small but had a window and a fireplace, and looked homely.

"Lady Bryan thought you'd like to wash and change after your journey," she continued, "so I've left you a bowl of water and a towel. When you're ready, come through to the nursery. She's looking forward to meeting you."

I sat down for a few minutes to recover because I was afraid I'd made a bad impression on Sir John. Then I knelt to thank God for my safe arrival, and ask for His support for my new position, and for friendly faces. When I was ready, I tapped on the nursery door and stepped through.

It was a big room: two nursemaids were folding linen, two others were playing ball with a little girl, and in a large chair by a window sat an elderly lady working at a tapestry screen. They all looked towards me. The nursemaids stood still and then dropped little curtseys as I walked towards the elderly lady, whereupon I also curtseyed. It was a nervous moment for me. I had to get on with Lady Bryan. Would I find it easy or not? She was of a different generation, and had been in her post for twenty years so was likely to be set in her ways. I, the junior newcomer, was the one who would have to adapt. Even if she was severe, I was the apprentice and needed to learn from her long years of experience.

Lady Bryan was rather plump in build (like me). She sat very erect in a brown linen dress and with a brown cap perched on her white hair. She told me later that she too had been anxious about taking a stranger into her nursery, but at the same time she was longing for a cheerful, supportive companion. Her face looked determined but kind.

"Welcome, Miss Champernowne," she said with a smile. "We've been expecting you. We saw you arrive in the courtyard some time ago, but I hear Sir John kept you waiting."

"Thank you, milady. Yes, I'm afraid he was out when I arrived."

"I hope he was civil to you."

"Well, I'm afraid I got off on the wrong foot with him."

"Don't let that upset you, my dear. I'm sure it was nothing personal. Sir John's manners are not the most sensitive. I hope he remembered them enough to welcome you as a gentlewoman."

"I think his budget was uppermost in his mind, milady."

"Yes, that's Sir John! Well, perhaps it's a good thing that you've got the measure of him so soon. He certainly hasn't been much support to me in these difficult months. More on that another time; little pitchers have long ears. Martha, bring a chair for Miss Champernowne. Come over here to meet her, everyone!"

The little girl came eagerly up to inspect me with a very direct gaze and no shyness. She had reddish-gold curls, fair skin and dark eyes.

"A curtsey please, Elizabeth, for Miss Champernowne," Lady Bryan prompted her.

The child held out her skirts and bobbed down and up. I curtseyed in return. "Have you come to live with us?" she asked.

"Yes, milady."

"Can you play chasing?"

I nodded. "Perhaps we can play tomorrow."

"Why not now?"

"It's too late, my dear," intervened Lady Bryan. "And Miss Champernowne is tired after her long journey. Now I must introduce the servants. This is Martha, who's the head nursemaid, and there's Sally, Meg, and Catherine – good girls all."

There was a knock at the door and two groomsmen brought in trays of food. The nursemaids sat down with the child and shared out the food.

"We'll be in my chamber, Martha," said Lady Bryan. She then led me to a room opposite the nursery, where we sat down.

"I won't bother you with a lot of information today," she said. "But you'll want to know about mealtimes. The Princess – oh, I must stop calling her that! – Lady Elizabeth eats in the nursery with the nursemaids, but you and I eat downstairs in the Great Hall with the rest of the household for dinner and supper. You, as a gentlewoman, will join me on the high table with Sir John and Lady Shelton. Sometimes Sir John will have a hunting friend or two as well. When Lady Mary is here, she sits with us, of course, but she's at Court at present. Now, you've met Sir John, but I must tell you before supper about poor Lady Shelton. She was aunt to Queen Anne, and had to go to the Tower to wait on the Queen before attending her niece's beheading. It was all a terrible shock to her, of course, and she's still having nightmares, and is very jittery. She told me about it when she got back here, and I've tried to calm her down, but she's not very cheerful company at present. So don't expect her to be a sociable hostess.

"There's one other vital thing to tell you," she added. "I've decided we must not mention the late Queen Anne at all, nor refer to anyone else's mother. It will be safest if Elizabeth forgets her mother. All she knows is that her mother is very ill. She doesn't often mention her any more. That's enough for now. Supper will be in an hour, and a maid will knock on your door then. Sir John is a stickler for punctuality, though he may not apply it to himself. He makes the most of any excuse to take me down a peg and criticize the nursery!"

Everyone stared up at me as I took my seat at the high table that evening. There were about thirty people in the hall, plus the servers. Sir John intoned the grace, and then everyone started talking, and the focus was off me and onto the food! We always had good food and plenty of it. I felt very thankful for being so comfortably provided for, and for finding Lady Bryan so welcoming.

After supper she introduced me to a pale Lady Shelton, who said, "We are at a low ebb here, Miss Champernowne. This establishment is not what it was. We have come down in the world."

Sir John interrupted her with, "It's a damn sight worse than that! When I undertook this post, I expected to be heading the Household of a Prince of Wales. Plus a Duke of York or two to follow. Now I'm stuck here with one female bastard."

Over the following weeks I was all eyes and ears, watching and listening to Lady Bryan as she confidently managed the nursery. She was respected by all the servants (women *and* men) and never had to raise her voice. What was rarer was that they all liked her, and the nursemaids often told me what a considerate mistress she was. I could see at once that Lady Elizabeth loved her, and wasn't a bit frightened of her, which was unusual in nurseries. My own dear parents (and others I knew of) used to pinch and slap us every day to train us in the way we should go.

And, I may tell you, that happened in the highest families in the land. Because, years later, when Lady Elizabeth and I lived with Lady Jane Grey (who was the daughter of King Henry's own niece) she used to tell us about her treatment at the hands of her parents: whatever she was doing when in their presence, they would taunt, threaten, pinch and cuff her, so she hardly had a moment's peace. Even if she was just sitting silently, that would happen! I was struck by a phrase she used, 'I think I am in Hell.'

But that wasn't Lady Bryan's way at all. She was most unusual, and I came to admire her for it. She taught me that very young children should not have force used against them, as they could not properly understand right from wrong. Even when they were older, words in the long run would be better than the whip!

Certainly little Elizabeth was a good advertisement for Lady Bryan's principles. At nearly three she was an outgoing, happy and confident child. She had a fine command of language, and was eager to learn; she already knew her numbers and was starting to recognise letters, and very much enjoyed doing so. But she was not just 'bookish'. She loved her riding lessons, and already had a good ear for music, which she danced to very sweetly. She really was 'a little love', as my granny used to say! Her manners were of a particularly high standard, and that was a department on which Lady Bryan put a lot of emphasis.

"It's important for all high-born girls," she said, "and essential for a princess." She paused. "And even though she's no longer a princess, she is a King's daughter, and she will need to show herself as such to stake her claim in the world."

Far-sighted words, Lady B, which I did not forget.

I don't mind telling you that I, too, learnt a lot about Court manners and formalities from Lady Bryan. I was keen to learn, as I didn't want to let down our establishment and its protégée by appearing too much of a Devon bumpkin! It was straightforward enough at the country manors, but when we had to go to Court I would certainly have been found wanting. The gradations of rank were so important there. If in doubt about someone's relative status, it was always best to show too much courtesy rather than too little.

By the way, I wouldn't want you to think that Elizabeth never misbehaved. Of course she wanted to have her own way, and was sometimes demanding, impatient or downright disobedient. When that did happen, Lady Bryan would calmly tick her off, and the nursemaids would give her disapproving and disappointed looks, so the child felt the weight of the whole room was against her. Sometimes Lady Bryan would then leave the nursery for a time to underline her displeasure. It seemed to be very effective, because Elizabeth craved love and approval.

I quickly became devoted to Elizabeth, and she accepted me as one of her 'family'. She was soon calling me Kat, and Lady Bryan followed suit. I was anxious that there should be no question of me being a rival to Lady Bryan for the little girl's affections, and I took care to take a back seat when we were both in the nursery. In fact Lady Bryan often called me forward to play with Elizabeth.

"I'm too old to get down on the floor and play skittles and suchlike as I used to do with Lady Mary," she would say. "You do the scampering and hiding, Kat!"

We had a few administrative nuisances at that time. There were the questions about Elizabeth's clothes, and where she should eat, and, last but not least (to me!), my salary. Elizabeth was wearing a very tight dress one morning, and I asked Martha to change her.

"There aren't any bigger ones, milady," she explained. "Lady Bryan knows about this and has taken it up with Sir John, but she's got no help from that quarter!" She then leaned forward and whispered to me, "Queen Anne used to send us the new clothes. We haven't had any for three months. To be honest, we're at sixes and sevens here, not knowing whether Lady Elizabeth (bless her!) is still royal or whether she can claim the grand sort of clothes she used to get. We servants have been afraid for our jobs but your coming, milady, has made us feel more secure. We heard you were appointed by Master Cromwell himself. Before that we feared the child might be packed off to live with the Boleyns in Kent, and our whole household would be disbanded!"

Soon after that, Sir John Shelton made a totally impractical demand that Elizabeth should eat her meals at the high table in the hall. She was much too young of course, and Lady Bryan refused. I well remember one dinner-time when Sir John began shouting and criticising Lady Bryan's suitability for her job! All the servants could hear, as he meant them to. I was seething. Lady Bryan went red, but she kept her dignity and convinced Sir John to retire to the private parlour to continue the debate. I went back upstairs to the nursery, and let off steam to the nursemaids. We were all ready with sympathy and praise when a flustered Lady Bryan rejoined us and sank into a chair.

"I'm too old for such altercations and insults," she burst out. "But there's only me to stand up for the child. And stand up I most certainly will." She put a firm comforting arm around Elizabeth, who had come up to her chair looking frightened.

She told me she was going to her chamber to write a letter to Cromwell, asking for official guidance on all her problems. "Then at least, we'll know where we are, Kat," she said. "I can't carry on like this!"

I said how much I admired her, and I was sure her letter

would be well received in London. "You'll win through, milady. Please don't worry."

She wrote an excellent, detailed letter covering all her difficulties, which she kindly read out to me before sending. It ended by praising Elizabeth, which I thought was courageous because the child seemed officially to be invisible at that time.

Within the week, she had a reply from Cromwell himself. It established Elizabeth's continuing high status, empowered the Lady Mistress to order all necessary new clothes, and agreed to the child eating in the nursery. Cromwell expressed regret that the Lady Mistress had suffered any anxiety on these matters. He hoped she was in her usual good health.

Lady Bryan opened and read the letter in private, and then entered the nursery beaming. "I have good news to share with you all," she announced. "Listen to Cromwell's words."

She read the letter to us, and I couldn't help clapping with joy! The nursemaids and Elizabeth joined in, and we all ended up laughing in relief and delight.

Our post-rider, Joseph, told Martha that evening that he had also delivered a letter from Cromwell to Sir John. We were never made aware of its contents directly, but we certainly inferred that Sir John had been put in his place. The next day a request (!) came for Lady Bryan to honour Sir John with her presence in the parlour. There he apologised to her for having encroached on her prerogatives, and assured her that there would be no more 'misunderstandings'.

I suspect that he said it through gritted teeth, but the fact is he never set his will against hers again. So, with two waves of Cromwell's pen, the whole atmosphere of our establishment lightened!

My own personal grievance was that after six weeks I had still not received any salary. Emboldened by Lady Bryan's success, I also wrote a letter to Sir Thomas Cromwell. I explained that a salary had been promised to me, and I couldn't manage without it as my father had a very small income and could not afford to subsidise me. Lady Bryan kindly (and probably crucially) added a note to say how indispensable I had become to her. I soon had a short letter from Cromwell's secretary promising that a regular salary would be paid. And so it was.

"Now I can afford some clothes suitable for Court," I told Lady Bryan.

"It's unlikely we'll be showing our faces at Court any day soon, I'm afraid," Lady Bryan replied.

There she was wrong. That October, news came of a rebellion in the North by those who wanted to restore the Catholic religion. One of their aims was to restore Lady Mary, a firm Catholic, as the King's heir. Lady Mary was staying with us at Ashridge at the time, and frightening rumours came thick and fast that the rebels were gathering forces to march South towards London. Our establishment was suddenly ordered to go to Whitehall Palace as soon as possible for security. In great haste we did so, taking three days on the journey. Fear was in the air, and the roads to London were full. When our convoy finally reached the Palace, Lady Mary and her retinue were swiftly bowed inside, while the rest of us waited at the gates in the rain. Lady Bryan sent a messenger to summon her daughter, Lady Elizabeth Carew. She came down, hugged her mother and spoke to the guards, and then led us to the apartments she had prepared for us.

"I'm sorry they're so small, mother," she said. "It's been such short notice and the Palace has had a great influx of people! I've done my best, but status counts for everything here, as you know. I'm afraid that at Court this little girl's status doesn't carry much weight now. I've had the fires going for you, so at least you will be cosy soon."

Our lodgings were a bit cramped, and towards the back of the Palace, but I had the advantage of being used to a small home. Poor Lady Bryan had been used to grander quarters on her previous visits to Court over the years, so for her it was quite a come-down. At least Lady Carew had managed to procure a bedroom for her mother. The rest of us female staff slept on pallets on the nursery floor. Lady Bryan and I ate in a huge dining-room with other Court officials. I felt rather a country cousin there, as I'd had no time to have smart dresses made at Ashridge before our sudden journey to London. I always sat next to Lady Bryan, but with different people on my other side at every meal. I saw it as an opportunity to get to know them, and to learn about how the Court worked. Some of them simply ignored me, and one lady said sharply, "Speak when you're spoken to, my girl!" Most of the Court officials were men, and as a new, unmarried arrival from the country I had to put up with a lot of stares, sly pinches and impudence. My Devon accent was much mimicked, and Lady Bryan's put-downs cut no ice with them!

But others were friendlier, and began to question me about my job and little Elizabeth and Lady Mary, and what I thought of the new religion. Lady Bryan would often nudge me then as a reminder to guard my tongue. She had warned me to take great care not to cast my opinions about.

"There are lots of ears at Court, Kat," she'd said. "Not all benevolent. There's money to be earned by informers, and your innocent words, my dear, could be twisted and used against you. Our little Elizabeth has enemies here, you know."

"Surely no-one could see her as a threat, milady?" I replied.

"Not in herself now. And, of course, being female she could never become a sovereign. But looking ahead, say, fourteen years hence, she will marry and may well have a son. That is her potential threat in competition for the Succession. This wretched Succession problem already has a lot of victims, as I have seen firsthand." She paused, and then went on with a smile, "Now, if Queen Jane can produce four or five sons, that will be an end of it!"

Poor Lady Bryan had a more immediate worry at that time. She was afraid that Elizabeth's memory of her mother might re-surface at Court, particularly if she encountered the King. Apparently, until Queen Anne's death, portraits of the King and Queen had hung in the nursery side by side, so their daughter had of course associated them together. We would all be in disgrace, she said, if the little girl blurted out any question about her mother.

To be honest, there was nothing we could do to prevent that completely. But I tried to reassure Lady Bryan by suggesting new topics to steer any conversation away from pitfalls. It was strange to me (and quite chilling) that she was so frightened of the King; I had gathered from Cromwell's consents to our requests that Lady Bryan was in high favour.

We spent several weeks cooped up in Whitehall Palace. It had some spacious and beautiful privy gardens, but our establishment was not permitted to enjoy them. Lady Bryan did manage to gain access to a small courtyard where Elizabeth could take exercise. I think we were all longing to get back to our country manors, though we knew we were in London for our own protection.

And then the King did summon Elizabeth to see him! The northern rebellion was over (at least for the time being) and the stressful atmosphere relaxed. I suspected that Lady Mary, now well back in the King's favour, may have suggested to him that, as Elizabeth was at court and much loved by Lady Mary, he might like to appraise her for himself. We had only an hour's notice of this royal summons. What a rush it was to get ready! Lady Bryan was very nervous, but bravely assumed an air of calm confidence. And she and Elizabeth set off hand-in-hand in their best clothes, led by a gentleman usher of the King's own privy chamber.

All of us in the nursery knew what a lot was at stake for us in this meeting. If the King's Grace was displeased, then our whole establishment might be dissolved and all our jobs gone. I'm not a natural worrier, but I remember the tense atmosphere that morning in our cramped quarters. Sally even began to cry as we waited. It was only about thirty minutes, but seemed much longer. Finally the gentleman usher banged on the door and announced, "The Lady Elizabeth and Lady Bryan," and we learnt the good news from Lady Bryan's face. She generously said we could all take pride in the way the child had acquitted herself.

"But it was Elizabeth's own delightful character, her poise and her forwardness in speech that won the King over," she explained. "She did so well, didn't you my dear? Thank heavens for that! Without realising how important those few minutes were, she's done herself a power of good."

We all petted and praised Elizabeth, and hugged each other and laughed with relief after the tension.

A few days later we were released from Whitehall and set off for Eltham, ready to rejoin the Court at Greenwich for Christmas. It was there that King Henry displayed his second daughter to the whole Court: her dinner was taken in the great dining-room with the King and Queen. They, of course, were at the high table with Lady Mary and members of their Privy Chambers. But Elizabeth was not far away, sitting between Lady Bryan and me. A lot of gazes were directed at her, and the point of her presence was not lost upon the observant Court. She had clearly been welcomed back into the royal fold. The King's Grace summoned her several times that holiday to visit and chat with him, and showed himself very fond of her.

At supper times that Christmas, Elizabeth ate in her nursery, and Lady Bryan and I did not eat with Their Majesties. But when we ate our supper with Court officials (as at Whitehall), I was no longer rebuked, pinched or teased. I began to enjoy Court life with so many new people to chat to, and all the news and gossip flying about. Anthony Denny sought me out, very pleased that Lady Elizabeth had been graciously received by the King. I seized his hands and thanked him for introducing me to my new life.

That was the time when I fell in love with a handsome gentleman usher who paid me a lot of attention. He had a very smart uniform too! I told Martha about him, but she found out on the servants' grapevine that he was married. So, with some tears, I had to forget him. My nomadic life gave me few opportunities to find a husband.

There was some whispered worry at Court that Queen Jane was not pregnant, and imploring prayers were said in Greenwich Chapel that Their Majesties would soon be blessed with male children.

We spent happy months at Hatfield after Christmas, and we were there when news came in March that the Queen was expecting a baby!

"Our prayers have been answered!" exclaimed Lady Bryan, and there was hope in the air again.

Those were peaceful, undisturbed spring days, with Lady Elizabeth growing, learning, and noticing more and more. That was when I got to know her Boleyn cousins, Catherine and Henry Carey, who sometimes came on short visits. They were fourteen and eleven, lively and energetic children, but also patient when amusing Elizabeth and playing childish games out-of-doors, which she adored. She had known them all her life, and she loved them and cried when they left.

"I want to come with you," she would sob. "Why can't I?"

The Carey children would look across at Lady Bryan, whose stock reply was: "It's because you're the King's daughter, my dear. You're too important to go visiting. You must stay safely at home."

Catherine and Henry would hug their little cousin and promise to come again before long. Their governess and grooms would then escort them home, and they would wave goodbyes as they rode away through the gatehouse.

Elizabeth, of course, was wonderfully looked after and cherished, but it struck me at those partings how deprived she was of the company of other children. It would have been so good for her to play with others of her own age, and she would have had such fun. She was very friendly, and sociable by nature, but spent her childhood only with us adults.

I remember saying to Lady Bryan, "She may live in a palace, but she's missing what children like best! Couldn't we ask the housekeeper's son and daughter to join her sometimes? She's been pleading with me to play with them."

Lady Bryan was quite shocked at the idea, and I apologised and bowed to her great experience of the royal rule-book. Fraternisation with the lower ranks of society could not be allowed. (Even gentlemen's children would be frowned on.) She explained that playmates from the nobility might in theory be allowed, but our wandering life was not suited to the building of friendships. She agreed that Elizabeth was unlucky in having no siblings or cousins of her own age who could have been allowed to share her household.

We moved on to Hatfield in April, and as the Queen's pregnancy slowly took its healthy course, Lady Bryan began to wonder whether the new baby would affect her own position.

"I'm well into old age now, Kat," she said one day. "I'm all of sixty-seven and I know I get more tired, and I fret more too. I can manage Elizabeth for a couple more years with your help and our good servants, but to take on a new baby would be a *very* different matter."

"I'm sure your age would excuse you, milady."

"The King's Grace doesn't like excuses. He naturally doesn't like faithful retainers to grow old and retire! And one doesn't refuse the King."

"But won't Queen Jane have someone she knows in mind?"

"No doubt she will," Lady Bryan replied. "But even she has to accept the King's wishes. I can but wait and see."

I could hardly suppose Lady Bryan would be asked to take on such an important new job at her age. One of her hips was giving her pain, and she walked with a slight limp. She had given up riding on our journeys, and travelled in a litter now. On the other hand she had known the King for many years, and I noticed she was usually right in gauging his views. So I started to think about my own position if Lady Bryan left us. Would some other noblewoman be deputed to take her place? Was it possible that *I* could be promoted to her position? Without her there to turn to, could I carry the extra responsibility? Elizabeth had no family to help or advise me. Would I have the authority to face down men like Sir John Shelton?

For a short time those questions alarmed me. But my hopeful nature soon won through. After all, there was plain sailing ahead! Lady Elizabeth was welcome at Court. The King's Grace loved her, and so did Lady Mary. There would soon be a new sibling to befriend her. And her godfather was Archbishop Cranmer himself. She had passed the rocky reefs of her mother's horrible fall, and had reached clear water. And so I reassured myself.

I was glad I had given the prospect some thought when Lady Bryan was suddenly summoned to Court in July. She returned to Hatfield a week later with the news that she had indeed been chosen by the King to be in charge of the expected baby.

"Well, it's happened, Kat," she said. "The Blessed Virgin knows I haven't sought this new post, but my dear son is most confident I can cope. And my daughter is going to help me get the nursery up and running at Hampton Court. So much to do! I'll miss dear Elizabeth so much and our happy household!

We'll just have to work it all out. At least you're in place as a successor to me here. If Cromwell approves, of course. I'll try to set that up for you, my dear. You would do it, wouldn't you? You'd get a higher salary, and I'd feel less miserable about deserting Elizabeth if I knew you were in charge."

Then she brightened up. "Actually, the likelihood is that, after the first few months of infancy, the new baby's establishment will be joined with Elizabeth's. So we'll soon be all together in one household again."

The good lady did write to Cromwell, and to my joy he approved my promotion. Then we moved to Richmond in August for Lady Bryan's last weeks with us so that we could be near Hampton Court. While we were there, I gradually began to take over the things that Lady Bryan had always done with Elizabeth, such as saying prayers morning and evening. One day I asked Lady Bryan how she was going to break the news of her departure to the little girl.

"Oh, I haven't had time to think about that, Kat! I know she'll be upset but I don't want to worry her in advance. I suppose I'll have to tell her the night before I go."

This was not what I wanted to hear. I foresaw great hurt to the child if her lifelong Lady Mistress didn't give her longer warning of their separation.

"Forgive me, milady," I said, "but, with respect, I fear that would be too sudden for her. It might make her always fearful in future that she was about to lose those dear to her. She loves you so much, milady, that it would be very hard for her to be unprepared for your leaving."

"I don't know", she said. "She may just grieve for longer if I tell her in advance."

"She will grieve for longer but, when the time comes to part, it will not be such a shock to her, milady," I said. "I'm sure it will help in the long run, and she won't lose her trust in us."

Lady Bryan turned it over in her mind. Many a

noblewoman in her position would simply not have listened to her young apprentice. She did. And I applaud you for it now, Lady B.

I tried again, "If you don't spring the bad news on her at the last minute, it means, milady, that you'd have time in the following days to reassure her about it – to say that you'd still be able to meet each other sometimes. Lady Elizabeth would have time to get used to the new plans for her household before you have to go."

"We can't be sure of anything, Kat. It's very difficult. But I know you love her, as I do, and we're both trying to do the best for her. I do have some misgivings. But, as you're the one who'll be left helping her adjust to the actual change, I will follow your advice."

I was so relieved that I lifted Lady Bryan's hand and kissed it!

She went on, "I'd like you to be with me when I break it to her. Bring her to my room after breakfast tomorrow. Warn her that I've got some very important news."

So, the three of us came together the next morning. I remember the scene so well: Lady Bryan, in her high-backed chair, broke the news as gently as she could, but Elizabeth quickly took in the harsh fact of separation, clung onto her, and sobbed into her lap. We let her cry for several minutes, while she flung away sweetmeats we offered. Then I showed her that Lady Bryan and I were crying too, and she was amazed and stared at us.

Lady Bryan couldn't speak, so I began, "We're all sad, my dear. None of us want Lady Bryan to go. But we have to make the best of it. We must show the King how brave we are."

Lady Bryan had been Elizabeth's loving rock and mainstay since her birth: in fact she had been a mother to her. I think when Elizabeth saw the tears running down her face, she suddenly realised that even Lady Bryan could not control everything; even Lady Bryan was not free to do as she chose. This parting was going to happen, and none of us could stop it. Perhaps I'm just being fanciful, but certainly the poor child's sobs subsided at that point, and she remained still and silent, as if the stuffing had been knocked out of her.

She wasn't the sort of child to be fobbed off easily with compensations. But I remember eventually we started talking about her forthcoming birthday, and she joined in. It was a tacit acknowledgement that she had understood the bad news, but would try to be brave.

Those last weeks of summer with Lady Bryan simply rushed by. The lady herself was often visiting Hampton Court to prepare her new nursery, so I was getting used to being in charge of her old one.

When she was at Richmond, she kept recollecting advice she needed to give me. "You've learnt all the practicalities of this establishment, Kat, and I thank the Blessed Virgin for that! But I must tell you about who's allowed to visit Lady Elizabeth, and who's not. Her situation is still not exactly 'de rigueur', so you will have to tread delicately. If in doubt, always refer to Cromwell, won't you? Try to uphold her high status and honour at all times – it will fall to you now, and it's so important in her case. I know you won't let her down."

Elizabeth's fourth birthday was a very happy day. I can see her now: slim and darting about excitedly in her deep blue dress and auburn curls. There were presents, songs and dances, plus her Carey cousins to play with. Lady Mary visited too, as did the Archbishop of Canterbury himself! I noted Lady Bryan's gracious short speech of welcome on Elizabeth's behalf. Later she took me aside to a window bay to introduce me to Matthew Parker, who was a priest accompanying the Archbishop.

"Now, my dear Kat," she whispered, "I must tell you that this reverend gentleman was Queen Anne's chaplain. You should know that only a few weeks before she died Queen Anne asked him to watch over her daughter. She also separately begged me to do the same, and I gave her my promise. But now that I've got to bow out of Elizabeth's life, I'm passing on to you the Queen's plea. I know you'll do your best to keep to it. And you and Father Parker here will help each other if you can."

I clasped her hands, and said I was proud to inherit such a solemn trust.

Father Parker put a kind hand on my shoulder and said, "I see you have a warm heart, Miss Champernowne. Lady Bryan is leaving the Lady Elizabeth in good hands. Thanks be to God, the King's Grace has taken his daughter under his wing, so we may hope that her future is secure now."

"Amen to that, Father!" I said.

I don't think I've mentioned it before, but I was a fervent supporter of the new reformed religion, even in sleepy Devonshire. Because of my excellent education I had always been able to read the Bible in Latin. But I thought it right that everyone should be allowed to read the Bible in our own language, or to have it read to them if (like most people) they could not read. I can't believe that Our Lord Jesus would not want His words spread far and wide, to high and low alike. Although, of course, I'd never met Queen Anne, everyone knew that she had strongly promoted the new religion. So I felt sympathetic towards her. And, because I loved her little daughter, I didn't hesitate to take on the promise that Lady Bryan had made to the frightened Queen.

Lady Bryan and half the nursemaids left us about a week after the birthday party. The rest of our household saw them off at the riverside. Elizabeth was in floods of tears, of course, and she and Lady Bryan had a final embrace, and she kissed each departing nursemaid too. Then they embarked, and the oarsmen struck out downriver. The child and I stood for a long time on the landing-stage, waving our handkerchiefs into the distance. I felt very sad, but I never doubted that we had done the right thing in trying to prepare Elizabeth for that great loss. It was a nervous moment for me: Lady Bryan had been my rock too in that new world of mine. I'd been extremely happy working under her, and had never been ambitious to move into her higher position. I recognised that day as a turning point both in Elizabeth's life and my own.

"Lady Bryan loves you very much, sweetheart," I ventured. "And she's going to write letters to you and me from Hampton Court. When she's settled in, she'll invite us to visit her soon, like she said."

"But I'm still sad," she said.

I knelt down and drew her to me. "You've every right to be sad, sweetheart. It's a sad day for us. Now what can we do to cheer ourselves up? I've got some good news: Catherine and Henry Carey are coming, and they are going to stay for two nights! What about that?"

Her face lit up. "Really? When?"

"After dinner. Dear Lady Bryan and I thought it would help comfort you when she had to go."

"Cathy and Harry are my friends!" she said, jumping up and down with delight. She gave them an extra warm welcome when they arrived that afternoon. Their mother had briefed them about Lady Bryan's departure, for they declared to Elizabeth that they were very sorry that Lady Bryan had had to leave.

"We know you must be missing her a lot," said Catherine as she put her arms around her little cousin. "We'll try and cheer you up, won't we, Harry?"

"That's right," Harry added. "And Kat here will cheer you up too, 'cause she's always happy. Can we go and talk to the guardsmen again, please?"

And we trooped off to the guard-chamber in the gatehouse, where Harry could admire all the weaponry.

Their visit certainly tided Elizabeth over the sudden reality of Lady Bryan's absence. Afterwards she helped me to compose a letter to Lady Bryan telling her about the Carey children's stay. 'And I am missing you, and I want to come and see you,' she added. Whenever she became tearful again, I would confidently hold out the imminent expectation of our being invited to Hampton Court. I'm afraid I was too optimistic on that score: Lady Bryan's first letter sent her love, but disappointed us by not arranging a meeting. I felt bad at having raised Elizabeth's hopes.

"Let's go in the morning anyway," she suggested.

"I'm afraid we can't visit the Court unless we're asked," I replied.

"But you said we could go soon."

"I'm sorry, sweetheart. I really thought we would be going any day now, but we'll just have to wait."

There were more tears.

When another letter came a few days later, I was less impulsive, and didn't tell the child it had come. I read it privately, which was lucky, because Lady Bryan wrote that Queen Jane's cold and formal manner towards her had deterred her from mentioning Elizabeth.

'I have a feeling she resents her stepdaughter,' Lady Bryan had written. 'I'm quite depressed about it, as you can imagine. It doesn't bode well for my seeing the dear child much in the future.'

Over the following few weeks I had to back-track over visiting Lady Bryan. I tried to keep Elizabeth occupied, and when she (frequently!) questioned me about the promised visit, I said that Lady Bryan was much busier than she had expected. The nursery at Hampton Court had been very dirty, and had a smoking chimney, so Lady Bryan had to get it all put right in a hurry in case the baby arrived early. I spun out that story, and, as the days passed, Elizabeth's misery tailed off, and she asked less about the visit. But she did cling to me, and often told me never to leave her.

In late September, quite out of the blue, I received instructions from Cromwell about the forthcoming christening. I was thrilled to hear that Elizabeth was to have an official role – a clear sign that her improved public status was to continue. She was to carry the special christening robe up to the font. The christening would take place when the baby was three days old, and I must be ready to take Elizabeth to the Palace when the summons came.

I remember running down to the garden with the good news, and enthusing Elizabeth with my excitement. Sally and Meg were beaming too, because all recognition of Elizabeth meant their jobs were more secure.

"She may not be *called* a princess, but she is being treated as one!" I said.

Elizabeth was twirling about on the lawn saying: "Is it a party? Can I wear my birthday dress?"

On 12th October we heard that the baby was the long-awaited Prince! It was a great joy to us all – thanks be to God! Church bells rang all day and cannons were fired. Cromwell immediately set the wheels of the christening turning, and a summons came for 'the Lady Elizabeth, Miss Champernowne and one nursemaid' to arrive at Hampton Court on the morning of the 14th. We'd been in a state of readiness for a couple of weeks, and duly arrived at the busy gatehouse. An usher ticked us off on Cromwell's list, and showed us to our chamber; he then instructed me to bring Elizabeth to the chapel that afternoon for a rehearsal. It was a most thrilling time; the vast Palace was bubbling over with high spirits and happiness!

Cromwell himself supervised the rehearsal. He knew exactly what order we were to process in, and even the Archbishop moved as he directed. I had expected to be walking beside Elizabeth, but no! Lord Edward Seymour, the Queen's brother, was deputed to carry her up to the font. She began to protest at that, but I quietened her. In fact it meant she could see and be seen. After the ceremony she was to walk back with Lady Mary, which pleased her. I was to stand back against a wall, ready to withdraw the child if she became fretful. For the baby's sake the ceremony was, luckily, not going to be very long. Some parts had to be practised several times, as Cromwell was a stickler for correctness. But sweet Elizabeth was extremely patient, if a little wide-eyed at all the grand people around her. Plenty of them stared back at her, for she wasn't often seen at Court.

Prince Edward himself (all of two days old!) was not at the rehearsal, of course, and a swaddled doll was used instead. I was told Lady Bryan couldn't be spared for the rehearsal, but would be at the christening, waiting in the wings like me in case the baby needed her. This was the first time I had been at Court in my own right, independent of Lady Bryan. It made me realise how much I had depended on her authority and status there. She was a noblewoman, with many grand connections, and I was only a rural gentlewoman (and a young one at that) with no standing at Court. However, I reminded myself that I was now the guardian of Lady Elizabeth, the King's daughter, whom I was devoted to, and as her representative I would hold my head high. My confident bearing would reflect her high status.

We wore our best dresses for the christening, and I put on my French hood. The chapel was absolutely full and humming, with everyone wanting a glimpse of the Prince. I handed Elizabeth over to Sir Edward Seymour and stood back. I spotted Lady Bryan, but I couldn't get near her for the throng. I couldn't see the ceremony, because I'm not very tall, but I saw Elizabeth held up by Sir Edward and her delighted wave at Lady Bryan. The infant Prince had a healthy cry, which thrilled us all!

Afterwards, Lady Mary and Lady Elizabeth walked hand-in-hand down the aisle, following their brother's procession. In the antechamber of the chapel, Queen Jane sat in state, pale but buoyed up by the universal congratulations of her grateful subjects. Lady Mary was the first in line to pay homage in a deep curtsey, and I saw her whisper to her sister to copy her. The Queen smiled at Mary and pressed her hands, and gave a nod to Elizabeth before they moved on. I stepped forward and curtseyed to Mary, thanked her, and took Elizabeth by the hand. She was looking around the room, and then caught sight of Lady Bryan coming towards us, and rushed up to her. Lady Bryan bent and embraced her and kissed her forehead.

"How's my sweetheart?"

"Will you show me your new room?" Lady Elizabeth asked. "Look at my dress –it's the one I had for my birthday! And Kat is very smart today too! We took a long time dressing up. Can I come and see Martha please?"

"My word!" Lady Bryan said. "What a torrent! That dress really is beautiful, dear. You played your part very well at the christening, and I was so proud of you."

"Can I come and see your new nursery?"

"Well, today is so busy with all these grand people that I – " she broke off in surprise as a lady-in-waiting tapped her shoulder.

"Lady Bryan," she said, "Her Majesty does not want you lingering here. You are to escort the Prince back to the nursery at once."

Lady Bryan was quite flustered. "Of course. I'm so sorry!" As she turned away, Elizabeth let out a wail and tried to follow her.

I had to pick her up and whisk her away from the celebrations through a crowd of disapproving faces. I took her back to our chamber, where Sally helped us out of our finery, and we comforted the tired child. The next morning we were rowed back to our own little world at Richmond.

A day or two later, quite out of the blue, Elizabeth asked me, "Where did the baby come from?"

"The baby?" I havered.

"Yes. You know. Baby Edward. Did he come from God?"

"Yes. Yes, he did. God sent him to our country, as the Archbishop said."

I paused, then took the plunge. "But the baby actually grew inside Queen Jane's tummy. That's why she is his mother."

"Her tummy must have been big."

I nodded. "Do you remember when Sheba had her kittens in the summer? She grew very fat first, didn't she?"

"Her tummy was nearly on the ground!" she said with a laugh.

"Well, she had three babies inside her."

"And Jess even had six puppies!" she said. "Can we do some drawing now, please?"

A few days later, the shocking news came through that Queen Jane was very ill. Prayers this time were not granted, and she died of childbirth fever nine days after the christening. I had to tell Elizabeth because she would expect to see her at Court in the future. It was the first time she had heard of someone dying whom she knew. I told her the Queen had gone to live with God in Heaven.

"But will she come back soon?" Elizabeth asked.

"I'm afraid not. No-one can come back from Heaven. But it's a lovely place, and she'll be very happy there."

"Will she have her shiny dress in Heaven?"

"I'm sure she will, sweetheart."

I didn't raise Elizabeth's hopes, but I wasn't entirely surprised to get a letter from Lady Bryan inviting me to bring Elizabeth to Court for a day.

"Lady Mary agrees and so does Cromwell," she wrote, "and I am so looking forward to seeing you both again!"

And so it was that we began a regular weekly visit to Hampton Court. I impressed on Elizabeth what an important baby her new brother was, and that we were very privileged to visit his nursery. She was so happy to have Lady Bryan's love and attention again, and fascinated by the baby. In fact on our first visit she tickled us all by asking what the difference was between a boy and a girl! I remember admiring Lady Bryan for her matter-of-fact answer and her use of Prince Edward as a model!

"It was an opportunity, Kat," she said later. "How's she to learn, otherwise? There's no mother to tell her."

The following week we were chatting in the Hampton Court nursery when Sir Edward Seymour (by then, I think, already Viscount Beauchamp, and still rising) strode in unexpectedly to see his valuable nephew. He immediately began bewailing his sister's death in a loud voice to Lady Bryan. His main complaint seemed to be that Queen Jane could supply no more royal nephews for him! But he kept dwelling on all the pain she had suffered and all the blood she had lost. I felt most indignant that he was holding forth so graphically in little Elizabeth's hearing. I could see he had all her attention, but none of us could interrupt his lament.

As soon as he'd left, Elizabeth's questions began about what exactly had happened to Queen Jane. Lady Bryan in her calm way answered very frankly about the perils of childbirth.

"I wouldn't have wished her to learn about it yet, Kat, but a nursery can't be shuttered from the real world", she explained. "Queens are in God's hands just like the rest of us, even more so perhaps, for queens have a duty to have children. I remember when King Henry's own mother died in childbirth when he was only eleven."

She warned me to be prepared for Elizabeth to start asking about her own mother. "It will surely come soon, Kat, but spare her the actual beheading until she's much older, won't you?"

And indeed a few days later Elizabeth brought up the matter: "Lady Bryan said Queen Jane was the baby's mother. But where's my mother?"

"I'm afraid your mother is dead, my dear."

She stared at me. "Did she die when I was born?"

"No, sweetheart. Not that. You were two-and-a-half when she died. But that's too young to remember her."

"What was her name?"

"Queen Anne."

"Was she very old?"

"No."

"Why is she dead then?"

"Well, she died very suddenly. I'm afraid it happens sometimes. But now she's in Heaven, and I'm sure you'll see her there one day."

"But I don't know what she looks like."

"Well, *she* will know *you*, my sweet."

It will seem strange to you that bright young Elizabeth took a long time to realise that she hadn't got a mother. I am sure it was because she had no experience at all of family life. Nor did she mix with other children, so she didn't know that they had mothers. The Careys had been warned not to mention her mother or even their own. Prince Edward was the first baby she knew. There were few other children at Court. Of course at the country manors she sometimes saw cottagers' or servants' children, but she must have assumed their mothers were their Lady Mistresses like Lady Bryan, or gentlewomen-in-waiting like me.

By January 1538 Prince Edward was three months old, so the time had come for him to travel to the royal manors. It was decided by Cromwell that Lady Elizabeth's household should join him at Hatfield, which delighted me. We were re-united with Lady Bryan and dear Martha and her helpers, and we formed our happy community again. I was really lucky because Lady Bryan mentioned then that if Queen Jane had lived, our households would not have come together at all.

"One of her ladies-in-waiting recently told me," she'd said, "that Queen Jane had considered Lady Elizabeth to be illegitimate and not fit to share an establishment with the Prince of Wales. 'It would be over my dead body' was how the Queen had expressed it."

That was a very happy year for Elizabeth. It was a year of stability surrounded by those she loved. She began to learn new skills of sewing and her letters, as well as improving her dancing and riding. It was no chore to her: she relished learning and was very quick at it. She continued to benefit from Lady Bryan's wonderful knowledge of royal etiquette and manners, which I had so little experience in.

On earthier matters too she quickly absorbed lessons. In the country manors we were surrounded by cats, dogs, chickens, cattle and horses. She was always asking questions, and soon grasped the facts of life, which were all around us! Later I expanded the theme by explaining that we humans (created in the image of God) had been given the sacrament of marriage to sanctify our sexual instincts. Until we married, divine laws insisted on chastity.

Lady Mary came to stay sometimes. Of course, I was never as close to her as Lady Bryan had been. I was not of noble rank, and she knew that I supported the new religion, so she was never going to warm towards me. But she always greeted me courteously. She was devoted to her younger siblings, and wrote favourable reports to the King's Grace on their progress. She was a lonely figure since Queen Jane's death, and, as ever, devoted a lot of time to prayer and studying the Bible (though not in English). It crossed my mind that the King would be well advised to seek a husband for her, so that he could hopefully be blessed with grandsons to bolster the Tudor line. But nothing happened.

I speculated about it to Lady Bryan, but she advised me to keep my thoughts to myself: "If you've learnt one thing from me, Kat, keep your mouth firmly buttoned up on royal matters, especially anything to do with the Succession. How often do I have to say it?"

Poor Lady Bryan! I must have been a disappointment to her sometimes, but she was very patient with my lapses.

Thank goodness she was still with us when another family question unexpectedly surfaced. It came about because Sally had been home to Gloucestershire for her birthday. It was a long journey from Hatfield, so she had been given a week's holiday. She was so excited to have seen her family again after a two-year absence; she didn't often have news of them, for neither she nor they knew how to write. Sally told us how her two grandmothers had wept with joy to see her again, and given her presents: one had given her a needle-case, and the other a skein of wool.

Lady Bryan said, "Sally, your grandmothers are women after my own heart."

We all laughed, and then Elizabeth piped up, "Are you *my* grandmother?"

"No, my dear," said Lady Bryan carefully.

"Where is my grandmother? Will she give me a present?"

Because the child was addressing her questions to Lady Bryan, I thankfully took a back seat in this conversation.

Lady Bryan visibly summoned her resources, and, playing for time, replied, "Well, Lady Elizabeth, your grandmother was, of course, er – naturally, a queen. She was His Grace the King's excellent mother. But I'm afraid she died a long time ago when King Henry was only eleven. May God rest her soul."

"But why did she die?" Elizabeth asked.

"She was having a baby, my dear. Sometimes that is dangerous, if you remember."

Silence.

Then she asked, "But where is the baby?"

"I'm afraid the baby died too," Lady Bryan replied.

"But it wasn't old."

"No, but babies do die sometimes if they are not strong."

"I'm strong."

"Oh yes, dear. Don't you worry about yourself."

Elizabeth's little face pursed up as she digested all this, and we had turned back to our needlework when she suddenly asked, "Where is my other grandmother then?"

The nursemaids and I instinctively flashed a look at Lady Bryan. The child noticed that, and it made her more determined to have an answer.

"Your other grandmother? Well, my dear, she lives a long way away," Lady Bryan replied.

"As far as London?"

"Oh much farther than that."

"Will she come and see me?"

"No, my dear, it's much too far."

"But will she send me a present?" Elizabeth asked.

"I'm afraid you must just take it from me that it wouldn't be suitable," Lady Bryan said. "Now, we must get on with our needlework. How about using this beautiful purple wool for your next row?"

News reached us later that year that Lady Boleyn had died. And Lord Boleyn died the following year in 1539. I had never met them, of course, but I felt sorry that they hadn't had the pleasure of knowing their clever granddaughter, nor she the love of grandparents. Still, they knew Catherine and Harry Carey, their other grandchildren, and would have been very proud that Catherine was appointed a Maid of Honour to the new Queen, Anne of Cleves, at the end of 1539.

So, pretty Catherine Carey made her début at Court. She soon caught the eye of Sir Francis Knollys, and they were married in April 1540 when she was just 17. Elizabeth was invited to the wedding, and I remembered to write to Lord Cromwell for permission. I was so thrilled when he agreed. We never went to parties, and it was a great excitement. We hugged each other in our wedding finery before we set off! Elizabeth drew a lot of attention in a red and gold dress, and the guests bowed and curtseyed to her. She took part in two dances very gracefully and thoroughly enjoyed herself. She gave loving kisses to the bride and to Harry Carey. Their mother (Mary Boleyn) was there, of course, but I knew I should keep Elizabeth away from her, and she didn't approach us. I noticed her watching Elizabeth a lot, and she must have been glad to have that one chance to see her sister's child again.

The bridegroom's country house at Greys Court was not that far from the royal manor at Ashridge, so from then on whenever we were living there, Catherine Knollys tried to visit. Because of her frequent pregnancies, however, we sometimes travelled to her.

But I've digressed a bit. I must bring you back to the new Queen, Anne of Cleves. Her marriage to King Henry was encouraged by Cromwell because it was a political move. The aim was to gain a Protestant, German ally to bolster us against the might of France and Spain. No doubt the intention was right, but the whole project collapsed when the King met his new bride. He found her so repugnant that he couldn't face having sex with her. So there was no chance of a Cleves brother for Prince Edward. The King had to go through with the marriage ceremony, but a divorce was quickly arranged on the grounds of non-consummation. In fact she probably never knew why she was divorced, because her English ladies reported that she knew nothing of the facts of life! It seems unbelievable, but Cleves was a straight-laced backwater, and her mother was so religious that she had kept her daughters in strict ignorance. No slap and tickle there! No come-hither looks! Nothing to excite a red-blooded male, let alone King Henry.

Queen Anne reported to her ladies that the King did kiss her goodnight, to which a bold lady responded, "Madam, there must be more! Otherwise we shall never get a Duke of York, which is what this Kingdom is longing for."

Anne of Cleves had the sense to relinquish her title for a big pension and no protest. She enjoyed a safe and wealthy retirement in England, which she probably enjoyed more than her cloistered upbringing in Cleves.

The end of her brief reign was marked by the beheading of Lord Cromwell. He had been such a powerful man that his fall shook us all. For me he had been an infallible oracle to consult whenever I had doubts about what Elizabeth could or couldn't do. He was a buttress I sorely missed.

On the day Cromwell died, the King, then forty-nine, married nineteen-year-old Katherine Howard. I had to keep Elizabeth informed about who was Queen, in case we were called to Court. She had noticed that Anne of Cleves was 'Another Queen Anne, like my mother'. We never met her as Queen, but I had to explain that she was no longer Queen because the King's Grace didn't like her.

"But now there's a new Queen called Katherine," I said.

"Does the King like *her*?" she asked.

"Yes, everyone says he adores her."

We did meet this fifth Queen several times. She was a petite, vivacious and light-hearted girl who looked even younger than her nineteen years. She loved music and dancing. She happened to be one of Anne Boleyn's cousins, and she made much of Elizabeth, telling her they were related. She once arranged for Elizabeth to sit opposite her at a Court dinner, and she also took her out for a river trip in the royal barge, where they giggled a lot together. Elizabeth at seven was captivated by this special treatment.

It made it all the harder for me to explain when suddenly the little Queen fell into disgrace because she had had two lovers before marrying the King. She was imprisoned in November, and her head was cut off in the Tower in February 1542. She was only twenty and had been Queen for just eighteen months.

I had to tell Elizabeth what had happened, and she was horrified.

"But she was the Queen! She couldn't be beheaded! The King wouldn't allow it!"

"Well, it's very sad, sweetheart. But she had deceived the King."

"How?"

"She pretended that she was a virgin when she married the King. But it later turned out that she had had sex with two lovers before she married. It was a terrible shock for the King."

"But why couldn't he divorce her like the last Queen?" Elizabeth asked.

"I think he must have felt so dishonoured by her sinful behaviour that she had to die."

"But did it hurt her?"

"I don't know, sweetheart. But we mustn't ask questions about her now."

I have to say that King Henry's many marriages were the talk of Europe. His subjects knew that it was not a topic for open discussion, but a lot of whispering went on all the same. Katherine Howard's death naturally reminded everyone of Anne Boleyn's execution, and phrases such as, 'Another Queen beheaded!' and 'History repeating itself' crept into conversations.

Elizabeth was eight-and-a-half by this time and she was quick to pick up on careless snatches of information. I was terribly on edge about all this. Eventually, very reluctantly I decided that the time had come for me to break the news of her mother's dreadful death. It was cowardly to put it off. The shock was bound to break over her soon. It would be far better for her to hear it direct from me in private than from just anyone, anytime, anywhere. I would spare her that.

Ever since I'd told her that her mother had died suddenly, she had mentioned her sometimes, and even asked if there was a picture of her. Whenever we'd been to Court since then, I had made her promise not to mention her mother because it was a sad subject and the King didn't like it. Fortunately for me (and possibly more by luck than judgement) she had kept her promise.

Unfortunately Prince Edward's establishment was not with us at that time, so I did not have Lady Bryan to consult. It wasn't a subject I dared put into a letter to her. I spent some sleepless nights, but I didn't doubt I would have to break the news to Elizabeth then.

So, later that February, I took Elizabeth to my room in Hatfield and we sat alone by a warm fire.

"I've got to tell you something important and very sad, my sweetheart."

She froze, then burst out, "You're not leaving me, Kat? Don't leave me! Don't leave me!"

"No, no, no!" I said, hugging her to me. I kept my arm around her. "This is something that happened a long time ago – when you were only two-and-a-half."

"That's how old I was when my mother died."

"This is about that sad time. It's about your mother." There was a silence. "I'm afraid this will be a shock for you, my sweet. But now you're growing up I think it's best if I tell you myself. Otherwise you will find out unexpectedly some day soon, and it would hurt you more."

"Why would it hurt me? What is it?"

"This is very difficult for me to say. You know how upset we were two weeks ago when Queen Katherine was executed?"

Another silence.

"Everyone has been talking about it," I continued. "And they can't help remembering your mother, Queen Anne."

I paused tensely, hoping that she might make the connection.

She felt her way. "What do you mean?"

"This is the very hard part. I'm afraid your mother died in the same way as Queen Katherine."

She stared at me stupidly for a few moments with her mouth open. "What?" she faltered, "What?"

"I'm afraid it's the truth, my sweet."

She kept staring at me. "Do you mean she was beheaded too?"

"Yes. That's what I have to tell you."

"I thought…, I thought she fell ill and then had a grand funeral like Queen Jane. Didn't you tell me that?"

I shook my head. "I just told you that she had died suddenly. You were far too young to be told about an execution. You're still too young to hear it, and I hate telling you! But the truth will out. Specially if it's about someone famous. Any day now you might suddenly hear or read something about your mother's death. I'm doing my poor best to forestall that. I'm trying to prepare you, so you can be brave and strong when it happens. I'm telling you because I love you. I'm so sorry, my sweet."

She was quite stunned. She couldn't help knowing by then that she was a person of great importance. People bowed and curtseyed to her wherever she went. Her father was great King Henry, and her mother had been Queen. But how could she equate her own status with a death of such disgrace? And what would she think of her mother? She was silent and breathing fast. I held her to me and kept quiet while the shock sank in. Then I had to continue.

"The important thing now, sweetheart, is not to talk about your mother to other people. Particularly at Court. The King would be dreadfully angry and I would be punished for it. I would not be allowed to serve you any more. I couldn't bear that. I've dared to tell you this because I know that you're old enough, and wise enough, to keep a secret now, aren't you?"

She nodded, with a frightened look.

"So our lips must be sealed," I stressed. "For our own good. It's been a terrible shock for you today I'm afraid. But when you're older, you'll understand it better. Meanwhile, we must remember to keep absolutely silent about it."

"I will, Kat," she whispered.

"That's my brave girl," I said as I kissed the top of her head.

"Shall we say the Lord's Prayer together now and think of you and your mother?" I asked. And we knelt down.

The next day I took Elizabeth for a short walk in the Hatfield gardens. I wanted to give her the opportunity to ask about her mother. And of course she did. She has always wanted all the information she can get.

"Kat," she said softly, 'Now that we're alone, can I ask you why my mother was executed?"

"I can only say that she lost the King's favour."

"But why? Queen Katherine had done bad things, hadn't she? But did my mother also do bad things?"

"I'm afraid we have to accept that she did." I suddenly imagined Lady Bryan at my elbow, and I quickly added, "We mustn't question that."

"But what bad things did she do?"

"It was said that she loved other men more than the King. Believe me, you're too young to understand it all now. Be patient. Don't worry about the reasons until you're grown up. Just remember never to talk about it."

"I'll be very careful, Kat. I know it's secret. I can keep a secret."

Mercifully my trust in her silence proved justified. For many years she did not mention her mother again. She had always seemed older than her age. Now, the knowledge of her mother's execution made her yet more mature, and a slight but definite wariness crept into her character. Specially when she was at Court.

That September, when Elizabeth was nine, the King's Grace invited her and Lady Mary to dine with him at a royal hunting lodge in Essex. I accompanied her on the journey from Hunsdon, and reminded her not to mention her mother.

"I'll never forget any of that," she assured me.

We met Lady Mary there and waited for the King to return from a falconry display. His Majesty was beginning to feel his years and no longer rode out hunting. When the usher called for 'Their Graces, the Lady Mary and the Lady Elizabeth', I watched them go down to the hall hand-in-hand to meet their father. My mind went back to that day six years before at Whitehall, when the King had sent for little Elizabeth, and how worried we had all felt in case she referred to her mother or made a bad impression. This time I was happily confident that she would acquit herself with the intelligence, courage and grace I knew so well.

The dinner lasted two hours, and His Majesty sat between his daughters. They told me afterwards how attentive he had been, and displayed great fondness to them both. He showed particular interest in Elizabeth, and asked a lot of questions about her lessons and accomplishments. He saw her far less often, of course, as Lady Mary was the first lady at Court now that there was no queen again.

A few weeks later at the King's command, several bales of rich velvet and brocades were sent from Hampton Court to Hatfield to be made into new clothes for Her Grace, the Lady Elizabeth. Elizabeth was thrilled with the gorgeous material. We saw it as a sign that she might be expected to be on display at Court more often in future.

In December news reached us that the King's nephew, King James of Scotland, and his French Queen had had a daughter. She was to be called Mary.

"You have a new cousin!" I told Elizabeth in the nursery. "Princess Mary of Scotland!"

"Why is she a princess?"

Sally and Nell glanced across from their mending, and I realised that another pitfall loomed, an awkward one at that. It fleetingly crossed my mind to say that the title was a Scottish custom, but I ploughed boldly on. "It's because her parents are a King and Queen."

"But my father is the King of England. And-" she stopped and looked at me. "Anyway, Lady Mary's parents were the King and Queen of England, but she's not called princess either."

"No. The truth is that you and your sister are in an unusual position," I explained. "It was decided a long time ago that the marriages of your mothers to His Majesty were not lawful. That means that, although the King is proud to claim you as his daughters, neither of you can be in line to the throne. So you can't be called princesses. But the important thing to remember is that you are both part of the King's family, and are honoured as such."

She was trying to take it all in.

"But why weren't the marriages lawful?"

"It's complicated. But I'm sure both marriages were made in good faith. Both your mothers (and the King, of course) believed at the time that the marriages were lawful, but sadly it turned out they were mistaken. I think you'll understand it better when you're older."

She was silent.

"Anyway, isn't it good news that you've got a new cousin? Yet another girl, like the Grey daughters!"

Although little Princess Mary of Scotland served as an opportune example of a truly royal child, she was actually a princess for only six days! Her father died suddenly and the baby became Queen in her own right. The Scots had never had a ruling Queen before, let alone a baby one. It was a very weak position for them to be in. King Henry launched several attacks on Scotland in the next few years, but was driven back each time.

I'm trying to highlight the important events and moments in Elizabeth's life but all this time her education was continuing in the background. She was beginning to tax my resources in languages! I was teaching my avid pupil Latin, Greek, and French. The local vicar would come to supervise her religious studies. And of course in the country she practised her riding and archery. When we were near London, a special dancing master would visit us. I began to teach her to play the lute, and when she was older and living at Court she had professional music masters. She had also begun to meet a few other children at Court, such as her second cousin, Lady Jane Grey, and the five sons of Lord Dudley.

And for all those years she and Prince Edward often lived together so they were getting to know each other well. She was playful and patient with her little brother, and they naturally became devoted.

Lady Mary was of a different generation and had an important role at Court by then. Although fond of her brother, she could never be close to him.

In fact Lady Mary's position as first lady at Court was soon to be handed on yet again. The King's favour had settled on a charming twice-widowed lady, Catherine Parr. Elizabeth was summoned to Court to meet her in June 1543. She was tremendously excited to be invited to the wedding at Hampton Court in July. She reported that her fourth stepmother had talked to her most warmly, and she was longing to see her again.

The next month all of the King's children were summoned to Windsor Castle, and they lived as one family for a couple of weeks. Prince Edward was nearly six, and about to leave his nursery household. The King and Queen were taking advice on the best tutors for him, and they also chose a Cambridge scholar, William Grindal, for Elizabeth's education. I was relieved to hand over the academic side of my job, but the question of my leaving Elizabeth altogether was never raised, as far as I know. I was to continue to manage her servants and be her closest attendant. Lady Bryan, however, at the great age of seventy-three, was then given an honourable discharge and a pension. I owe her a huge debt for all I learnt at her side.

Before we left Windsor the good old lady made a final plea to me to stay with Elizabeth and always try to uphold her status and reputation. In fact I felt full of confidence at that parting of the ways. I would miss Lady Bryan as a dear friend, but I had been with Elizabeth for seven years. Her household was sailing serenely along in the wake of the Prince of Wales. We had reached safe havens indeed, thanks be to God! The friendly and sophisticated new Queen was another ally for us, and would no doubt eventually take the fledgling Elizabeth under her wing at Court.

Elizabeth's days became much fuller with her many lessons, but she still wanted to see her Carey cousins. The older she got, the more persistent she became, and I somehow managed to arrange visits whenever possible. Catherine (now Lady Knollys) had two babies by this time, and Harry was a captain in the army and beginning a career at Court. They were due to come that August, but had to cancel because their mother had died.

Elizabeth was terribly disappointed: "But I thought their mother died years ago! I've never heard of her. They've never even mentioned her. Why not?"

"Calm down, my dear. I'm afraid Catherine and Harry were instructed long ago not to mention their mother to you. It was all done for the best. Their mother was the sister of your mother. Lady Bryan feared that if you heard about her, it might lead you to ask dangerous questions about your own mother. It was to protect you. You were too young then to keep a secret. You might have blurted out something at Court."

"What was her name?"

"Her name was Mary. Mary Boleyn before she married."

"Have I got any more aunts or uncles I don't know about?"

"No. There was one uncle. But he died a long time ago, and he didn't have any children. Mary was the only one left from your mother's side of the family."

"I can keep a secret now. I wish I'd met her. I could have asked her so many questions!"

"That was impossible, my sweet. The King's Grace would not have approved."

She was silent for a bit, then said: "Well, at least I'll always have Cathy and Harry. They're allowed, aren't they?"

"Yes. But do be careful not to discuss your mother with them. Otherwise I'm afraid they might not be allowed any more."

She stared at me, shocked, and her mouth quivered. "But they're my oldest friends. I can't lose them!"

I said nothing. I thought, "They are really the only friends you've ever had."

"I'll just be very careful, Kat. I've learnt to be careful, you know, haven't I?"

The year 1544 was an 'annus mirabilis', a joyful landmark in Elizabeth's life. His Grace the King issued through Parliament a new Law of Succession. It established Lady Mary and then Lady Elizabeth in line to the throne after Prince Edward and after any children of the King's most recent marriage! An official notice from the King's Privy Council was sent to Lady Elizabeth to inform her. His Majesty's two daughters had been disinherited for many years with an undefined status. Now here it was in black and white at last: restoration to the royal line! I was overjoyed and our whole household felt re-invigorated and confident.

I wrote and told dear Lady Bryan. I knew what it would mean to her after all the ups and downs of Elizabeth's childhood. She replied that her prayers had been answered.

She also wrote, 'Here's a word of advice from an experienced old lady: now that Elizabeth's place in the Succession has been formalised (and she is approaching adulthood), you should gradually increase the respect you show her. I suggest you curtsey to her morning and evening. And I'm afraid your endearments should gradually give way to 'madam'.'

I followed that up with a talk to Elizabeth. I explained how important she had become now that His Majesty had restored her to the Succession.

"Am I a princess now then?"

"No. Not that. And the King (in his wisdom) has not even pronounced you to be legitimate. Maybe that will follow one day. Lady Mary has been treated the same. But those are minor questions compared with the Succession. Every king has to ensure and determine his Succession, and that is what His Grace has now done."

"Who else is in the Succession?"

"I think I'd better draw a family tree for you, to show you how your relations fit in."

I spread some paper on my table and sketched it out. There was only King Henry and his two sisters (both dead by then). His elder sister Margaret's two descendants were her granddaughter, the baby Mary, Queen of Scots, and a daughter, Lady Margaret Douglas, by her second husband.

"That baby Queen comes next after you in the English Succession," I told her. Then King Henry's younger sister, Mary, had had two daughters, Frances and Eleanor, and between them they had four daughters.

"What a lot of girls in the Succession!" she exclaimed. "There's only Prince Edward and then ten girls!"

"You can see here you come ahead of all those girls except Lady Mary. So you are a very important young lady. In fact, my dear, from now on I'm going to curtsey to you at the beginning and end of the day."

"You don't need to do that. It would feel funny."

"It's kind of you to say so, my sweet, but it will be good for me to get into new habits straightaway. It will then set the tone for other people. But you might have to remind me at first!"

The next month, on 26th June 1544, the King gave a lavish party at Whitehall Palace. His purpose was to set the seal on the new Act of Succession, by displaying his heirs to all the greatest in the land. Not only was there the six-year-old Edward, but his two elder sisters now stepped out of the wings onto centre-stage to buttress their young brother in the Succession. It was an assertion of confidence and of continuity in the great Tudor dynasty.

What's more, work was started on a large painting with His Majesty, Prince Edward and his mother, Queen Jane, in the middle. At a little distance from those central figures are Lady Mary on one side of the picture and Lady Elizabeth on the other. Yes, to some extent they are sidelined, but there they stand!

The King's Grace had included them in this permanent witness of his dynasty. That painting hangs to this day in the Audience Chamber of Whitehall Palace, and my Queen ensures it is prominently displayed.

From then on we were at Court more often. Queen Catherine much enjoyed the company of both her stepdaughters. She was a great disciple of the reformed religion, but she still won Lady Mary's warm affection. And Elizabeth just basked in the love and interest shown to her. Her previous three stepmothers had not had time to get to know her.

Looking back fifteen years I can see that those three years,

1544-7, were a halcyon time. With the Succession established, the kind Queen, and seeing the King more often, we simply felt safe. After a doubtful past there was now an assured future. We had no anxieties at all, and after an uncertain voyage we had reached the Promised Land. By 1546 Elizabeth, at thirteen, was officially top of the list of the Queen's ladies-in-waiting, and she was beginning to live at Court more often than in the country manors. Very confident and poised she was, holding herself proudly like a princess. She was well aware of her place in the Tudor line. She accepted (and expected) courtiers' homage as her due, but she was deeply respectful to the four people with higher status than herself. She knew by then that most Catholics, and perhaps some Protestants, still considered her to be illegitimate. But, enfolded by the King's Act of Succession, she bore herself with truly royal dignity, to confound those who would demean her. Out of the public eye, she remained loving and loyal to me, Martha, Nell and Sally who had served her as long as she could remember.

She was, of course, very worried when I told her in 1545 that I was going to get married! At thirty-two I had given up any thought of marriage, but John Ashley persuaded me to change my mind. He was a newcomer, along with several others, to Elizabeth's growing household. A well-educated gentleman, he had served as a secretary to the Duke of Norfolk, and was later attached to Prince Edward's household, which is how we met. He was in fact one of Queen Anne Boleyn's many cousins. His mind had an academic turn, and he was cheerful and optimistic, like me. We quickly became great friends, and were soon a courting couple. I braced myself to tell Elizabeth about my wedding plans.

She had been so busy with all her lessons, extra Court visits, dressmakers and painters that she hadn't noticed John's and my attraction, or heard the household gossip. It was a jolt for her. At first she shed tears and years. Like a child again, she begged me not to leave her.

"Stay with me, Kat! Please stay with me. Don't get married!"

"My dear, you know I would never willingly leave you. John and I will be proud to serve you together. Nothing will change."

"But then you'll have a baby and you might die – or you'll love the baby more than me!"

"As for any baby, I must accept God's will. But to me, my lady, you've been like my own child all these years. I'll always love you. Although you're so busy now, I'm still always there when you wake up and go to bed, aren't I?"

"Yes." Pause. "But I don't like change."

"I know," I said, as I put my arm firmly round her. "But life is full of changes. Specially now you're growing up. In a few years' time you'll be getting married yourself. Then I'll be well placed to give you advice, won't I? I have to keep a step ahead of you!"

She wasn't convinced. It was a small dent in her new sense of self-importance, and she sulked for a few days. It was the first time we had had a rift, and I won the day. The only other time was far ahead in the future, when she was Queen, and she couldn't lose then.

"Anyway, Kat," she retorted a few days later with her chin raised defiantly, "*I'm* never going to marry!"

She had said the same thing, at intervals, for two or three years. But now that she was eleven, I made a snap decision to acquaint her with the reality.

"I know you think that, Your Grace." She shot me a look. "But now that you're growing up, you'll need to change your tune. It's because you're the King's daughter, you see, and third in line to the throne. The King's Grace will undoubtedly *require* that you marry in a few years' time."

"Why?"

"It will be your royal duty. To help our country with a marriage alliance with a foreign prince – like the King's sisters did."

"But that didn't work," she pointed out.

"Well no, perhaps not then. But the hope and expectation were there, which had to be tried. And then there's the Succession. It will be important for King Henry to have plenty of grandsons. I'm sure you'll want to strengthen the Tudor dynasty, won't you?"

She was silent.

"It will be your main role in life, my dear. It's what you were born to do."

"But Mary hasn't had to get married."

"No," I racked my brain. "But I think Lady Mary is a special case. She's so devoted to the old religion and – . But it's not my place to talk about the Succession. Matters of state are beyond me. I just wanted to warn you that one day you will have to marry. All the more so if Lady Mary doesn't."

My memories of Elizabeth in the last years of King Henry's reign are happy and proud. When she reached thirteen in September 1546, His Grace the King commissioned a grand portrait of her, standing alone, dressed in scarlet and gold. Sumptuous is the only word that can describe her scarlet gown, with its underskirt and slashed sleeves of figured gold. The neckline was edged with pearls, and she wore a matching French hood, necklace, rings, pendant and a girdle of pearls and gold. But this girl is not dwarfed by the magnificence of her attire: it is her calm poise and steady gaze that rivet the viewer's eye. The painter, Master Meynert, had been a friend of the celebrated Master Holbein (who had tragically died three years before).

This magnificent portrait now hangs in Windsor Castle. If you ever get the opportunity to see it, you will surely agree that the sitter can only be a princess.

King Henry probably had plans for that painting. He may well have intended it to be displayed at foreign Courts to attract a royal betrothal: behind Elizabeth are the bed-curtains usual in such pictures. I know that His Grace was delighted by the outcome of his commission, and took pride in showing it off to ambassadors and the Court.

But that beautiful picture was one of the last pleasures of the King's life. That autumn his domineering character was as strong as ever, but his huge body was failing. He could barely walk for pain in his legs, and he was escorted about on a special chair with wheels. Christmas festivities were very subdued, and Elizabeth and Edward were not invited to Court. News soon reached us that the King was getting worse.

Then, at the end of January 1547, Elizabeth was at Enfield Manor when Edward and his entourage arrived unexpectedly from Hertford Castle. The Prince's uncle, Edward Seymour, was in charge of him, and he broke the news to the two children that King Henry had died. Elizabeth and Edward burst into tears and hugged each other for comfort. But there was hardly any time for grieving. It was vital that the little Protestant King and his uncle get to Westminster quickly, and they were soon on the London Road.

King Henry's death at fifty-five was a sudden shock to the country. Kings' illnesses are not widely publicised. He had reigned for thirty-eight years. Certainly one of our strongest Kings. He was greatly feared, yes, but he was also a mighty defender and champion of his country. He left a vacuum: a nine-year-old boy not nearly ready to assume his father's vast mantle. Our enemies, both abroad and within, would observe our ship of state drifting, with its masterful captain gone.

Thanks be to God, only two days later the Council of Regency announced that they had chosen Edward Seymour to be the Protector of the Realm and the young King Edward's governor. The speed of the handover of power offered no opportunity for France, Spain or the Catholic people here to attempt anything different. So England as a whole felt reassured of stability.

But in our own household King Henry (terrifying though he could be) had been the foundation and guarantor of our world. I hadn't realised what an abyss he would leave. He had become proud of Elizabeth and restored her to the Succession. At the time no-one had dared to question that. But without her all-powerful father, could this thirteen-year-old girl maintain her high position? The Seymours were in charge now, and they had no reason to champion her. We knew that many people still held that she was illegitimate. Catholic Europe still referred to her as 'The Bastard'. We felt suddenly exposed and vulnerable. I told John it reminded me of when I first came to serve Elizabeth, when her household had been fearful for their future.

By God's providence we were not left long in limbo. Catherine Parr, now the Queen Dowager, warmly invited Elizabeth and her staff to live with her at her manor in Chelsea. The Queen also welcomed nine-year-old Lady Jane Grey into her home. The Council approved those proposals, and it seemed an ideal arrangement. Elizabeth was very fond of her stepmother, and could learn a lot from such a charming and experienced royal lady. In happy relief we settled in Chelsea under the Queen's wing. I knew she would be a huge help to me in overseeing Elizabeth's adolescence.

But we hadn't reckoned with Sir Thomas Seymour, now Lord High Admiral. I heard it from my dear brother-in-law, Anthony Denny, that a few weeks after King Henry's death, the dashing Admiral had asked the Council for permission to marry Lady Elizabeth! His brother (the Lord Protector) and the whole Council at once vetoed his ambitious scheme. Unabashed, he then began courting Queen Catherine. In fact they had wanted to marry before she became Queen. But when

King Henry became attracted to her, even Tom Seymour had the good sense to leave the field. Now, in 1547, he renewed his attentions, often visiting her Chelsea manor. The Queen, who had not had an enviable life with the ailing King Henry, was soon so in love with the handsome Admiral that she agreed to a secret marriage with him as soon as April. When the Lord Protector and Council heard about it they were angry, and indeed the general opinion was that such a quick re-marriage showed scant respect for King Henry's memory.

However, the marriage was lawful. And, of course, the Admiral came to live with us at Chelsea. What can I say about him? He was thirty-eight then, a hot-blooded, high-spirited and impulsive man – definitely a risk-taker and very full of himself! He was attractive to women – me included, I must admit. My dear John couldn't stand him, and managed with difficulty to maintain a courteous attitude. The Admiral took liberties with female servants, and even with married gentlewomen. He was a persistent bottom-pincher and would roar with laughter when reproved:

"I can't resist a Devon dumpling! You should be flattered, Mrs Ashley!"

What he really relished, though, was a challenge. He had set his cap at the Queen and won her. Not content with that, he started to lay siege to Lady Elizabeth. It began with his often coming to her bedchamber. I felt I couldn't bar his way, but I did remonstrate.

"I'm disappointed in you, Kat," he complained. "I've never put *you* down as a prude. What a spoilsport you are! I'm just playing. The poor girl needs some fun in her life. You let her stand on her dignity too much. In fact I'm an important part of her education. An experienced man like me has a lot to offer."

"Pardon me, sir, but –"

"No 'buts', Kat. You know I mean no harm. You'll have to allow me my games. After all, I am the master of this manor now."

He would give me a dazzling smile and a mock bow as he left.

It seemed to begin as play, but as it continued I felt there was a purpose to it. He went so far in his fun as to slap Elizabeth on the back or even on the bottom, and he would often chase her. If she was in still in bed, he would pull back the curtains and lean in towards her, while she squealed and backed away. Once he even tried to kiss her in bed! At that point my indignation burst out, and I actually ordered him to leave the room.

Elizabeth herself, nearly fourteen by then, was apprehensive of these morning visits, but also excited. We knew it was the Admiral when we heard the handle of her privy chamber being turned without a knock first. She would giggle nervously and run to me or the maids. There's no doubt she was attracted by this man of power, authority and boldness. She had never received any male attention, because no-one would have dared approach her in King Henry's lifetime. She had always been treated with great deference and respect, and she didn't know how to deal with the Admiral's brazen challenges. He seemed to knock her off her pedestal.

Word of his imprudent teasing began to circulate in the manor. I became more uneasy and button-holed him quietly one day. "Excuse me please, my Lord Admiral, but I must beg you to stop your visits to Lady Elizabeth's bedchamber. They are being talked of now, and much criticised."

"For Heaven's sake, woman, you know it's just a game! Don't listen to such gossip."

"I must protest, sir, because Lady Elizabeth's honour is at stake. It's my job to safeguard her good name. You know how vital that is to her."

"Don't be ridiculous, Kat! My friendly visits are part of family life. I won't put up with malicious slanders on me. In fact, I'll complain to my brother!"

I could see I would get nowhere with the indignant Admiral, so I reluctantly mentioned my worries to the Queen.

"My dear Mrs Ashley," she demurred, "Surely you're making too much of this? You know how my lord always loves a game. He just wants to be an affectionate stepfather to an orphaned child."

"I'm sure his intentions are good, Your Majesty," I lied. "But I'm concerned how outsiders could view this. Rumours can't be stopped, and they get worse in the telling. I must keep her name above reproach, madam."

"Of course we all want that, Mrs Ashley. If any false rumours start, it's best to ignore them."

"Unfortunately, madam, they've already started. Forgive me if I beg Your Majesty to accompany the Lord Admiral when he next visits Lady Elizabeth's bedchamber. Your Majesty is so respected that your presence by his side would give the lie to such gossip."

"I really don't see the need for this. However, since it is you, Mrs Ashley, who is begging this of me, I will come with my lord a few times."

I thanked her, knelt and kissed her hand.

"What time do you say he calls on Elizabeth?" she asked.

"It is early, madam. Usually about seven o'clock."

"What? As early as that? I'm asleep then! Never mind. I'll tell my lord to come to my chamber and wake me before he goes visiting." She stopped and smiled. "He'll be good at that!"

The Queen did come with the Admiral a few times after that and I was most thankful to see her. They were both in a very good humour. They would tease and joke with Elizabeth, and we all had a good laugh.

The Lord Admiral, however, was not a man to be easily deflected. Later, when we stayed at his house in London, he began to call alone again, dressed only in a nightgown! I had to confront him about that, and my anxieties re-surfaced.

In the new year of 1548 the Queen informed us all that she was pregnant. Tongues had been wagging in Chelsea since Christmas, when she had been sick, and news of the coming child brought great joy.

However, I could see that Elizabeth was upset by the news. She burst out to me one day in private,

"When she has the baby, I won't come first with her anymore! That's the trouble, Kat. I can see it coming. I know Lady Bryan did love me, but she loved her own granddaughters more. And look at the Careys now! Catherine Knollys has a baby a year, so we hardly ever meet. And now Harry's got two babies as well!"

"Life moves on, my dear," I said. "New generations have to spring up. One day soon, God willing, you'll have your own family to love."

"I'm so glad you haven't had a baby yet, Kat. I'm sorry to say that, because I know you'd like one. But I still come first with you, don't I?"

"You do, my dear; you know that."

"And I hardly see Mary now," she added. "She disapproved of the Queen marrying the Admiral, didn't she? So she hasn't been to see us. And she keeps away from the King's Court because it's Protestant. As for the King, we're separated now. We write, but it's not the same."

"We did see him at Christmas," I said.

"Yes, but he was so busy. Everything's changed! And now the Queen's going to change too!"

"But she'll always be very fond of you and look after you, my lady."

"But I won't come first any more."

She wasn't easy to comfort now she was growing up. She saw things too clearly. And she was right. For someone of her rank, she was unusually lacking in family and powerful supporters.

The poor Queen suffered from sickness and exhaustion throughout her pregnancy, and the Admiral no doubt felt rather neglected. He increased his visits to Elizabeth's rooms in spite of my protests. He seemed well-informed about the few times that I was elsewhere, and Elizabeth told me that he would then order her maids to go. Although flattered by his attention she was luckily also nervous of him, and she had the courage to remind the maids that they had promised me not to leave her alone with him.

"Mrs Ashley is getting above herself as usual," he said once. "How can she set herself above the Lord High Admiral of England? What does she mean by it, my dear?"

The maids stood their ground and reported it all to me. I was very awkwardly placed at that time. I couldn't enlist the Queen's help, because of her sickness, and Sir Thomas was, after all, the master of the house and 'in loco parentis' while the Queen was ill. Matters came to an unhappy head some weeks later, when the Queen happened to see her husband embracing Elizabeth in a corridor. She was so furious that the Admiral was worried for his unborn child, and did his best to soothe her by acting the injured innocent. The Queen, however, had seen him in that role before, and was not easily placated.

She sent for me later that day. She looked miserable and expressed her disappointment over my care of Elizabeth. "I have decided that Her Grace and her household must leave this house for the time being. Her Grace is not old enough to head a household, so you must consider where she may now lodge. I expect you, Mrs Ashley, to arrange somewhere suitable as soon as you can. I must approve it. And the King, of course, must give his consent."

The Queen also summoned Elizabeth to see her privately, and gave her a sad and serious lecture. She said that her forward behaviour had been unworthy of her, and would undermine her status. "You, of all people, need to maintain the highest moral standards."

Elizabeth came back to her rooms weeping. She loved the Queen. She didn't want to be sent away. Between sobs she complained that the Admiral had not treated her with the respect she was owed. He had kept intruding on her. She hadn't known how to handle it.

Now that she was nearly grown up, I didn't often put my arms round her, but I did that time. She needed comforting, and I knew that the Admiral had been the troublemaker, not fourteen-year-old Elizabeth.

I too felt wretched. I blamed myself for not having opposed the Admiral more defiantly. But with the Queen sick and Elizabeth alone in the world, who could I have turned to? I felt I was inadequate in this complex situation. I found myself wondering how Lady Bryan would have dealt with the Admiral. Would she have repulsed him more staunchly than I had? As a noblewoman she had always had more status than me. I cried for some time on John's shoulder, feeling out of my depth. John was a great support and comfort. He pointed out what a relief it would be to get away from the Admiral. He suggested we should propose moving to my sister Joan's house at Cheshunt in Hertfordshire. You may remember she was the wife of Sir Anthony Denny. He had earned a very high reputation at Court, having become Chief Gentleman of the Privy Chamber to King Henry. They would certainly be approved by the Council as an appropriate lodging for Lady Elizabeth.

And so it turned out. In consultation with the Queen we gave the reason for the move as the Queen's sickness, rather than the Admiral's reprehensible overtures to Elizabeth.

At the end of May we all moved to Cheshunt, taking with us Roger Ascham of Cambridge, who had recently become tutor to Elizabeth. He was a most scholarly man, but also excellent company, and our small household was much enlivened by him. Elizabeth's academic talents flourished, greatly applauded by Master Ascham. He and John got on particularly well, and they had endless happy debates on the classics and the new religion. Another newcomer about that time was Master Thomas Parry, who had been appointed Treasurer to Elizabeth. Under King Henry's will she had inherited several royal manors and an income of £3000 a year. So she now needed someone to manage her property.

My beloved sister made us extremely welcome. She and Sir Anthony had had nine children in as many years, but their grand house was very large, and room was found for our household. It was an undemanding refuge for us from a time of great uneasiness at Chelsea. I remember hoping that Elizabeth might make a friend of one of my nieces. But they were all a bit too young. And, in any case, Elizabeth by then had a fair amount of self-importance and would not have thought them suitable.

Elizabeth soon wrote to the Queen from Cheshunt expressing how sad she was to leave her. She stressed that she had taken the Queen's advice to heart. In fact they kept up a happy correspondence all that summer of 1548. The Queen wrote sometimes from Sudeley in Gloucestershire, where she had travelled to await the birth. She missed Elizabeth and wished she was with her, writing: 'Gloucestershire is so far away. It is very peaceful but dull! I'm longing to get to the end of this pregnancy and feel well again. When I can travel, I will return and summon you at once to Chelsea to meet our baby.'

As the weeks drew on, Elizabeth wrote that if she were at the birth she would have the baby smacked 'for all the trouble he has put you to!' She sent good wishes from us all at Cheshunt for a safe delivery.

We were so delighted to hear that the baby, though a girl, had arrived safely at the end of August. Our letters of congratulation were sent by a fast rider, but by the time he reached Sudeley Castle the graceful Queen was dead from childbed fever. She had died two days before Elizabeth's fifteenth birthday, which we had celebrated with such joy.

It was a tragic shock. Particularly for motherless Elizabeth who had become so attached to the kind Queen. Another support had been kicked from under her.

She wept, but rallied surprisingly fast. "I can see I must be strong, Kat. I must fend for myself soon. I've got no real family now to shelter me."

At that time, of course, we did have the shelter of the Dennys' home. However, in October the King's Council of Regency judged that the Lady Elizabeth was now old enough to head her own household. She was to reside at the Royal Manor of Hatfield, which had recently been granted to her. It must have been a relief to Joan that Elizabeth and her servants were not to be billeted on her any longer. But when it came to our departure, Joan (after a deep curtsey to her royal guest) clung to me in tears assuring me what a cheerful support I had been. I hugged and kissed her for all the hospitality she had given us, and because I loved her.

"Your sister is a good woman," Elizabeth said (rather enviously) as we rode away. "You will always have a home there, Kat."

We had barely settled into Hatfield, when I myself was summoned to London to a most humiliating interview with the Lord Protector and his powerful wife, Duchess Anne. They were obviously suspicious of the Admiral's intentions towards Lady Elizabeth now that his wife had died. It was the Duchess who spoke, while the Lord Protector simply stared at me grimly.

"You may be wondering, Mrs Ashley, why you are being honoured with our valuable time? And you a mere gentlewoman. We have brought you here to warn you very sternly to take more care in watching over the Lady Elizabeth.

Disgraceful rumours have reached us that the Admiral was paying improper attention to her even while the Queen Dowager was alive."

She paused to hear my response.

"Your Grace," I said, "I have done my humble best to keep the Lady Elizabeth from any harm."

"Then your best is not good enough. We hear that you are on the Admiral's side in this matter of state? What do you say to that?"

"Your Grace, I am always on Lady Elizabeth's side."

"Whatever that means. You can be quite certain, Mrs Ashley, that the Council would never give their consent to the Admiral marrying the second in line to the throne. That is forbidden territory. He is far too ambitious for his own good."

I bent my head.

"Last but not least, Mrs Ashley, you will certainly be replaced by someone more suitable, if we hear anything more to suggest that you are unfit to look after the King's sister."

I felt weak at the knees at that threat, and couldn't get away from London fast enough. I had to relay it all to Elizabeth, and she was furious at the Duchess's 'presumption', as she put it. But we both knew where the power lay.

I reported it all to John in some distress.

"My dear Kat," he said, "you must take care to have no communication whatsoever with that dreadful man. I'm sure Her Grace is half in love with him. I watch her. She can't help smiling when he's mentioned, and she even blushes. For God's sake keep them apart and stop talking about him."

Thus began some turbulent months. The Admiral was a man who created turbulence. He didn't grieve long for his Queen, but apparently began to scheme secretly to secure Elizabeth as his wife. He knew that he needed the Council's permission. He should have known that it would be impossible for him to get it.

He was fuelled by a great jealousy of his brother and a sense of injustice: "I am kept back. I am kept down," he growled to Thomas Parry, whom he had summoned to London several times to itemise Elizabeth's property and lands. He proposed that Elizabeth should acquire grand Durham House as her London residence by visiting Duchess Anne and trying to persuade her to lean on the Council!

Elizabeth was outraged at the idea that she should be a supplicant to the Duchess. "I won't do it. You must tell the Admiral so. I won't go to London, let alone sweet-talk any Duchess!"

When Parry put to her the Admiral's question of whether, if the Council agreed, she would marry the Admiral, she replied very warily,

"If the Council agreed, I would do what God advised me."

Parry's visits to the Admiral had been noticed, as had the Admiral's rash talk of recruiting soldiers in the West Country, where he owned a lot of land. His visits to the Royal Mint in Bristol to raise money were also common knowledge. He wrote to me asking to visit Elizabeth at Hatfield on his way to his lands, but I told him not to come for fear of gossip. We heard that London was full of rumours that the Admiral would seek to marry Lady Mary or Lady Elizabeth. Old Lord Russell was deputed to warn the Admiral off such an idea.

"Why, what's wrong with it?" retorted the Admiral. "They will need to marry, and it's much better if they marry a high-ranking man from this Kingdom rather than abroad."

"The Council would never stand for any man setting himself so high," said Lord Russell. "It would be seen as opposition to the King's Grace. You'll ruin yourself!"

Suspicion was swirling about London, and swelling fast. Fears of a power struggle and even civil war were being voiced. But the impetuous Admiral spurned humility and retreat. He was summoned to see the Lord Protector, but refused to go. On

17th January 1549, the Council decided that he should be committed to the Tower for 'disloyal practices'.

We had a few hours' warning from one of our post-riders of the Admiral's fall. "The traitor's friends are being rounded up too," he whispered. "No knowing where it will end…"

Parry turned pale at that, and I seized his arm and hurried to Elizabeth. She was appalled to hear that the Admiral was in the Tower, and she was struck by Parry's fear.

"But I can't be tainted by this," she insisted. "I took no part in anything he may have planned."

"Certainly not, milady," I said. "But we may be questioned. There are rumours that he wanted to marry you. We must support each other. None of us would have gone behind the Council's back. We would never have agreed to a marriage without the Council's consent."

"I've never promised to marry him at all!"

"Of course not, milady. And there's no need to mention all those stupid games he played on you at Chelsea."

"We've all forgotten that," she said.

"Exactly."

"Anyway, as the King's Grace's sister I am hardly likely to come under any suspicion."

"It's best to be prepared, milady. The Council of Regency is very powerful. Until His Grace the King comes of age, the Council rules us, and we have to obey its commands."

"We are safe in the truth that we've never disobeyed the Council," she said flatly.

"Yes that's the truth, and it's what we must all maintain. Come on, man," I said to Parry, "get a grip on yourself. You look condemned already!"

"You can say that, Mrs Ashley," he whispered. "You haven't served at Court and seen what I saw in King Henry's reign! The purges swept up the innocent as well as the guilty."

"But you haven't been at Court for a long time now," I said.

"The Admiral kept summoning me to his London house, didn't he? That'll all come out. I can tell you I'm trembling in my shoes."

"That's enough!" said Elizabeth sharply. (I had noticed her eyes narrow when Parry let slip that innocent people had been condemned in her father's reign.) "You're a man. You should be fortifying us women, not trying to frighten us. Take him away, Kat, and calm him down."

I led Parry quickly to his chamber, and advised him not to appear before the servants until he could put a better face on things. Rather apprehensive myself by then, I went to look for John in the Great Hall. There I suddenly stood still as several guards officers tramped loudly in and demanded that Mrs Ashley and Master Parry be produced. Everyone in the hall was struck silent. I stepped forward and made myself known. They soon collected Parry.

"Orders from King Edward's Council to take you both to London. No questions. Fetch their cloaks."

I found my voice.

"Sir, I must tell Her Grace the Lady Elizabeth that I have to leave her to go with you. Otherwise Her Grace will be most displeased."

"I have specific orders not to permit any words between you. Into the courtyard now. The horses are waiting."

Quite dazed I followed the officers out into the cold where an escort of guards was standing by. We were soon mounted and set off at once. I saw Parry ahead, slumped in the saddle, but we were kept apart for the whole journey. It took three days because of the short daylight and the atrocious winter roads.

I was exhausted when we reached London, and terrified when I learnt we were being taken to the Tower. I could only think of Signor Dante's *Inferno* and its dreadful warning: 'Abandon hope, all ye who enter here!' I was left alone in a small, cold room for several days for my fear to feed on itself. I thought of how worried poor John would be for me. I didn't know that he too had been imprisoned for questioning, though not in the Tower. I tried not to dwell on what sort of panic Parry would be in by now. My mind kept returning to Elizabeth. I knew she was strong and courageous, but she still needed me. She had grown up under my care. I had no children. I dare to claim I was like a mother to her. She was closer to me than to any of her few relations. We still put our arms around each other sometimes. If the worst happened to me, who would there be to love her? I found myself crying as I imagined her loneliness.

After a few days three men came to interrogate me on behalf of the Council. They sat facing me across a table, and fired questions at me about the Admiral.

"You are in some danger, Mrs Ashley," they said. "It will be wise for you to answer us truthfully. The Lord Admiral is suspected of having designs to marry the Lady Elizabeth. What do you know about that?"

"I know, sirs, that rumours were around in London last month," I replied. "But personally I heard nothing ever from the Admiral to that effect."

"But we have heard that you favoured the Admiral's suit."

"Not so, sirs."

"I suggest that the Admiral took trouble to win you over to his treacherous schemes, because he knew what great influence you have with Lady Elizabeth."

"No. It wasn't like that at all. I respected the Admiral as a member of the Council, and as the Lord Protector's brother, but I swear he made no proposal of marriage to Lady Elizabeth. If he had done so, the Council would have been the first to hear about it. Neither Lady Elizabeth nor I would have considered a proposal unless it had the Council's blessing."

"You say that now, Mrs Ashley, in this place, but we have information that you were a supporter of the Admiral's designs on Lady Elizabeth."

"I never encouraged him to go behind the Council's back."

"So you *did* encourage him?"

"No, sirs. I've had no influence on him in any way. Certainly not in respect of the Lady Elizabeth's Grace."

"But you sent a letter to him recently."

"That was just a reply. And I turned down his suggestion of visiting Lady Elizabeth at Hatfield."

"But you admit to corresponding with him."

"I was trying to keep him at a distance, for fear of fuelling the London rumours."

"What about the rumour that Lady Elizabeth is pregnant by the Admiral?"

"What?"

"You heard me, Mrs Ashley."

"I can't believe there's such a wicked slander. It's a cruel lie! It's been invented to bring my lady into disgrace. It must be denied immediately!"

"There would certainly be no future for *you*, Mrs Ashley, if the story turns out to have any foundation."

I felt tears welling up. Not for the threat to me, but for Elizabeth's reputation. She was so proud of how popular she was with the people. She didn't deserve to be dishonoured by such scandalous fabrications.

The questioning went on for several days. I had nothing to hide, except that I had been rather dazzled by the Admiral's flamboyant and dashing personality. I was not going to mention his foolish pranks at Chelsea; they wouldn't do Elizabeth's reputation any good, even though they had not been her fault.

I was shocked a week later when my interrogators said Parry had written a confession about his own meetings with the Admiral, and about the misbehaviour at Chelsea. I demanded to see Parry and hear it from his own mouth. He was led in, looking stricken, and babbled on about the

Admiral's rude impertinence in Elizabeth's bedchamber. He also dredged up all he could remember of private conversations he, Parry, had had with me!

In one of those private moments I had sighed, "I'd rather the Lady Elizabeth marry the Admiral than any other man! But I daren't talk about it now, because I've had such a ticking-off from Duchess Anne."

I felt he had been a despicable coward in volunteering such information, and I shouted at him that he was letting Lady Elizabeth down, and breaking his own promise. Then I burst into tears again.

The interrogators stepped up to the table with pen and paper. "There's a lot you haven't told us, Mrs Ashley. That puts you in a very bad light. If you value your safety, you will write us your own complete confession. Here and now. Pray that The Lord Protector is a merciful man."

I had to do it. I found out later that our confessions were sent to Hatfield to confront Elizabeth. I was told that she was terribly upset when she first saw them, and that she wept for a long time. I was also informed that the Council had dismissed me from my post as Elizabeth's Lady Mistress, because I had shown myself to be totally unsuitable. Lady Tyrwhit was appointed in my place.

So I was disgraced. I lost my home and the girl whom I had brought up with a mother's love.

But I had my life. Thomas Seymour was beheaded on March 19th, but amazingly Parry and I were released! In spite of our 'inappropriate gossip' no evidence had been found that we had conspired with the Lord Admiral to deceive the Council, or participate in any of his 'disloyal practices'. We were small fry, caught up in the twisted net which the turbulent Admiral had wrapped around himself. The Tower spewed us out. 'Out of the valley of the shadow of death', as I kept repeating. I spent a large part of the following weeks on my knees thanking God for answering my desperate prayers.

John had also been released from the Fleet Prison, and we were kindly taken in by his brother Richard in Berkshire. We couldn't go back to the Dennys because Sir Anthony had been sent by the Council as one of Elizabeth's interrogators. I didn't dare write to Elizabeth, but I managed to send word to dear Martha, who was still in her service. I just told her that we'd been freed, and where we were now living. As I'd expected, I received no reply. But my courier reported that the gatekeeper at Hatfield had recognised my writing and smiled, "Martha shall have it."

We were glad to put distance between ourselves and London. I felt exhausted and very low. I'd been terrified, publicly rebuked and sacked. We had no home and no income, and I was missing Elizabeth badly and all of our friends at Hatfield. On my worst days I imagined her heart had been turned against me.

In fact quite the opposite was true, as I learned later. She was fighting defiantly for my safety and my return to her. To her chief interrogator, Sir Robert Tyrwhit, she would not hear of any blame upon Parry or me, even on his promise of a free pardon for herself. In a letter to the Lord Protector she begged him to 'be good to Kat Ashley'. She raged against Lady Tyrwhit being appointed her Lady Mistress. She wept all night and sulked all day: "Mrs Ashley is my only Mistress", was her refrain. Sir Robert reported that it was astonishing how much she loved me, and how she stuck up for me angrily whenever I was criticised.

I had usually drafted her letters for her, but she now had to compose them herself. And the three letters she wrote to the Lord Protector then were respectful, but firm and very mature. She too had heard from her interrogators the rumours that she was pregnant with the Admiral's child.

"My Lord," she wrote, "These are shameful slanders."

She asked to come to Court to show herself there. When she did not get a satisfactory answer, she wrote again demanding that the Council should issue a direct proclamation that the rumours were lies.

In early March she took the initiative again in pleading to the Lord Protector for my release. When she eventually showed me a copy of that letter, it made me cry. She wrote that she had a duty to speak up for me because I had been with her for many years, and had taken great trouble in bringing her up, not only in education but also in moral standards. "We are, of course, grateful to our parents," she wrote, "But in bringing us into the world, they are only following their natural instincts. We should be even more grateful to those who spend years bringing us up."

Elizabeth went on to say that whatever I might have done in the matter of a marriage between herself and the Lord Admiral, I would have done it in good faith, knowing that the Lord Admiral himself was a member of the Council. She had often heard me say that I would not want her to marry anyone without the consent of the Lord Protector and the Council.

Her final reason for my release was this: if a woman whom she loved so much was kept in the Tower, people would think that she, Lady Elizabeth, was not innocent, but had simply been spared imprisonment because she was so young.

She did not forget my husband either, and ended her letter by asking for his release too, because he was related to her.

So. She had been fighting for us. Fifteen years old and all unsupported as she was.

We didn't know that at the time, however. We kept a low profile, and had to rely on the generosity of John's brother to support ourselves. But that autumn the Lord Protector himself was ousted from the Council and sent to the Tower. The new strong man was John Dudley, Duke of Northumberland. Soon afterwards, to our great joy, we received a letter from Elizabeth asking us to come back to Hatfield to serve her again.

We had an emotional reunion there, thankful to God for preserving us all. Elizabeth and I were simultaneously crying and laughing with the happiness of being together. It felt so good to be in the country with all of our old friends after the cold terror of the Tower and then our homelessness.

And yet it was not the same as before. I had been away for eight months. Elizabeth was suddenly taller than me. She had just reached her sixteenth birthday, and she had developed a new authority. It had been growing upon her ever since the Queen had died. She had braced herself then to be strong, and she had soon needed to be so, when I too was snatched from her side. Then she had faced down her interrogators over many weeks, standing up for herself, alone. It had been a huge shock to her to be under suspicion. Her high rank had been no protection, and she told me Sir Robert Tyrwhit had stressed that she was in danger and that she was 'only a subject'.

She had persevered through that dark tunnel, using only her natural bravery, loyalty and intelligence as her defence. She had withstood the pressure to incriminate herself or her servants. As a result, she now felt even more confidence in her own abilities. She was self-reliant. She drafted her own letters and she inspected her own household accounts.

I recognised the change in her. She still loved me – and I like to think she still needed the warm devotion I gave her, and the loving respect she received from Martha, Nell and Sally, her life-long nursemaids – but she had graduated from my care to taking over the reins of her own life. She had learnt great faith in her own judgement. So that, when she decided on something, it was an uphill struggle indeed to persuade her otherwise!

That Christmas we went to Court. King Edward was delighted to see his sister again, and she was given a lavish royal welcome. In fact she was by the King's side for most of her visit. I remember she chose to wear particularly plain clothes and no jewels on that visit. She wanted to show herself to the Court and Londoners as the chaste virgin she was, so that no fuel could be added to the old slanders. The King (a very pious boy) admired her simple appearance, and called her 'My sweet sister, Temperance'.

Lady Mary did not come to Court that time, although she had been invited. A religious chasm separated her from her Protestant siblings. That year the Council's Act of Uniformity became law: Cranmer's marvellous new English Prayer Book became the only permitted form of worship, and the Latin Mass was therefore banned. Lady Mary appealed for help to her cousin, Emperor Charles of Spain, and he asked the Council to allow her to practise her Catholic religion. The Council refused to make Mary an exception to their law, but so far had taken no steps against her. It was a delicate situation that was left unresolved.

But the following Christmas of 1550 Lady Mary did come to Court and sparks began to fly. The King was thirteen by then, and a strong promoter of his father's reformed religion. He criticised Mary in public for still holding the Mass. Mary was hurt and wept, but then retaliated by telling the King's Grace that he was far too young to pronounce on religious matters! She soon left London for her estates in East Anglia, where a lot of people were Catholic sympathisers. (In fact, only the year before, the Council had subdued a religious rebellion there.)

The next year the Emperor of Spain actually threatened us with war unless Lady Mary was allowed to hear Mass! The Council finally capitulated and permitted her to do so. Lady Mary (with her powerful relations) had fought her corner and won. I remember complaining to John that Lady Mary had overruled the laws of England, and it was a bad omen.

John soon calmed me down. "Take the long view, my dear. Lady Mary is now thirty-five, and will soon be past child-bearing. She will then lose most of her importance in the Succession. Luckily time's not on her side."

Lady Elizabeth wisely took no public part in debates about Lady Mary's religion. I can't believe that her brother wouldn't have sought her opinion in private on the festering problem. But she never mentioned it to anyone else. John and I didn't have high rank at Court, and we only saw Elizabeth in her private apartments there. But we did have the honour of accompanying her into London that Christmas of 1550. The procession formed just outside the city walls. The King had sent a hundred of his royal guards to escort her, and many of the nobility had also joined her there. Cheering crowds had gathered along our route, and Lady Elizabeth, in a bright green cloak on a splendid black horse, turned this way and that to thank them. She has always made the most of such occasions, winning her audience with her high spirits and grace of manner.

I remember Elizabeth told me later that Lady Mary had been informed by her friend, the Spanish Ambassador, about Elizabeth's grand welcome. "The King's purpose," he had said, "is to show the people that Lady Elizabeth has become a very great lady because she has embraced the new religion."

Most of the year, of course, we were not in London. We lived mainly at Hatfield or Ashridge, where Elizabeth took great pleasure and pride in managing her estates. She was keen to extract the maximum income from her farms and forests, and asked sharp questions about any failings. She had appointed Mr William Cecil as the surveyor of her estates. He was a rising star as secretary to the Duke of Northumberland, now leader of the Council. Unusually for a young lady, Elizabeth relished her business meetings. But she also loved reading, music, dancing, riding and hunting, and was talented at them all.

Those years were a time in which she was able to reconnect with her Boleyn cousins, Catherine and Harry. And their families! Catherine by then had, I think, nine of her eventual fifteen children, and Harry four of his twelve! Catherine was often summoned to stay at Ashridge and Harry became a gentleman of Elizabeth's household in 1551. Elizabeth always felt at home with those two, whom she'd known all her life. She looked up to them (as she had as a child) and didn't stand on her dignity as much as usual.

It was in April 1552, soon after another of Lady Elizabeth's grand visits to Court, that King Edward first fell ill. He caught the frightening disease of smallpox. He recovered, by God's grace, but his narrow escape made everyone suddenly think about the future. I'm sure it was the reason that Lady Elizabeth, then aged eighteen, decided to try to find out about her mother.

"Come to my bedchamber, Kat," she said one evening. "I want to talk to you alone." Her words then poured out as if they'd been held back for a long time. "I've been thinking about this for many months, but my brother's illness has made up my mind. I've been questioning Cathy and Harry about my mother. They knew her, of course, but they were surprised and reluctant to talk about her. Apparently their own mother, Mary, and Lady Bryan had impressed on them never to mention her to me. But they did admit that their mother strongly believed that her sister was innocent. What do you think of that, Kat? I was amazed."

She didn't wait for me to answer. "I know my mother was in disgrace. It was safest for me to forget her. I can't remember her at all. That's why I want to listen to people who knew her. My brother, the King, would sympathise. I know he's often asked his family and courtiers about his own mother. It's a natural thing to do, isn't it?"

"Yes; yes it is, Your Grace. But in your case –"

"Don't interrupt me, Kat. You must hear me out. I'm not

going to be put off now. Don't worry. I'm not going to shout anything from the rooftops."

"The point is," she continued, choosing her words slowly and carefully, "There are some people who perhaps in the future might not look kindly on me inquiring into my mother's life and death. And perhaps I could come under closer scrutiny one day. So, I've made up my mind to do it as soon as possible. Don't mention this to anyone, Kat, not even John. It will be a secret between you and me, and the few people I intend to interview. I want you to arrange for these people to come here. We must get on with it. But I'm not going to put anything into writing, and I don't want anyone else to either. Letters can go astray. These are the people I want to see: Lady Bryan, Archbishop Cranmer, Lady Shelton, Lady James Boleyn and one or two of my mother's ladies-in-waiting. I've heard that Mary Zouch was close to her. Can you think of anyone else who could help me?"

"I do think the fewer the better, Your Grace. Having a lot of visitors will attract attention."

She waited in silence tapping her foot.

"But I suppose you could see the Reverend Matthew Parker. He was Queen Anne's chaplain, and she asked him to look after you."

"Did she, Kat? Did she ask that?"

"Lady Bryan told me," I said. "Queen Anne asked her to do the same. It was shortly before the Queen was arrested. But she must have been very frightened."

"So. She was thinking of me. It's nice for me to hear that." She turned and looked out of the window while she absorbed what I had said. "You see, I know nothing at all. I've never seen a picture of her. I've hardly spoken of her. You stressed it would make my father angry. I took that to heart."

"Thank God, Your Grace. We were so worried about what you might say."

144

"And later I knew not to mention her, not to remind people of her. Even after King Henry had died. Because some people thought – and still think – that her marriage to the King was not valid. So, in their minds, I should have no place in the Succession. You explained all that, Kat. I even felt ashamed of my mother. But now I'm grown-up I want to find out more. I owe her that. I owe myself that. After all, the Bible says, 'Honour thy father and thy mother'."

Then she gave me instructions to go to London and track down the people she wanted, and fix dates.

"The only one whose visit will be noticed is the Archbishop," she said, "and he can say that he's coming here as my godfather to check on my knowledge of the scriptures. And I know from her letters that Lady Bryan isn't well. I'll write to her myself today. If she can't travel, I'll go to see her. No one could criticise me for visiting my old Lady Mistress. I'm impatient about all this, Kat. Be as quick as you can, won't you?"

"I will. But it's all very sudden to me. Please remember that this is the first I've heard about it. I can see you've been thinking about it for a long time."

"I have. But the King's recent illness has made me think it urgent."

"Yes. I understand what you mean. I'll leave tomorrow. But I haven't the status to approach these people on my own. Could you write me a short note introducing and vouching for me? Say that I'm conveying your wishes."

"Very well. If you think it will speed matters up."

I told John I was being sent on a private mission.

"As long as it's nothing to do with matters of state," he said.

"No, it's a family matter."

He laughed dryly. "Royal Family matters *are* matters of state. Don't we know it! Be discreet, my dear, and keep a low profile. Whatever it is, I don't want to know anything about it."

I set off for London with Sally and four guardsmen. We stayed in magnificent Durham Place, which now belonged to Lady Elizabeth. She had commissioned me to buy materials for new dresses, and some new chairs for Hatfield. That was the reason I was in London, if anyone should inquire.

I began with Matthew Parker and Lady Shelton, as they knew me a little. The priest was delighted to accept an invitation to Hatfield. Lady Shelton was reluctant to get involved, and I had to remind her that Lady Elizabeth was close to the King's Grace, and would not take kindly to a refusal.

Lady James Boleyn, on the other hand, was well aware of her great-niece's current status, and preened herself on the summons to Hatfield. She also enabled me to track down Mary Zouch.

I had known that Archbishop Cranmer would be difficult to approach. So many petitioners waited at the gates of Lambeth Palace. I had to dig deep in my purse to persuade the gatekeeper to let me in with Lady Elizabeth's letter, as he grumbled about forgeries. But, after a long wait, I was ushered in to Cranmer's office.

"I'm sorry you weren't given priority, Mrs Ashley," he said. "I have great respect for my goddaughter, and high hopes for her. Is she well?"

"Very well, Your Grace. I must tell you that she is a great admirer of your new English Prayer Book and we read it every day. But she has sent me to ask you to see her at Hatfield as soon as convenient. She has an urgent private matter she wants to discuss with you."

"I see," he said slowly.

"Her Grace knows that you are busy, sir, but she is confident that – as her godfather – you will do her the honour of visiting her."

He paused, then said, "Yes, Mrs Ashley, the honour will be

mine. Please tell Her Grace that I look forward to it. And thank you for bringing her message. Now I will leave you with my secretary to find the earliest convenient date. I'm afraid it may be a month or so."

I felt surprised and elated that I had achieved this important visit so readily. It made me more aware of Lady Elizabeth's very high status at that time.

Back at Hatfield, Lady Elizabeth waited in nervous excitement for the visits to start.

"I don't know what I'll find out, Kat," she said. "I must steel myself to hear bad things, but I pray for some good. I want these people to tell me their memories. Otherwise I'll never know what she was like. Most of these people are quite old now."

The visits soon began. She interviewed each visitor alone. She impressed upon them never to mention what they had discussed. My only duty was to show them in to her presence, and show them out again when she rang. In June she paid a short visit to Lady Bryan in Essex, and reported that she still had clear memories.

"I was shocked to see how weak she is," Elizabeth said. "She told me she had made her will. But I know she was pleased to see me. She said her lips had always been sealed about Queen Anne. But now she was so very old (and her dear son had died), she would talk freely, at least to me. And she did. I'm just so glad I went. She sent her best wishes to 'Kat Champernowne', too!"

I don't think news of Elizabeth's quest ever reached the Court. The few people involved knew it was not a topic to be mentioned. I believe the nursemaids (who had been with Elizabeth all her life) must have put two and two together, but they were totally loyal.

One day that summer as we walked in the garden, Elizabeth did confide in me a little.

"About my mother, Kat," she began in a low voice. "All those people I saw think she was innocent. Three of them heard her swear it on the damnation of her soul the day before she was killed. What a horror for her. How could such a miscarriage of justice happen? I can only think my great father's mind must have been poisoned by evil counsellors. Her execution was obviously planned ahead, because he was betrothed to Jane Seymour the very next day!"

Elizabeth paused a moment, and then went on.

"Lady Bryan was the only one to offer an explanation. She said, 'It was mostly about the Succession, of course.' I feel sad now, Kat. But I've done the right thing. I'm convinced she wasn't an adulteress. I know she loved me very much. My great-aunts said how amazingly brave she was on the scaffold. And at the end she said if anyone investigated her case, she hoped they would think well of her. *I* think well of her, Kat."

"That's just as it should be, my lady," I said. "I remember there were ballad-sheets in London at the time claiming Queen Anne was innocent."

"Really?"

"One was thrust into my hands in a crowded street. My mother threw it on the fire when we got back to the Dennys' house because she said it was dangerous."

"It would still be dangerous today. That's the trouble: I can't champion my poor mother. I can't cast aspersions on Queen Jane, or on anyone else. I mustn't stir up the religious divide. This subject is now closed, Kat. I'll never forget it, but I must keep silent. And so must you."

"And that reminds me, Kat," she went on. "When the Archbishop came last week, he warned me in confidence that there might well be spies in my household. 'Most great establishments have them', he said. 'They're not assassins, but they can be dangerous. They're listeners. They get paid for relaying unguarded conversations, opinions perhaps, about high-up people or religious practices. Walls have ears, and so do screens and hedges. I know, my dear goddaughter, that you are already the soul of discretion, but you must also impress that lesson on those who serve you.' He then added emphatically: 'Particularly those closest to you.' So, Kat, I am passing on his words to you. Be very careful – for my sake as well as yours."

"I know, I know, my lady. I'm just not wary by nature. But since the Tower I have tried to curb my chatter. John keeps on at me! But I can't believe we could have spies among us."

"Well, you'll *have* to believe it. The Archbishop has taken the trouble to warn me, and that's that."

I must record now that dear Lady Bryan died at the end of the summer. At eighty-two she'd had an exceptionally long life and we were certain that she had earned a place in Heaven, where she would be re-united with her husband and children. I owed so much to her experience. And the little Elizabeth had flourished under her wisdom and kindness. Our household had a special service to pray for her soul.

Around that time we saw a lot of the Knollys family. Sir Francis was a fervent Protestant (like John and I) and we had many happy private discussions about the virtues of the new religion and the vices of the old one. Lady Elizabeth took great care to distance herself from religious debate. She, meanwhile, would be basking in the company of her much-loved cousin, Lady Catherine. The many Knollys children were usually left at home at Rotherfield Greys during these visits, as Elizabeth liked to have her cousin's full attention!

Harry Carey, now an MP for Buckingham, also used to call in at Ashridge. He was doing well, and had been on two embassies to France. Elizabeth always called him 'My Harry' and preferred his wife and children to stay at home.

That Christmas of 1552 we were expecting to go to Court again. But a letter came from the Duke of Northumberland that the King's Grace had decided to moderate the Christmas festivities, so that he did not overtax his strength. Regrettably, this meant that neither of his sisters could be entertained at Court.

Elizabeth was disappointed and worried. In the New Year, she made up her mind to go to Court in February instead, for the Candlemas feast. We set off in late January, in spite of the weather, but we'd only got halfway when we were stopped by a detachment of cavalry in the royal livery. The Duke of Northumberland was instructing Lady Elizabeth to return to Hatfield, as the King could not see her at that point.

Elizabeth wrote anxious letters to her brother, but no replies came. We heard from our London contacts that the King was very ill. He was suffering the slow and fatal disease of consumption.

As the poor boy grew weaker, the Duke made hurried plans to perpetuate his own power. In May he arranged the marriage of his son, Guildford Dudley, to the Protestant Lady Jane Grey (who was third in the line of Succession under Henry VIII's will).

In June, the Duke, with the dying King, drew up a secret document setting out the new Succession, which would countermand King Henry's will. It declared that Lady Jane Grey (now Dudley) would inherit the throne, because the King's half-sisters were both illegitimate and might marry foreign princes to the detriment of our country!

When King Edward died aged fifteen on 6th July 1553, the Duke immediately announced the changed Succession. Elizabeth was appalled that her father's will had been overturned. Succession rights, in her mind, were immutable. Indeed they were virtually ordained by God. Her head and her heart were both on Lady Mary's side.

The Duke summoned both sisters to London, but Mary retreated from Hunsdon to her East Anglian estates, and

Elizabeth stayed at Hatfield saying that she was ill and couldn't travel. It was a critical time of great suspense. Riders kept arriving with the latest news.

Jane was proclaimed Queen on 10th July but Mary, undaunted, raised her standard in East Anglia. Countless lords and common people rushed to join her, angry at her unjust treatment. The Duke led his troops against her, but most of them deserted. On the 25th the Duke was arrested and sent to the Tower. His coup was over, and Mary was Queen.

The two sisters – with Mary leading – rode together into London on 3rd August surrounded by cheering crowds and pealing bells. A wrong had been quickly righted. There was an atmosphere of euphoria.

I remember it felt very strange to have a woman as our monarch. In all our long history no such phenomenon had happened. Quite by chance, all those in line to the crown were female. Now, if there had been a male among them, I suspect he might have been promoted over any females ahead of him; but there was no such man. And (unlike some European countries) we had no Salic Law, which specifically banned females from the throne. So Mary assumed the supreme power.

In her triumph she had no doubt that God had brought her to the throne. He had watched over her through all the hardships she had endured over her religion. It was His plan to use her as His instrument to bring the one, true, Catholic religion back to her realm. She was utterly dedicated to that goal, and became more and more intolerant of any dissent.

You must remember that Mary and Elizabeth had seen very little of each other for the six-and-a-half-year reign of their brother. They had kept in touch with occasional, rather formal letters. Now, at the start of Mary's reign, Elizabeth was continuously at Court. The three Grey girls were tainted by the Duke's attempted coup, so Mary and Elizabeth embodied virtually the whole Royal Family!

They were both regal and self-confident. But in looks and manner they were a complete contrast. Mary at thirty-seven was short and thin-lipped with a deep voice and a severe and penetrating gaze. Elizabeth, now nearly twenty, was taller than average with her father's auburn hair; she was vivacious, quick-witted and full of smiles. Observing the admiration which Elizabeth attracted, it was no wonder that the Queen began to feel jealous.

And, of course, there was the history. Mary was still fiercely devoted to her mother's memory. In her eyes both she and her mother had been ousted by Anne Boleyn. She was convinced that the wrongs Queen Catherine had suffered had hastened her death. Although she could not rationally blame Elizabeth for that, Elizabeth by then no doubt bore a likeness to her mother which brought bitter memories back. What's more, Elizabeth's life had never been blighted, as Mary's had, by being banished from Court for five years by her father, and only rarely received there by her brother. Elizabeth had had an easy life, yet she had still disgraced herself over her dalliance with the late Lord Admiral.

All those faults, however, would have been redeemed if only Elizabeth had been a true Catholic. That was her real sin. One of the new Queen's first proclamations asked her subjects to accept Catholicism peacefully. (There were street protests in London about that. After 20 years of the new religion most young people were Protestants.) From the start of her reign, Queen Mary put pressure on her sister to attend Mass, which was then celebrated at Court several times a day. Elizabeth stalled and procrastinated for a few weeks, but dared not hold out longer. On 8th September she did attend her first Mass, but claimed to be feeling ill and assumed a pained expression. She knew that the Court would correctly infer that she was only conforming because she felt threatened. After all – unlike Mary – she had no powerful foreign King to defend her religious beliefs.

"The Queen is so hostile to me, Kat," she said. "I can't tell anyone but you. I'm sick with worry. All her advisers are against me too. Specially the Spanish Ambassador, who's always with her."

"We can all sense the atmosphere, Your Grace," I said. "It makes me so angry."

"It's full of menace. But I have to speak up for myself. I must keep in with her. I can't just sit on my hands while they poison her mind against me. There's no one to help me – I'm alone."

It was the truth. I couldn't offer comfort.

"I'll have to see the Queen," she added. "I'll kneel before her and ask her directly why she dislikes me so, and what I can do to heal the rift."

Elizabeth was granted a private audience with the Queen. In tears, she said she feared that it was for religious reasons that Her Majesty had taken against her. She pointed out that she had never known the Catholic faith, and asked for instruction in it.

"The Queen looked down at me sourly, Kat," she said when she returned, "but she promised to send a priest and books tomorrow, and will pray for me to see the error of my sinful ways."

In public the Queen accorded Elizabeth her rightful place, as the people expected. At the coronation on 1st October, Elizabeth rode in a coach covered in silver cloth immediately behind the Queen's coach. By her side was the ex-queen, Anne of Cleves, (now speaking English quite well): two royal ladies together.

But, a few days later, Parliament, at the Queen's instigation, repealed the Act that had divorced King Henry from Catherine of Aragon. Queen Mary was therefore no longer illegitimate. This meant that King Henry's marriage to Anne Boleyn could not have been valid, and Elizabeth's position as a bastard was implicitly underlined.

At Court, away from the public eye, the Queen began to complain that Elizabeth could not possibly be the heir to the throne: she was not only a bastard but a heretic and a hypocrite too. Elizabeth's mother had been a scandalous woman, and it was even probable that King Henry had not been Elizabeth's father! All these slanders, of course, got back to Elizabeth. She felt so insulted and wounded that she asked the Queen's permission to leave Court, but that was refused. I was seething on her behalf, but she ordered me to keep calm, and not let off steam to anyone.

"I'm completely helpless in the face of these attacks," she said. "I can only try to give the lie to them by bearing myself as the King's daughter I am."

She certainly looked the part. We heard later that the ambassador of Venice (who was a Catholic) said her face and figure were very handsome, and she had a great air of dignified majesty in all she did. Indeed, he said, she looked like a Queen.

Even she, though, showed her resentment when she was further humiliated that November. Over Elizabeth's head, the Queen promoted two of her Tudor first cousins, Lady Frances Brandon (Jane Grey's mother) and Lady Margaret Douglas. Those ladies (both of Mary's age) were to take precedence over Elizabeth at Court! Elizabeth was horrified: she knew this was a challenge to her position as heir to the throne. She refused to take part in Court ceremonies, and remained mostly in her own apartments, unhappy and resentful.

The Queen, meanwhile, had lost no time in planning her own future. It was above question that a Queen's prime duty was to marry and have sons. This was urgent for her anyway at thirty-seven. It was also essential to her divine mission to embed Catholicism permanently in England once more. She had decided to marry her cousin, Philip of Spain, as soon as possible. Her enthusiastic negotiations were put in hand through Senor Renard, the Spanish Ambassador. He was

Elizabeth's worst enemy and had kept urging the Queen to send her 'clever and cunning' Protestant sister to the Tower.

In early December, Elizabeth again asked to leave the Court, which she found unbearably oppressive. To our surprise, this time Mary granted permission. I think she regarded Elizabeth's presence as a blight on her happy involvement in the wedding plans. She knew that Elizabeth had a lot of support among the people and in Parliament, and (whatever might be done in Spain) she could not send her to the Tower without a good pretext. Before we left Court, Elizabeth bravely met her sister in private. Fearful of the future, she extracted a promise from the Queen that if any accusations were made against her, she would not be condemned without proper evidence.

Dear Ashridge awaited us with a warm and familiar welcome. Our whole household had been under great strain at Court, and we felt released and happy that Christmas. John and I were well content to be home in a country backwater.

But my poor Lady Elizabeth could not relax. Even Catherine Knollys, bringing her usual comfort and kindness, couldn't soothe her. And it turned into a time of great foreboding.

"I'm not safe here, Kat. Or anywhere!", Elizabeth said. "The Queen can pluck me from Ashridge at any moment. There's the religious unrest. And now there's the Spanish marriage. The people hate that betrothal. They don't want a foreign King. And they don't want to become part of the Spanish empire like Holland. There'll be trouble. And because I'm the second person in this Kingdom, any rebel might claim my support. I can't stop anyone from using my name as a rallying-cry. And then I'd be the scapegoat, dragged down with them. I'm just a helpless pawn but my enemies will never believe that, will they?"

She grew ill and pale with her fretting. She lost her appetite and couldn't settle to any activity. She paced up and down, feeling trapped, and waiting for a storm to break over her head.

Sure enough, unrest over the Spanish marriage grew throughout January, and a revolt led by Sir Thomas Wyatt was planned. At Ashridge, Elizabeth received the dreaded summons to Court. She sent word that she was too ill to travel. The Queen sent doctors to assess her, but they couldn't persuade her to leave. Meanwhile, Wyatt led an army against London, but the royal forces won the day and the revolt collapsed on 3rd February. A week later the Queen commanded her sister to come to London and – ill as she was – she had to go. I took a body of her servants with me as I accompanied her. She was sick several times in the litter, and our cold journey took three times as long as usual. I kept her wrapped in furs and tried to persuade her to eat.

When we reached Whitehall Palace, the first news we heard was that Lady Jane Grey and her husband had been beheaded. When Queen Mary came to the throne she had mercifully spared their lives because of their youth. But this rebellion had hardened her heart against any potential enemies, and it seemed a frightening omen for Elizabeth. Hundreds of rebels were hanged.

Only ten of Elizabeth's staff were allowed in to the Palace, and for three tense weeks we were confined to our guarded rooms. Then one day a group of Councillors headed by Bishop Gardiner came in. They told Elizabeth of her suspected involvement in the treasonous rebellion. It was the Queen's pleasure that Elizabeth should be imprisoned in the Tower. We were all terrified, and I moved close to her side. But Elizabeth, after weeks of fearful inaction, rose to this direct confrontation. She stood up and steadfastly proclaimed her loyalty to her sovereign, and said that she couldn't believe that the Queen's Grace would send her to such a notorious place. Gardiner cut her short and warned her to prepare herself to move to the Tower the next day.

Then I and five other attendants were marched from her side and kept under guard in another room. There was no time to protest. We who had been expelled were her closest and longest-serving women. We were there for two days, so that we could not tell the outside world that Lady Elizabeth was to be taken to the Tower.

Once she was immured there, we were formally dismissed from her service and escorted out of the Palace into a bleak March day of rain and wind. The usual errand-boys were waiting outside the Palace, and I sent one to Elizabeth's nearby mansion of Somerset House to fetch us transport. Once safely there, I collapsed in sobs. Martha managed to tell the steward what had happened, and in no time word got out to the London Street.

I found myself thinking back seventy years to the Little Princes in the Tower. One of them was the true King of England, Edward V, aged only twelve. The other was his ten-year-old brother, the next in line. Their usurper uncle, Richard III, confined them there and they were never seen again.

The servants at Somerset House feared for their jobs as well as for their mistress. But I mourned only my mistress. Of course I had treated Lady Elizabeth with the great respect due to her rank, but to me she was also the girl I'd brought up for eighteen years. She was the child I'd never had. I deeply loved her and helplessly craved to protect her. I felt very bitter towards Queen Mary.

We stayed on in London to be near our mistress: so near and yet so far! To cheer me up, Nell and Sally would bring me pamphlets they'd been given in the streets, which were fiercely protesting against the Spanish marriage. Soon I revelled in other texts demanding that the Lady Elizabeth should be set free. I blessed the brave printing presses, which enabled opposition to circulate so fast.

There was a nine-day-wonder in the city then, when a wall

was heard to talk! When people said, 'God save Queen Mary', it made no reply. But, to 'God save Lady Elizabeth', it responded: 'So be it.' It turned out to be a con trick on gullible crowds, but was very popular until the authorities got to hear of it.

Sir Thomas Wyatt was beheaded at Tower Hill on 11th April, and word soon got round that on the scaffold he had specifically exempted Lady Elizabeth from any knowledge of his conspiracy.

That was a huge relief but it didn't stop Senor Renard from urging the Queen to execute Elizabeth as well: "Your Majesty will never be safe while your heretic sister lives. Her very existence gives hope to your enemies. For the sake of our religion you simply must harden your heart, madam."

Much later, Elizabeth told me something of her time in the Tower, seared into her memory. She admitted to being terrified. She couldn't stop thinking of her mother: "Lady Shelton had told me that my mother was executed not with the axe but by a swordsman from France. It was said to be more efficient. I decided that I too would ask for a sword. Every day I could see the chapel where she is buried."

She was interrogated by the Queen's Councillors several times, but could not be shaken into any admissions.

"I lived on my nerves, Kat. If a bell tolled, I thought it was for my imminent execution; the same when a new troop of guardsmen arrived; or I heard hammering outside; or even a knock at the door. I felt so close to death. Do you remember that line of Virgil we read with Master Ascham: 'Noctes atque dies patet atri janua Ditis? The door of dark death stands open every night and every day.' I couldn't get it out of my head. It kept coming back."

"But I prayed, and that calmed me a bit. I even composed some prayers of my own. They did give me pen and paper, you know, although I wasn't allowed to write letters. Perhaps they hoped I'd write a confession!"

The fact was that no evidence was found to convict Elizabeth of treason. Of course under King Henry's rule just to be suspected meant death. But I must grant that Queen Mary did have a respect for justice, which may have stayed her hand. Her Councillors were divided (and quarrelling by then) on the question of Elizabeth. They all knew that she was admired by a lot of the people, especially in London. So her execution would have caused angry protests. Queen and Council couldn't ignore vox populi in London. Only recently Sir Nicholas Throckmorton (one of the gentlemen of our household) had been acquitted by a jury of any involvement in the Wyatt plot. The Council had immediately sent all the jurymen to prison, but they dared not re-arrest Sir Nicholas. There was public rejoicing. It was a straw in the wind.

The Queen and Council were already bracing themselves for fierce dissent over the imminent Spanish marriage. It would not have been wise to add fuel to those inevitable flames by executing Elizabeth. But they couldn't justify keeping her in the Tower without charge. It was decided to keep her under house arrest, far from London in the country.

We heard of her release from the Tower on 19th May after two months of imprisonment. We fell on our knees in thanksgiving. News came that she had been rowed to Richmond Palace. The next day I set off with Martha in a Somerset House barge. But by the time we reached Richmond we found that Elizabeth had already been moved on westwards. She was being taken to Woodstock Manor near Oxford; and no-one was allowed to communicate with her.

This archive is not about me. Up till now you have heard a lot about me, but for much of Queen Mary's reign I was separated from Elizabeth. I missed her dreadfully. And I've heard her say that in that most dangerous time of her life it greatly added to her misery that I wasn't with her. So I can only pass on to you what she (a year-and-a-half later and bit by bit) told me about her eleven months under house arrest at Woodstock Manor:

"Before I left the Tower," she said, "I was put into the care of a most irritating man, Sir Henry Bedingfield. He was a country squire from Suffolk, a captain of the guard, and devoted to the Queen. Apparently none of the other Councillors or noblemen would consent to be my warder, so Sir Henry was leaned on. On 19th May, Kat, (the anniversary of my mother's death!), he and his guardsmen led me out of the Tower and by river to Richmond. When we got there, my servants were barred from going into the Palace with me. Suddenly I thought I was about to be assassinated! I turned and in desperation shouted to my gentleman usher, 'I think I'm going to die tonight!' I stayed awake all that night, so at least I couldn't be smothered in my sleep."

"For the next four days our convoy moved on towards Woodstock. To my astonishment, it was a glorious journey, a sunny interval between two awful places. The glory of it was the people: I hadn't been forgotten! In every village people came out to cheer and bow. They called, 'God save Your Grace!' Church bells were rung. Women brought presents of cakes and flowers to my litter. The welcome took me by surprise and made me so happy. The memory of it kept me going in the isolated months that followed."

"You'd hardly believe how dilapidated Woodstock Manor was. We lived in its small gatehouse with its broken windows and leaking roof. In winter my fingers were too cold to do embroidery. No-one had been managing it properly. You'd never see such a place on my own estates. I did at least have some of my servants there. And Parry was allowed to come and administer our expenses, but Sir Henry wouldn't let him live in so he stayed in the village pub – in very good spirits, I may say."

"Of course I asked for you to join me," she added. "But Sir

Henry had obviously been briefed on that one and immediately refused. He was a most annoying man! I soon got the measure of him. He was the sort of person who had no authority of his own. All my requests had to be referred to the Council. I wasn't allowed to communicate with anyone else. I used Sir Henry as my secretary and dictated letters to him. He was most reluctant and I'm sure he didn't send them all. One day he burst out that he was between a rock and a hard place. The Queen and Council were his rock, and I was the hard place with all my 'arrogant demands': 'You, madam, are only a prisoner. You should thank God for the Queen's mercy, and behave in grateful submission,' he said."

"I retorted that I had been deprived of my liberty but not charged with any crime. How was I supposed to resign myself to that? I wrote as much to the Council in an appeal to them. I asked either to be charged with a crime, or to be released to meet the Queen. No reply came. I was allowed to write one letter to the Queen, and I set out my loyalty and my grievances. Her reply was short: she would receive no more of my exaggerated and disingenuous letters. I felt completely abandoned then because there was no end in sight to my captivity."

"I was cut off from news of the real world. But, in July, Sir Henry did tell me that the Queen had married Prince Philip of Spain. And in November that the Pope had received England back into the Catholic Church. Then, in February 1555, we heard the cruel news that six Protestants had been burned at the stake for their faith."

"I was also told that the Queen was expecting a baby in May, which made my heart sink. Sir Henry was overjoyed at the momentous news, and he became even happier when he was told to take me to Hampton Court in April, where the birth was to take place. He would then be relieved from his duties as my warder, which he declared was the best news he'd ever had! Perhaps it was the only point on which we were of one mind."

"Of course I couldn't leave Woodstock fast enough," she continued. "But I was terribly depressed by the Queen's pregnancy. Was this child to force our kingdom under the yoke of Spain one day? How many more burnings would there be?"

"I still wasn't free at Hampton Court, you know, Kat. I had to stay in my rooms. The Queen and Council had summoned me so that I would be under their control if the Queen were to die in childbirth. I was the true successor, but I suspected the Queen and Councillors had other intentions."

"A deputation of Councillors visited me and advised me to ask the Queen for mercy, and she would then be good to me."

"I said, 'I don't want mercy, I want justice. If I asked for mercy, I would be admitting that I had wronged the Queen, which I have never done.'"

"Bishop Gardiner returned the next day and said the Queen was amazed I wouldn't confess. She said I would have to change my tune before I could be set free."

"A week afterwards, late at night, I was suddenly called to see the Queen alone in her bedchamber. I knelt and declared my innocence and loyalty."

"'You won't admit guilt,' said the Queen gruffly. 'You stubbornly persist in your claims. I suppose you assert that you've been wrongfully punished!'

'I mustn't say so, Your Majesty, to you,' I replied.

'But you will to other people.'

'No. I have borne this burden, and I must continue to bear it. I only beg you to think well of me as your faithful subject.'

'Leave me now,' she said abruptly."

"She then added something in Spanish, which made me think Prince Philip must have been within earshot, and that perhaps the Queen had given me the interview at his request."

"The whole of May dragged by, but the baby was still not

born. The midwives and cradle waited, as did our whole country. It wasn't until early August that the Queen had to face up to the fact that her pregnancy had never been genuine. You know, Kat, how practised I am at concealing my feelings? Well, that time it was a real struggle. My huge relief had to be completely hidden. It was a revelation to me how much I must have been dreading that baby. Not for my own sake but for my country's."

"The Queen, of course, was distraught with grief and disappointment. Less than a month later Prince Philip left England to visit the Spanish territory of Holland and she felt quite deserted. I'd met Prince Philip fairly often while we waited for the birth. He was kind and courteous to me, you know, not hostile like the Queen. I'm sure he liked me. I heard he had strongly advised the Queen to keep on good terms with me. Certainly I was gradually given more freedom. And then came the great moment in October when I was allowed to go back to Hatfield! I can't forget all the crowds who cheered me through London. It was overwhelming. I asked my officers to calm the people because I was afraid of the Queen's bitterness."

"And then at last you came back to me, Kat! God had delivered me from all my tribulations. I was full of thanksgivings, wasn't I?"

Elizabeth was certainly even fuller of self-belief than before. She had once again stood firm, alone, against powerful forces, and come through. She had made no concessions, and she had survived.

What a joy it was to get back to Hatfield that autumn with our old team, even though we were really under house arrest. Parry ran the finances and Roger Ascham occasionally stayed to read the classics. William Cecil, who had lost his official post at Court, was still Elizabeth's surveyor, and as such he visited her several times. Finally, my John came back from Padua

University. He had taken himself there when the old heresy laws were revised, but he hadn't been able to persuade me to go that far from my mistress.

We often heard terrible news of more burnings. In the end over three hundred Protestants – including sixty women – met that cruel death in the reign of Queen Mary. Most of them were humble people, but in the autumn of 1555 the ex-Bishops Hooper, Latimer and Ridley were burned, and the following spring Archbishop Cranmer met the same fate. All this torture bred a simmering anger against Catholicism, the Queen and Spain. We didn't want the Spanish Inquisition here! Elizabeth carefully kept her feelings to herself and cut short my bitter indignation.

One piece of good news was that our old friend Matthew Parker had been expelled from the priesthood, but otherwise came to no harm.

In January '56, quite out of the blue, Elizabeth received a letter from Catherine Knollys announcing that she, Sir Francis and their large family were about to leave England. She didn't spell out the reasons, but they were prominent Protestants and were joining a steady stream of frightened self-exiles. They were going to the Protestant city of Basel in Switzerland, and would be away indefinitely. Elizabeth was devastated and only just had time to send a letter in her own hand trying to offer comfort and signing herself 'broken-hearted'. All her life she had been deeply attached to Catherine. She looked on her like an older sister. She often wept about that loss. They both knew that any future letters to or from a foreign Protestant country would throw more suspicion on Elizabeth.

The Queen then introduced a Bill to confiscate the estates of those who had fled abroad, describing them as heretics and traitors. She resented them being spoken of as 'exiles'. Fortunately for the Knollys family and many others, Parliament bravely refused to pass the Bill. So Elizabeth had that small comfort at least.

I'm no politician, but John kept his ear to the ground and heard from his Court contacts that Prince Philip had a strong restraining influence on the Queen's treatment of Elizabeth. The Prince was motivated by politics more than by religion: his overriding aim was to subdue Spain's old rival, France. It was providential for Elizabeth then that the heir to the throne after her was Mary, Queen of Scots. She was only 14, but had been brought up at the French Court, and was engaged to the Dauphin of France. It must have been a terrible prospect for Spain that one day the Queen of France and Scotland could inherit the English crown. In Philip's eyes, Elizabeth (though probably a Protestant at heart) was the only barrier to that scenario. So the last thing he wanted was for Elizabeth to be bastardised, let alone executed. Queen Mary, as a submissive wife, referred important decisions to Philip and bowed to his wishes. Even when they conflicted with her own antagonism towards her sister.

The result was that we breathed more easily at Hatfield, aware of a measure of protection from the threatening storm of Queen Mary's reign. Nevertheless, fear was always present. Elizabeth, with great self-discipline, rarely let complaints pass her lips in those days.

But she was by nature energetic and active, and she did occasionally express her frustration: "I just feel so hemmed in, Kat! I want to get to my other estates and see my people. I want to keep in touch with the Court, but courtiers are frightened to visit me. It's as if I'm a leper. I know my correspondence is all checked, and any visitors are reported on. I can only sit on my hands nervously, waiting and praying for things to get better. At least I'm allowed to go out riding now and let off some steam."

In March '56 yet another conspiracy came to light. It was led by Henry Dudley with backing from France: Queen Mary was to be exiled to Spain, and Lady Elizabeth to be made

Queen. The revolt was nipped in the bud and, by the mercy of God (and Philip's influence too, we suspected), no harm came to Elizabeth. The Queen in fact eventually wrote to her expressing her esteem and goodwill, as long as Elizabeth continued to behave well.

But investigations continued and in June I myself was struck down again. A troop of guardsmen arrested me and three other senior members of the household. We were rushed from Hatfield to the Fleet Prison in London. The reason for my arrest was a small pile of 'seditious' broadsheets and pamphlets which I had kept in a box in my room at Somerset House. Somerset House had been searched from top to bottom after the recent conspiracy. My papers had nothing to do with any conspiracy. They dated from the time when Lady Elizabeth was in the Tower. I'd been so angry and miserable then that I'd found comfort in those anonymous protests from the street. I cursed myself for having forgotten them, and not having burnt them. I dreaded that my stupidity might be used to incriminate Elizabeth. It was my worst nightmare that my adored, ever-prudent mistress could be brought down by my carelessness.

Mercifully, it was obvious that the ballads and papers were too old to have any connection with this Dudley conspiracy. And Elizabeth's imprisonment in the Tower gave her the perfect alibi: she clearly knew nothing about them. Also, thank God, my husband John couldn't be blamed, as he was away in Italy then.

After four horrible months my prison interrogators severely censured me: "We are appalled that someone so close to the Lady Elizabeth's Grace should have collected these wicked papers. They claim not only that the Lady Elizabeth was wrongly imprisoned, but that the Queen's Grace should not marry the Prince of Spain. Although not linked to a specific plot, such opinions sow poison and unrest. If you were not a gentlewoman, you would be whipped through the streets. But your malign influence is now over. This is not the first time you have been in prison. You are dismissed from Lady Elizabeth's service, and must never approach her again."

What would I have done without my dear John then? He came to collect me and we went to the small house he'd rented in Bishopsgate, where we lived for the next two years. I ought to tell you here that my beloved sister, Joan, and her husband, Sir Anthony Denny, had both died by then, so there was no comfort from that quarter. I did keep in touch by letter with some of their nine young children. But they were lucky enough to have wealthy Denny aunts and uncles who divided them up between them.

John was shocked to see how much weight I'd lost, and he knew how desolate I was feeling at being parted from Elizabeth.

"My poor Kat," he said. "I'll never go abroad again. I wouldn't have let you gather those underground pamphlets, let alone store them! Let's just thank God that you're free and safe. We need a quiet life to recover."

I begged him for news of Elizabeth, and whether she could forgive me.

He had to admit that she had been angry. "She was very frightened when you were all arrested. When the panic died down, her fear changed to exasperation that you could have kept those papers. She burst out to me, 'What in God's name was Kat thinking of? I even remember once specifically warning her that such printings were dangerous!' She was scathing about her own servants letting her down. She said: 'I'm walking on thin ice at the best of times, John. Heaven knows I don't need my own household to bank up suspicion against me!'"

I wept when I heard that, but I wasn't surprised. My Lady Elizabeth had a sharp tongue. It was just that *I* didn't usually feel its lash. And she was justified.

John put his arms round me as I cried. "The very next day," he said, "Lady Elizabeth came up to me and said, 'You know, John, that I love Kat, and I always will.'"

That only made me cry the more!

We kept a very low profile that winter. John said that my movements were probably being watched, and any attempt to contact Hatfield could be harmful to Elizabeth.

"She knows where we are," he said.

Even we heard about it when she visited London through cheering crowds in November. But her stay was short, and she unexpectedly went back to Hatfield after a few days.

John had a keen interest in politics, and a good many useful contacts. He's an excellent listener, and people warm to him because he's such a cheerful, sympathetic companion, as well as being discreet. He was curious about Elizabeth's brief visit, and he found out that the Queen had summoned her to say that Philip was calling for her to be married to his cousin, the Duke of Savoy. Elizabeth had refused even to consider that proposition, and had returned to Hatfield very upset.

"The word is," explained John, "that Philip wants Elizabeth to be in the Spanish camp in the future. Left to her own devices she might choose an unsuitable husband, such as a Protestant or a Frenchman. So he must pre-empt that as soon as possible."

"She's often said that she doesn't want to marry at all," I said.

"Princesses don't have that choice, my dear. They're too important in the Succession, and in the diplomatic marriage market."

"I'd hate it if she had to marry abroad!"

John was silent.

"Anyway," I said, "surely he'd want her to marry a Spaniard, not this Duke of Savoy."

"You're right. But Philip is pragmatic. He knows his marriage to the Queen was unpopular here. Another Spanish marriage would be too much for us to swallow."

"It most certainly would!"

Prince Philip had been in Holland all this time, although the Queen kept begging him to return. He must have wanted an heir, as she desperately did, but he was rumoured to be sulking because the Queen hadn't been able to persuade Parliament to have him crowned as King.

In February '57 the Queen reached forty-one and, in March, Philip finally returned. He wanted a lot of our money to fight France. The Queen, thrilled to have him back, pressurised the reluctant Council into granting it. So we were dragged into someone else's expensive war.

His other reason for coming back to London was to arrange Elizabeth's marriage. John heard about it from our old friend Roger Ascham. He held the office of the Queen's Latin secretary so was often at Court. He was a brilliant linguist and got on well with ambassadors and other foreigners, and they sought his opinion because he knew Lady Elizabeth well.

Philip had been urging his wife not to drag her heels on Elizabeth's marriage but Mary resisted. Her old grievances surfaced: Elizabeth was a bastard and could never be her successor. Her mother had deeply wronged Mary's mother. If Elizabeth married an important foreigner, she would seem to be legitimate.

But eventually she couldn't hold out against Philip's personal pressure. He called in lawyers and had a marriage contract drawn up (under which the Duke's lands between France and Genoa would be transferred to Philip).

Then, at the eleventh hour, Mary suddenly and obstinately dug her heels in. For once, her hatred of Elizabeth weighed even more than her devotion to Philip. She would not consent to any marriage. Elizabeth had no right to the Succession, and her character was unworthy of it. The Queen's conscience had known that truth for twenty-four years (ever since Elizabeth had been born!). Her conscience was God-given and she could not oppose it, even for Philip.

Here, for once, I'll give you my own view: I accept that the Queen's conscience was one half of her reason for rejecting the marriage. But I believe that another, unspoken reason, was personal jealousy of her much younger and more popular half-sister who was likely to have children as soon as she married. I'm barren too. I can recognise the instinctive envy the Queen must have felt. It all accorded with her religious mission. If she, the true Catholic sovereign, could not have any children, then she must strive to deny any children to heretical Elizabeth.

Prince Philip left England that summer after only three months, and, in fact, he was never to return. He had been worsted in the power struggle with his wife and did not take kindly to it. But his influence from abroad over the Queen was still great, fortunately for Elizabeth. Meanwhile in the spring of 1558 Mary, Queen of Scots married the Dauphin and was poised to become Queen of France. She had already started to include the royal arms of England on her personal standard.

I was desperate for news of Elizabeth. But people were fearful of visiting me then because I'd been in prison for having those wretched papers. News did filter through to me via my John, who was not shunned. I had a stroke of luck there. That spring an Italian professor he'd known at Padua University came to London. He was a friend of the Venetian Ambassador, Signor Michiel, and introduced John to him. They got on famously, and John gleaned something of his impressions of Lady Elizabeth. He was a relatively impartial observer of the English Court. Venice had no pressing agenda in England, and, although he was Catholic, he was not on the Spanish or the French side. He was obviously a perceptive person and told John that when Elizabeth came to London, Queen Mary always tried to hide her hatred and scorn, but couldn't manage to do so. He described Elizabeth as very clever and proud – which was certainly true! And he'd noticed that she had managed to acquire Philip's goodwill. We were encouraged to hear via Signor Michiel that most of the nobility were now trying to get a foothold in her service 'because of the affection they felt for her'.

The ambassador also said that Lady Elizabeth had indignantly disputed the Queen's claim that she was illegitimate. She pointed out that King Henry's will had given them equal rights (according to seniority) in the Succession. She was also certain that her mother, Queen Anne's, marriage was clearly lawful, as it was authorised by the church and sanctified by the Archbishop of Canterbury. She knew that her mother would never have lived as Queen with King Henry unless that had been so.

I was astonished that she had openly spoken about her mother for the first time. But John pointed out that it was imperative for her to challenge the bastard accusation. If she'd let that pass, she might well have lost her place in the Succession.

In early 1558 our country suffered a shameful defeat: we lost Calais to the French. What would King Henry have said! It was our last territory in France, and we lost it because we had been dragged into Spain's war. Public resentment simmered against Queen Mary. The religious and political burnings and hangings never stopped. And taxes were rising. We were sliding downhill under what felt like a foreign Queen and King.

Far worse for Elizabeth's supporters was the news that the Queen was pregnant! She had waited six months before announcing it 'so that there could be no mistake'. On 30th March, 'Aware of the great danger of childbirth' she made her will. It left her throne to the child, with Philip as Prince Regent. There was no mention of Elizabeth. I felt in helpless despair at that point. There seemed no hope for our country. My life had lost its purpose. Elizabeth had been my raison d'être, and I was missing her terribly. As a mother would miss a lost child. I'd also lost all my friends in the household I'd been part of for twenty years. I was mourning them all. I didn't see how I could ever join them again. I was in that dark forest of Signor Dante's, where my path was lost.

Thank Heaven for my dear John. He was my loving support through those sad days. I often cried on his shoulder.

Then, miraculously, news came through that the Queen's pregnancy was again just wishful thinking, another mirage for the wretched woman. Sudden relief washed over us. We thought of our friends at Hatfield, and of the silent prayers of thanksgiving that Elizabeth would be offering. From then on Queen Mary never seemed well. She went into a slow decline, without any obvious symptoms. There was a swarm of speculation and rumours as to whether she would overcome the malady. For Elizabeth, the menacing clouds that had hung over her for five years were starting to dissolve. More and more noblemen began to visit Hatfield, and offer their help 'to maintain Elizabeth's royal title and dignity'.

"What they mean," said John, "is that if there is any question over her succession, they will have their men ready to back her."

Throughout that summer, as the Queen's health continued to weaken, momentum gathered behind Elizabeth. By October there was a public debate about when the Queen would die. More and more eyes were turning to Hatfield.

I was in a state of tense excitement. Was it really possible that my Elizabeth could sit upon the throne? Would someone harm her? What would Spain do? What were the English Catholics planning? Would Mary, Queen of Scots claim the crown? Or would Lady Catherine Grey under King Edward's will? I didn't dare believe in a smooth transfer of power.

Suddenly, on November 17th 1558, the news was being

shouted all over London that Queen Mary had died. That same day the Lord Chancellor announced firmly in Parliament that Lady Elizabeth would inherit the crown,

"Of whose most lawful right and title to the crown, thanks be to God, we need not doubt."

I collected more news-sheets over those happy days, and John didn't stop me! Bonfires were lit in the streets, and tables set up for drinking the health of our new Queen. Such an atmosphere of relief and rejoicing! It took me back to when Prince Edward was born. I found myself laughing and crying a lot as all the fears of the last five years fell away.

Our new Queen stayed at Hatfield for six days to set up her Council. It was no surprise to us that she immediately chose William Cecil to be chief secretary. He was a wise and outstanding administrator, whom she greatly admired and trusted.

We joined the excited crowds in London to welcome her procession, led by heralds and trumpets. I had to keep pinching myself! Then, in accordance with tradition, she lodged in the Tower for another week. The presses were churning out ballads and broadsheets, and we read that at the Tower she made a short speech, saying: "Some people have fallen from being sovereigns of this land to being prisoners in this place. But I have been raised up from being a prisoner here to being sovereign of this land. It is all the work of God's justice and mercy."

When I read that, I felt she must have been thinking of her mother.

All the talk was of hope and a new beginning. The Succession dominated most conversations: our Queen was young and strong and would need to give us princes for our future security. Who would she marry? She would have to put this essential task in hand very soon. King Edward had died too young to give us heirs. Queen Mary had done her best, but

Providence had denied her. King Henry's dynasty now depended solely on his younger daughter to perpetuate it. We never doubted that she would secure her royal line: the great Tudor dynasty must be her destiny!

When the Queen moved to Somerset House in early December, she sent for us. Dear Martha brought the message. I clung to Martha silently for several minutes.

"It's been so long, Mrs Ashley," she said. "So long without you. We didn't dare write. So many spies around. But we hoped Master Parry's money got through sometimes."

"It was manna from heaven," said John. "By a very circuitous route."

Two days later we were escorted through the Palace, thronged with grand people. I had no Court dress and I felt quite shabby as they stared at us. It was slow progress through the bustle to reach the private apartments. In the privy chamber were four or five elegant noblewomen, whom I didn't know. Martha and Sally met us there and led us into the Queen's bedchamber. It felt like a miracle to be with her again. We sank in deep reverence.

"My dear, dear Kat," she said and she put her arms around me. "I've missed you so much. You mustn't leave me any more."

I kissed her hands but couldn't speak, and she put a thin, strong arm around my shoulders.

"It's alright now, Kat. It's alright. It's been a rough road, but God has brought me to my father's throne. Now at last I can reward my faithful servants. I've had several months to prepare for it, you know. I want you to be chief lady of the bedchamber. And I appoint John as a gentleman of the privy chamber and keeper of the jewel house! No more living in your little house in Bishopsgate. You will be at Whitehall Palace as soon as you can."

"Your Majesty!" I said, overwhelmed. "Thank you for your

kindness. I've never thought of such a position. But-" I hesitated. "Everything will be much grander now. I'm really a country-manor person, not a Court person."

"Well, from now on you will *have* to be a Court person!" Then she burst out, "I'm so excited, Kat! It's such a joy to be free. You know how wary and guarded I've had to be all these years. I couldn't do anything I wanted. I can't quite take it in that *I* give the orders now. No-one can overrule me!"

"So many people are queuing up to see me, and I have to display dignity and authority. But underneath it all I'm just incredibly happy."

She was so flushed and thrilled, that a sudden memory of her as a child flashed across my mind. Her natural joie de vivre was being released again. She had surely earned the right to that now.

The following weeks were a whirlwind of activity – such a contrast to our recent, subdued life. There was a joyful Christmas, with stout Thomas Parry revelling in his knighthood and his new post as controller of the household. Robert Dudley became Master of the Horse.

Harry Carey was summoned to be created Lord Hunsdon and captain of the Queen's bodyguard. "Who would have thought it, Kat?" he said. "What dark days we've been through, but now the sun is bursting forth. What a glorious Queen she'll make, eh? Wouldn't Lady Bryan have been delighted? You know Catherine and family will be home very soon. The Queen's longing to see her."

Sure enough the Knollys family arrived back from exile just after Christmas. The Queen clung to Catherine (who looked exhausted and older) and hugged her close.

"Welcome home, my cousin. Now you won't be able to desert me again. It's all arranged. You're going to be a lady of my bedchamber! And Sir Francis will be vice-chamberlain of my household. I'll look after you, and you'll look after me!"

I remember the frenzied rush to get ready for the Coronation on 15th January. People were working day and night making fine clothes, rehearsing the pageants and processions, preparing banquets and issuing invitations: Thomas Parry certainly had his work cut out!

On the day before the ceremony, the Queen was borne on an open carriage of cloth of gold through the city. She was followed by her entourage, which included John and me. At the start the Queen looked up to Heaven and thanked God for his mercy in sparing her. She compared herself with Daniel, whom God had delivered from the cruelty of the greedy and angry lions. The streets were hung with silks and flags, and crammed with cheering onlookers. The Queen stopped at each of five tableaux to hear their messages. The first one displayed her ancestry, and, to my great surprise, included a figure representing her mother, Queen Anne, with her crown and sceptre sitting next to King Henry on a high arch. It meant a lot to Elizabeth to see her birth legitimised and her mother honoured in this way. In fact she ordered her carriage to be moved back so that she could view that tableau more clearly.

At the next tableau the Queen was given an English Bible which she ostentatiously held up, kissed and hugged to her heart. Then a boy from St Paul's School read a prayer that God would bless this virtuous Queen with dear children, and that she would become a joyful mother. We all said a fervent Amen.

What a spectacle it was, and the Queen reinforced the people's love by constantly waving and smiling to people in high windows or at the back of the crowds, as well as stopping the carriage to speak with individuals or accept flowers. She was brilliant at courting the public. And it wasn't just an act: she genuinely loved her people and wanted to thank them for supporting her.

The following day the Coronation itself was another triumph. When the ceremony was finally over she stood outside the Abbey door dressed in gold with a purple cloak, wearing the crown, and laughing and waving in delight to the crowds. John later told me that he had been chatting with an Italian envoy who'd disapproved of the Queen's exuberance, saying that she was overstepping the boundaries of gravity and decorum.

"Maybe she is," was John's reply, "but the people don't look troubled by it, do they?"

The Queen was tireless at winning the hearts of her people, and was convinced she owed her throne to them.

"You know, Kat," she told me. "A week before Queen Mary died the Spanish Ambassador called on me at Hatfield. Would you believe it, he claimed that Prince Philip was the cause of my being named as the Queen's successor? He said I should be grateful to the Prince! I soon put him right. I told him I owed my position not to Prince Philip, nor even to the nobles, but to the people of England: they have always supported me, even at my lowest ebb."

She was unshakeably convinced of that.

And yet, and yet, she would not give her beloved people what they most wanted! However grateful she felt, she would not promise to marry and secure the Succession.

Only two months after her accession Parliament presented her with a petition asking her to marry. She sent a wordy reply saying it was her wish to remain unmarried. However, she vowed she would never do anything prejudicial to her country, and if she ever did marry, her husband too would have to be concerned for the good of our Kingdom. There was no need for her to have children, since Almighty God would, in any case, provide a suitable heir to the Succession in due course. She ended pointedly by expressing hearty thanks to her House of Commons for their good intentions rather than their petition itself.

Well. That was a shocking dash of icy water. It was out of the question for any sovereign not to marry – specially one with no siblings. One of the M.P.s was outspoken enough to say that nothing could be more harmful to her people than Elizabeth not marrying: the safety and peace of the kingdom were dependent on her marriage. William Cecil himself prayed for God to send our mistress a husband and, in time, a son. He did not hesitate to speak to the Queen about it. I was attending her once when he said, "Your Majesty, I'm reminding myself of the impressive command you gave me not long ago, when you graciously appointed me as principal secretary of your Council. You generously said to me then, 'I charge you to give me the advice which you think best, regardless of what I might wish to hear.' So now, in that spirit, I recommend you to turn your mind to marrying and having children. That would be the greatest comfort to all your subjects."

The Queen paused, and then said in a forbearing voice,

"I refer you, Mr Secretary, to my long response to the Commons' petition last month. I am amazed that I need to repeat it. I do not have an inclination to marry. I intend to wait and see where God will lead me."

Throughout Europe it was taken for granted that our Queen's priority would be to find a husband. King Philip of Spain was the first to offer his hand. Elizabeth was prompt to reject him because she was a 'heretic' (as she styled herself) and because her people did not want another Spanish marriage. Prince Eric of Sweden was another suitor – and a Protestant one – but the Queen claimed to be averse to the uncouth manners and heavy drinking of the Swedish deputation. Then there were the two Austrian Archdukes who put themselves forward. The Queen did make enquiries about the younger one, particularly about his looks and his way of life.

"For," she said, "I don't want a man who sits at home by the fire all day!"

The fact was that she was only toying with those Princes. She was prevaricating and posturing, and had no intention of actually choosing one. Her delaying tactics kept Parliament and her Council at bay for a time.

Part of the truth behind it was that she had fallen in love with Sir Robert Dudley. He was a good-looking, ambitious and masterful character. Most attractive to women! He had known Elizabeth a little on and off since she was eight, but they had hardly seen each other during Queen Mary's reign. Now he was prominent at Court and treated the Queen in a most familiar way. He would hold her gaze, unabashed, and would even tease her and tell her what to do!

Elizabeth was excited by his boldness, which was in such contrast to the deference of the other courtiers. He cut through the flummery and obsequiousness and treated her as a woman as well as his Queen. She'd had no experience of flirting or courting since Tom Seymour's time when she was a child. Other men didn't dare to make such approaches to their autocratic Queen. So Robert Dudley had the field to himself. And they did suit each other: they were both self-confident and brave; they laughed a lot together; and they loved riding and hunting. I think she craved adventure having been confined for so long. She was always complaining that her horses were too slow, and challenging her handsome Master of the Horse to find her 'the good, strong gallopers from Ireland'.

Elizabeth began to show her feelings to the Court. She would slip her arm through Sir Robert's, or smooth his cloak over his shoulders. They were small gestures, but intimate and proprietorial. It was the talk of the Court and gossip swelled, as it always does.

For Sir Robert was a married man. In 1550, aged just seventeen, he had married Amy Robsart. It was a childless marriage, and she never came to Court, but lived at their manor in Oxfordshire. It was said that she had a disease of the breast.

So the Queen's love for Sir Robert was much criticised. The ambassadors were particularly scandalised by it, and they spread the word throughout Europe. Our own nobility were jealous of Sir Robert anyway for his influence over the Queen and they referred to him insultingly as 'the gypsy'. Rumours sprang up that the Queen was going to bed with Sir Robert. I know that they were quite untrue, as the Queen was never alone. Her other ladies corroborated that. But gossip has a life of its own, and it doesn't want to hear the honest truth.

I was deeply upset for her reputation. She had always been so proud and careful of her good name. I couldn't bear to hear of her being held in dishonour so soon after attaining the throne. What's more, she was wasting precious time dallying with Sir Robert, when she should have been concentrating on the Succession.

"What should I do, John?" I asked. "What should I do? It's all unravelling!"

"Now, it's not that bad," he said. "It's early days. She's been doing well on the religious front: she's made Matthew Parker her Archbishop and she's brought back Cranmer's English Prayer Book. She'll soon come to her senses about Sir Robert."

I wasn't particularly comforted, but I was too nervous to take any action, and I remember Sir Francis Knollys buttonholing me one day, in July.

"Surely you could convince her, Mrs Ashley? I've tried but had the brush off. The fact is that I'm under a bit of a cloud with Her Majesty: she resents my criticism of the statues and candles in her chapel. Anyway, she simply *must* marry! It's vital to ensure a Protestant Succession. There's another Bloody Mary waiting behind her. I've asked Catherine to use her influence, but she doesn't want to. Between you and me, she's in the early stage of pregnancy yet again, and I don't want to pressurise her. So when you get the chance, Mrs Ashley, please, please try!"

I undertook to try, but didn't find an opportunity. Then, a

few weeks later at Richmond, I was summoned to see Sir William Cecil. He has always been most courteous, and he stood up from his busy desk.

"Good morning, Mrs Ashley," he said. "Please sit down. My spies tell me that the Queen has gone hunting."

"Yes, sir."

"Again?"

"It is a great passion of hers, sir."

"Yes. Well, Mrs Ashley, after some very precarious years our prayers have marvellously come true, and we now have a young Protestant Queen. So far so good, I think you'll agree?"

I nodded.

"But we can't stand still. I have to secure the long-term safety and peace of our country. That means the Succession. In my view it's our biggest problem: bigger even than our empty treasury or our need for allies abroad."

"Did you hear," he went on, "that the King of France died last month? It means Mary of Scotland has become Queen Consort of France. She's a devout Catholic and next in line to the English crown. In fact she claims that, as our Queen is illegitimate, she, Mary, should by rights be Queen of England already! If that ever happened, I am convinced that it would cause a bitter civil war with much bloodshed and anarchy. The only way to prevent that happening is for our Queen to have children."

"You know this to be true, Mrs Ashley, and so do all Her Majesty's supporters. She alone seems to have lost sight of that crucial fact. Of course she knows it, but she seems unwilling to face up to it. As her principal secretary I have repeatedly raised the subject with Her Grace, but to no avail."

He paused. Usually, on the rare occasion that I heard the Queen criticised, my defensive instincts would spring up. But that morning I couldn't take up the cudgels on her behalf. I rather miserably nodded my agreement.

"I now come to the not unrelated matter of the Queen's

affection for a married man. I can tell you that it is causing an embarrassing scandal throughout Europe. Yesterday I received a despairing letter from Sir Nicholas Throckmorton, our ambassador in France. He reported that the new Queen Mary of France greeted him with, 'Bonjour, Monsieur Throckmorton. We hear that the Queen of England is going to marry her horse-keeper!' And the whole Court burst out laughing at him."

I could only shake my head unhappily.

"But," he went on, "Apart from the immorality of this infatuation, it is, I believe, causing her to drag her feet over choosing a husband. The Succession question is becoming more urgent by the day – or should I say 'by the *month*' – but she will not attend to it. Again, I have spoken frankly to Her Grace about Sir Robert, but she does not appreciate the advice. At least, not from *me*."

He waited a moment to see if he was carrying me with him. But I had suspected all along what he was building up to.

"So, Mrs Ashley, having made no headway myself, I've decided to ask you to try. Everyone knows that she's devoted to you. I'm hopeful that words from you will influence her."

"She honours me with her trust, Sir William. But I sense that I have very little influence these days."

"Will you try?"

"I haven't yet dared remonstrate with her. But, knowing you approve, I'll do my best. She doesn't often capitulate, you know! I'll have to choose my moment. It won't be easy."

"Thank you, Mrs Ashley. You will be doing our country a great service."

I felt extremely anxious at the prospect, but at least I could stop fretting impotently. I was going to take positive action – which suited me better. I kept wondering how to approach the thorny subject. I knew she would resent it.

Then one evening as we were helping her to undress, she said, "You're unusually quiet, Kat. Whatever's the matter?"

"You're right, ma'am. I *have* got something on my mind."

"Well?"

"Ma'am, may I beg a quarter of an hour of your time one day in private? As a great favour?"

She suddenly looked watchful.

"You may beg it." Long pause. "And yes, I'll grant it. I don't like to have you out of spirits. Not tomorrow. Friday morning will do. I won't be riding then. Before I sit for the portrait."

"Thank you so much, Your Majesty."

On the Friday my interview was not private, as the Queen kept several ladies with her in the bedchamber. I think she wanted her rebuttal to any criticisms to be made known round the Court.

I knelt in front of her chair in silence, my head bowed and my pulse racing. It didn't help that she was looking particularly regal in an elaborate black and gold dress for the portrait sitting.

"Right, Kat. What have you got to say?"

"Your Majesty," I began tentatively, "you know how proud I've always been of you? And I love you so much. I hate to hear disrespectful talk about you. But such talk is growing because of the familiar way you treat Sir Robert. Yes, I must speak plainly. It's leading people to think you are committing adultery with a married man. If it continues, your people will soon lose their great love and respect for you. Civil war might break out, and it would be blamed on you. If I'd ever thought that would happen, I'd have strangled you in your cradle!"

"For God's sake, milady, please give up Sir Robert! For your country's sake you need to choose a suitable husband as soon as possible to give us an heir."

The Queen stood up sharply and walked slowly round the room to compose herself after my lecture. The ladies remained by her chair as if frozen to the spot.

"Strong words indeed to a sovereign," she said eventually.

"Who would have dared to speak to my father like that? It amounts to Lèse-Majesté!"

There was a very uncomfortable silence. Then she seemed to unbend a little, and came back to me with an exasperated sigh.

"However, Kat, I know your shocking outburst comes from a good and loyal heart. Of course I will consider marriage, but marriage is a serious matter and needs a lot of thought. Anyway, as you well know, I would prefer *not* to marry."

Then she very deliberately turned away to close the unwelcome subject.

I had to challenge that.

"But, ma'am, this is such an urgent matter! Life is uncertain. What would happen if – Heaven forbid – you died young with no child to succeed you? You would leave us in a state of civil war. Or even religious war. For the love of God, ma'am, please decide very soon on one of the suitors seeking your hand – I beg you!"

"Don't upset yourself, Kat. Have faith in the God who made me Queen and who will continue to look after me and my country."

"As for Sir Robert, there is no foundation for any of this scurrilous gossip, as you and these ladies well know. I've had a lot of troubles in my life and my Robin's company makes me happy. That's all. I would never commit adultery."

"In any case," she added emphatically and defiantly, keeping her eyes set on mine, "Even if I were to behave badly, I don't know anyone who could tell me not to."

She turned away, beckoned to two of her ladies, and swept off to the portraitist. I stayed on the floor, sitting back on my heels, my heart thumping. Catherine Knollys gently led me to a chair and fanned my face.

I was overcome with relief that the confrontation was over. But I knew that I hadn't gained any ground. The Queen had fended off my rebukes with her characteristic, vague generalisations. It would cause a bit of a rift between us. But I had done it for her sake, and in her heart she knew that was true.

The story of our encounter soon spread round the Court. A lot of important people congratulated me quietly, and urged me to keep up the pressure to marry. But I couldn't face another direct confrontation, and she would not have tolerated it. She wouldn't forget my words. I could only hope that she would come round to fulfilling every queen's first duty to her subjects. It was so obvious!

When I wrote those last words, I didn't think that this memoir was coming to an end. But it is!

I started writing while we were living in Bishopsgate – in that dark time after I was released from prison. I was lonely. I had no role, and no future. It doesn't suit me to be idle. It cheered me to look back at happier times, and it gave me a purpose.

John was full of encouragement. "As long as you stop at King Edward's death, sweetheart," he said. "Don't cross *that* line!"

So I didn't touch Queen Mary's reign back then. And I also judged it best not to include Elizabeth's inquiries into her mother's life and death. You see I have learnt some caution! But as soon as Elizabeth came to the throne, I knew I must bring my memoir up to date, add an introduction and a few insertions, and then round it off with its triumphant ending. I wrote it in my rest days, mostly in John's quarters by the Jewel House.

It was John who gently advised me recently to stop writing.

"I think you're overrunning yourself, my dear. You've achieved so much. No-one else has been so close to the Queen for so long. Only you could have written such a personal account of her life. And you've done it out of love and pride, which shines through it all."

"But?" I said.

He smiled. "But! The risk is that you'll stray into matters of State. Now that she's Queen, you needn't worry that her life won't be chronicled. She'll always be on centre stage, with lots of historians to report her sayings and doings. They'll take up the tale now, so you can put down your pen. In fact, it might be wise to turn the clock back a little and remove your last few pages."

"Do you mean my appeal to the Queen?"

"Yes. The Succession is a sensitive subject."

"But you mentioned my love and pride in her. And they were the motivation for my appeal. She knows that. And I'm sure she'll soon *have* to come round to producing a prince or two! Anyway, my great plea to her wasn't secret – the whole Court knows about it already. So I'd like to leave that in."

"Well, you do know her best."

"I do." I paused for thought. "But I can see that my memoir could easily become too political now, so I'd better stop. How about that?"

"There's my wise wife!" he said, laughing and giving me a hug. "We don't want to jeopardise our royal home, do we?"

So the time has come to leave you, my unknown readers. Thank you, gentlemen, for your patience in following this account. I don't have the talents or style of professional historians like yourselves. But my facts are first-hand. It's been a great pleasure to look back over my long and extraordinary journey with my beloved Lady Elizabeth. Just as her character is very strong and vivid, so are my memories of her.

Katherine Ashley
Whitehall Palace
September 1559.
The First Year of the reign of Queen Elizabeth

PART 3

Lady Catherine Knollys

My dear family,

I am writing this memoir from the vantage-point of a high position at Court. It is 1568, the tenth year of the reign of my first cousin, Her Grace, Queen Elizabeth. How I long to write 'the *glorious* reign'! But the Succession vacuum blights it. For ten long years it has cast an ever-lengthening shadow over her subjects.

I, Lady Catherine Knollys (née Carey), am one of four ladies of the bedchamber – the women closest to the Queen. In fact I'm now the chief lady. Two by two we take turns to wait on her. It is not always an enjoyable role, but it's highly respected. It brings prestige and opportunities to my large family. My dear husband, Sir Francis, also serves the Queen, and is treasurer of the chamber. We have eight sons, seven daughters and now six grandchildren. No shortage of heirs for us!

God has shown great mercy in preserving me through so many childbirths. I'm forty-five now, and my youngest child is five, so I'm overwhelmed with relief that I won't have to face those dreaded dangers again. Francis has found it a great financial burden to have so many children but, as he has often emphasised to me, it is God's will.

This year (due to a foot injury) I've not been selected to attend the Queen on her annual two-month summer progress travelling the country. So, most unusually (and thankfully), I have some leisure time. Francis is still guarding the Queen of Scots in the north, so I've decided to use this time by jotting down my memories of Her Majesty. They're not to be published, but I'll store them privately with our family papers as a historic keepsake for my children, grandchildren and later descendants. It is for you, my darlings, that I have always tried my best to care for the Queen and laboured long hours in her service.

I was born in 1524, the first child of Mary Boleyn and Sir William Carey, a gentleman of King Henry's privy chamber. My brother, Harry, was born two years later. I can only just remember my father; he died of the sweating sickness in 1528.

You may have heard the old rumour that King Henry himself was our real father? I'd better deal with that. Mama certainly always denied it, although she admitted the occasional liaison with the King during those years. She liked men, and they were attracted to her prettiness and sensuality. I'm quite sure that my brother couldn't have been the King's son, or the King would surely have proudly acknowledged him. The King did have one illegitimate son (born in 1518 and died in 1536) whom he made much of and ennobled as the Duke of Richmond, the Duke of Somerset and Lord High Admiral! Maybe he hoped that son would be viewed as an acceptable successor. Harry would surely have been singled out in the same way if he'd been the King's son, wouldn't he?

As for me: I can't be so sure. I'm the wrong sex so there'd have been no point in His Majesty seeking to make me a candidate for the throne. But I like to think he'd have shown occasional interest in me as I grew up, which he never did. So I accept Mama's word that I'm a Boleyn and a Carey – not a Tudor!

My grandfather, Sir Thomas Boleyn, held several important offices at Court, and also served the King as an ambassador. He was a talented, energetic man who had married a daughter of the Duke of Norfolk. Their son George, Lord Rochford, was the apple of their eye. I remember him as a dashing, quick-witted and playful uncle. He and his wife had no children, so he took a special interest in me and Harry. He always gave us a great welcome, particularly as we had no father. He was a gentleman of the privy chamber, and the King enjoyed his lively company.

Sir Thomas sent both his daughters, Mary and Anne, to the French Court when they were twelve. It must have been hard for them leaving home. I remember saying that to Mama (rather anxiously!) when I was about ten.

She gave a shrug. "It was time for us to grow up, ma cherie. Would you have had us stay in the schoolroom? We were so naive then. You can't imagine. But we were ready to learn more worldly lessons. The French Court was rich and sophisticated, and the ladies were an eye-opener to me. They were obsessed with their appearance and the latest fashions, and always presented themselves with great poise, perfume and glamour. They had graceful, feminine manners, but were also very bold and confident in their dealings with men. They were never downtrodden, and freely expressed their opinions. Twelve is a most impressionable age, and I suppose I absorbed their norms and tried to adopt them. And Anne did the same when her turn came. And you see where *she* is today!"

We Careys lived in Lambeth, opposite Westminster near my Boleyn grandparents' large house. We spent a lot of time there, and Uncle George and Aunt Anne were sometimes there too, giving plenty of high-spirited fun to me and Harry. George would play-fight and kick a ball around with Harry, and Anne would bring her lute and teach me songs and dances. Some of those I remember to this day. I like the one about the snows of yesteryear which she often sang:

Dites-moi où, n'en quel pays,
Est Flora la belle Romaine,
Archipiades, ne Thaïs,
Qui fut sa cousine germaine,

Echo, parlant quant bruit on mène
Dessus rivière ou sur étang,
Qui beauté eut trop plus qu'humaine?
Mais où sont les neiges d'antan?"

"Come on, Cathy, sing up!" she said. "We Boleyns don't do half-measures!"

Anne was the King's favourite from the late '20s. Everyone said he was captivated by her vivacity, wit and style. She must have stood out among the demure, modest ladies of the English Court in their old-fashioned gable head-dresses. Mama used to say Anne was very full of herself. She wasn't as pretty as Mama but she attracted more attention, and she courted it.

In 1533 King Henry at last managed to divorce his Spanish Queen, and he was then able to offer marriage. Anne became Queen, and my grandfather was raised to the nobility as the Earl of Wiltshire. In June, rejoicing in her visible pregnancy, we saw her crowned by Archbishop Cranmer in Westminster Abbey. You can't imagine how proud we all felt! We fervently joined in the Archbishop's prayers for a prince.

Three months later I first met 'The High and Mighty Princess Elizabeth'. Harry and I were allowed the privilege of entering Queen Anne's bedchamber at Greenwich, and we silently peeked into the glorious purple cradle at her bedside, quite awed by the little scrap of new life.

"I'm sorry it wasn't a boy," Harry blurted out.

Mama cuffed him.

"She's very sweet," I said swiftly.

"She's not just sweet," retorted the Queen fiercely. "She's the heir to the throne of England and Wales. You two must learn – fast – to bow and curtsey to her." She then fell back on her pillows and turned away from us.

Mama chivied us out, and I felt a twinge of unaccustomed anxiety.

"Aunt Anne's eyes were red," said Harry.

"Hold your tongue, young man!" snapped our grandmother.

She was speaking in a low voice to our mother. My sharp young ears picked up "...sent us all out..." and "...sounded furious..." I could tell my grandmother was very upset, which made me feel frightened.

We visited the baby a couple more times that autumn (always on our best behaviour!) And then, at three months, she was whisked away to the country manors under Lady Bryan. We saw her when she came back to Greenwich, Eltham or Hampton Court. By then she was smiling and I loved playing baby games with her.

Mama re-married in 1534. Our stepfather was Sir William Stafford, and Mama loved him very much. I'm afraid our Boleyn family (particularly the Queen) disapproved because they expected her to marry into the nobility. But our grandfather gave them one of his manors, Rochford Hall in Essex, and we lived happily there. Sir William was good to Harry and me, and we made a lot of childhood friends among the neighbouring gentry. And Uncle George still made a point of coming to play with us.

We continued to visit Princess Elizabeth regularly at Hunsdon or Hatfield, and occasionally at Court. She got to know and remember us, and was all smiles when we came, which was endearing. Babies always love children, don't they? I don't think she met many others.

With hindsight I can see that I was lucky to be sheltered in Essex from the tragedies of Queen Anne's three further pregnancies. My poor aunt had a stillborn baby in August '34, another one the following year, and a miscarriage in January '36. Mama went to see her each time, and came back thanking God that she wasn't a Queen, and that she had a loving husband. I remember her saying that one of her Howard cousins had had a succession of stillbirths after a healthy firstborn.

"But she was far luckier than Anne," she said, "Because her first baby was a son."

Each time Mama came home she was worried but trying not to show it. That last time I found her crying on her bed.

I knelt beside her. "What is it, Mama? What's happening? Let me help you."

She needed comfort so much that she responded to me. She lay there whispering:

"It's poor Anne. She's failed too many times. She's sure the King will cast her off now. She says she'll be sent abroad or to a convent. She's terrified of losing Elizabeth. She says it's a judgement on her for treating Lady Mary unkindly."

It was a shock to me because I'd naturally been proud to be the Queen's niece. "But you don't think there'll be another divorce?"

"What else? And soon. The King doesn't need to wait for the Pope's consent this time. She's helpless. Helpless. Just keep quiet about it."

She started crying again, so I kissed her hand and crept away.

I saw Queen Anne once more. We went to Hampton Court in March on a family visit. She was pale and thin – a shadow of her old vivacious self. But she rallied and taught me and Harry a new card game, and played the lute for us to dance to.

As she kissed us goodbye, she said,

"Now promise me you'll be good friends to Princess Elizabeth, won't you? I know she loves you. Isn't she a brilliant talker now? She's coming to see me next week – I'm counting the hours!"

I've never got over the horror of Queen Anne's death – the suddenness of her arrest, trial and execution. And Uncle George too! My grandparents were completely shattered, and only lived a couple more years. I was thirteen, and I remember not being able to keep my food down. It terrified me that they could have been beheaded. I couldn't stop myself imagining the bloody scenes. And how could the King be betrothed to Jane Seymour the very next day?

Mama was distraught, but she wisely wouldn't answer my questions and ordered me and Harry never to talk about it: "I couldn't bear it, sweethearts, if you were put at risk! For God's sake keep quiet!"

We cowered, full of nightmares, at Rochford Hall, cold-shouldered by our neighbours. Mama was on edge whenever we heard horsemen on the road.

Gradually our immediate terror subsided. We heard that Princess Elizabeth had been declared a bastard, but her household seemed to be intact. Mama decided then to write to Lady Bryan to ask if Harry and I could still visit 'Lady Elizabeth' sometimes. After some delay (and to Mama's surprise), Lady Bryan consented, but on the condition that Harry and I must never mention Queen Anne (or even our own mother or grandparents) to little Elizabeth. Mama drilled those rules into us before every visit.

We used to visit about four times a year, depending on the locations of Elizabeth's household. We'd stay a few nights and put ourselves out to entertain our cousin. It was a bit boring amusing a three-year old, but Mama had impressed on us that in the long run it might help our family. Anyway, I adored children. And Elizabeth was always so thrilled to see us. She was a brave little thing too at riding, and I felt deeply for her having no mother. She has always been thin. With her pale skin she looked to me then like a waif, and I felt an urge to protect her. I gave her lots of hugs and cuddles to show I loved her. I'm sorry to say that Harry didn't always pull his weight, and would wander off to talk to the guardsmen about soldiering!

When we re-started our visits, we found that Lady Bryan

had been joined by a young lady called Kat. Harry and I had been rather in awe of Lady Bryan, who was quite old even when we first met her. She was kind, but we sensed that she was a person of authority and we had to be on our best behaviour. The newcomer, Kat, was great fun. She was plump, with dimples, and full of smiles. She would happily join in our games with Elizabeth, and make a big effort to amuse and interest us at our own level too.

Mama kept an ear to the ground about Elizabeth's status. In that tragic year it cheered her that Elizabeth had been summoned to Court at the time of the northern rebellion, and was also at Greenwich for Christmas with the King. Later, Mama was very proud when Elizabeth had an official role at Prince Edward's christening. And when the two royal nurseries merged, she felt confident about her niece's future.

"Yes, alright, she's outside the Succession." she said. "But: the King recognises her as his daughter. She lives with our Prince of Wales, as his sister. Mark my words, the King will find a highborn husband for her one day, and bestow a big dowry too. She'll have lands and an honoured place at Court. You two can only gain from her friendship. Heaven knows our family needs some luck!"

In 1538 our dear grandmother, Lady Elizabeth Boleyn, died after a long wasting sickness. As usual, we had been to stay at our beloved Hever in August. I like to think our company gave her some comfort. And we could tell her about her other grand-daughter too. I drew her a picture of Elizabeth, and she smiled.

In November we went to her funeral at Lambeth, and there met her brother, the Duke of Norfolk, a powerful man at Court. Grandmother had written to him asking him to help me and Harry find positions at Court when the time was right. I here record that he honoured her request.

It was solely through his influence that in November 1539, aged sixteen, I was privileged to be appointed a maid-of-honour to the Queen-to-be, Anne of Cleves. The future Queen did not actually arrive in England until the end of December, so I had time to be trained in my role. The Queen's chief lady-in-waiting, Lady Browne, supervised the maids-of-honour, and was quite particular about duties, dress and the niceties of Court etiquette. It was a much sought-after placement for well-born young girls. It was an opportunity to see and be seen in my big new grown-up world at Court. In practice it was a starting-point for many marriages. Mama had already pointed that out to me, and given me a lot of advice on how to be graceful and alluring without cheapening my reputation.

"Be prepared, cherie," she said. "Tongues will wag. People will whisper about you because of my poor sister. You'll have to live down that disgrace – undeserved as it is."

I'd had an early teenage crush on a neighbour's son. But after the Queen's execution we'd been shunned like the plague, as I told you, so I'd had no chance of meeting possible suitors. Suddenly I was propelled into a dazzling world full of attractive young men! Lady Browne, of course, was a strict chaperone, and I needed to please her. She had her work cut out with some of my fellow maids, Katherine Howard (my mother's cousin) for one. Poor excited little Katherine! I remember her failing to smother her giggles when Lady Browne told us that Anne of Cleves was ignorant of the facts of life.

My first Court career was short – unlike my second one, which has lasted ten years now. The Queen I served then was kind, modest and gentle. She spoke only German but was keen to start learning English, and laughed at her own mistakes. I remember teaching her to play cards, which she'd never seen! She was a very easy mistress, and I look back on my service as a time of great happiness. Of course, that was mainly due to my having fallen in love with Sir Francis Knollys! He was then a Member of Parliament and a gentleman pensioner at the

Court. My dear Francis courted me for several months (with the approval of his family and mine) and we were married in April '40, when I was seventeen and he was twenty-eight. It's amazing to think that we're nearing our 30th anniversary.

It was a most suitable marriage, as we were of the same rank. We were not nobility but gentlefolk who served the Court. Although my family had been tainted by Queen Anne's execution, our kinship to the King's daughter was now beginning to count for something on the social scales.

We invited Lady Elizabeth, then six and a half, to the wedding, and the attention paid to her almost put me in the shade. She was wearing scarlet and gold – quite the princess! – and enjoyed being the focus of all eyes. But she was still my adoring little cousin, and flung her arms out to embrace me and Harry.

I stayed in London through that summer of change, which saw Anne of Cleves cast aside, Katherine Howard marrying the King, and mighty Lord Cromwell dying on the block.

In the autumn we were thrilled to be expecting a child, and I moved out to Oxfordshire where our country manor, Grey's Court, waited at Rotherfield Greys. If I thought at all about my future, I expected to be living half at the manor and half in London. But in fact my great fertility was to tether me then mainly to Rotherfield. Our son, Henry, was born in April 1541. I can't tell you how relieved we were to have a son. A boy to carry on the family name and, above all, to inherit the estates. It had been a desperately sad day for me and Harry when Hever Castle had reverted to the King, because Grandfather Boleyn had no son to inherit.

Lady Elizabeth soon visited, but she wasn't very impressed with my beautiful baby.

"He's quite boring, isn't he? But you've got the nanny and wet-nurse to look after him. Prince Edward's wet-nurse stayed till he was two. Do you know how good I am on the lute now? Let's go in the garden, and I'll show you how fast I can bowl my hoop."

That was the time she told me her mother had been a great Queen who'd died young, and she asked me if I'd seen her. I managed to say that I hadn't; I added that I didn't want to talk about her because it was so sad. Luckily she didn't follow it up. As soon as the subject had been broached, Kat stiffened and said, "We mustn't talk about that. Remember?"

So began my twenty-two long years of child-bearing! Mary (named after Mama) arrived in '42, and Lettice in '43 – just too late for Mama to meet her. Mama died that July from a disease of the breast. She'd been the mainstay of my life. On her deathbed (past caring about treason) she told Harry and me that she was quite sure her sister and brother had been innocent.

"It was all planned," she whispered. "The King got betrothed the day after her cruel death. He didn't have to kill them. I can't forgive him. Kings can always pronounce a pretext for a divorce. I can speak freely now. I must pass that on to you, my darlings"

I was lucky to have my new life as wife and mother to soften my grief. I made a home for Harry, then seventeen, with us at Grey's Court. But Harry was eager to start out in the world, and soon strode off to a commission in the army.

Lady Elizabeth, meanwhile, was kept busy with her academic education from learned Cambridge tutors. But she still summoned me. We began to correspond regularly, especially in winter when the roads were bad. She wrote elaborate sentences in an elegant hand, often showing off with a French or Italian phrase. I tossed off cheerful replies about my children and any funny domestic incidents to amuse her.

We were overjoyed in 1544 when the King reinstated Elizabeth in the line of Succession. What a turnabout! I wished Mama could have known. I felt that it was a tribute to Elizabeth, but also a tiny vindication of her mother. And, selfishly, it could be no bad thing for Harry and me.

"The trouble is," said Francis, "that His Grace has also reinstated Lady Mary. And her offspring will be senior to Lady Elizabeth's."

"Well, at least he's set out his Succession firmly. We'll hear no more speculation about that Scottish baby or the Grey girls."

The next year there were two weddings which Elizabeth attended. In May my dear brother Harry, an officer of the King's guard, married Ann Morgan, a gentlewoman from the Welsh Marches. When Elizabeth arrived, we sank on one knee in recognition of her new official status. She received our homage with dignity. But she wasn't too grand to embrace Harry and me lovingly, and show all the guests how fond of us she was.

Then in July Kat Champernowne got married. She had found a good man in dear John Ashley, a distant cousin of mine on the Howard side. Years later Roger Ascham, Elizabeth's tutor, told me that his main gain from a distinguished Court career was his friendship with John. John had a warm, cheerful nature, but also added some prudent ballast to Kat's impulsive character. Francis became very fond of him, and they always enjoyed debating the virtues of the new religion.

Elizabeth, now nearly twelve, honoured that wedding with her presence, but I saw she was not in rejoicing mode.

"What's troubling you, milady?" I asked quietly.

"Oh Cathy! I'm so worried Kat will leave me when she starts having babies."

"But Kat would never leave you. She loves you too much."

"Not enough to stay unmarried for me!"

I squeezed her hands. "We mustn't begrudge her a chance of marriage – and to a relation of ours."

"But what about the babies?"

"Well, I suppose she would have to have the babies at Hatfield or Ashridge. So she'd always be on hand for you. Except for the four-week lying-in period. After all, she hasn't got any other home, has she? And anyway, how old is she now?"

"She's thirty-four."

"Well, there you are. There won't be time for her to have many babies. She's quite lucky in some ways. Look at me – three already, and another well on the way. I sometimes wonder if I'll ever go riding or dancing again."

She didn't smile.

King Henry's death in January '47 was a turning-point for our country. Few people could remember life before his reign. Although he'd been a terrifying ruler, we were proud of his stature in the world, and felt suddenly diminished and nervous without him.

Francis fretted terribly at having a child as our King.

"If only he could have given Edward another ten years to grow up! At least there *is* a boy and he's been brought up a Protestant. Thank God Protector Somerset installed himself so fast. No chance for the Papists to seize power."

I was so beset with babies by then that I couldn't give much concern to anything beyond my nursery. Except, of course, when Elizabeth summoned me to one of the royal manors. I was very fond of my young cousin, but my own children had naturally become closest to my heart. It certainly wasn't always convenient to visit her, but I remembered Mama's counsel. Elizabeth always gave me a most loving welcome, and I would devote myself to her for several days. I was very conscious that Harry and I meant a lot to her as, by then, she rarely met her royal half-sister and half-brother, and she never seemed to have any friends of her own. It was sad, but I suppose she didn't know what she was missing. The fact was she needed our love more than we needed hers.

At thirteen she was very aware of her high rank by the time King Henry died. She had become quite imperious, and I felt I was too much at her beck and call. Harry was often away in the army and on embassies, which usually enabled him to get out from under her little thumb.

So when we heard that in future Elizabeth would be living with the Queen Dowager, Catherine Parr, I must confess to feeling some relief. The Queen would not expect to entertain Elizabeth's non-royal, non-noble cousins. So I was let off the hook! I kept up a light-hearted correspondence with Elizabeth, and she sounded happy in her new settled home in Chelsea.

Francis had been appointed Master of the Horse to King Edward, so he was often at Court. I occasionally came up from the country to join him. Gossip always swirled about in London, and I used to relish its titbits – far more exciting than the local news in Rotherfield. The Lord High Admiral, Tom Seymour, was often whispered about. I remembered how we maids-of-honour had been warned by Lady Browne to keep him at arm's length! This time it was his political machinations. But then Lady Elizabeth's name began to be drawn in. She was living under his roof at the time, and he certainly wasn't a suitable guardian for a fourteen-year-old girl. Stories leaked out from the Chelsea Manor that he was treating her too familiarly, and even invading her bedchamber! A few bitchy courtiers – full of innuendos – would try to draw me into some unguarded comment.

"You know her well, don't you, Lady Knollys? What's she like? Growing up fast I hear. I'd hate to think she took after her mother…"

I would brush aside the rumours, and give a brief description of the virtuous girl I knew.

"Delighted to hear it, Lady Knollys. We do miss you at Court, you know. You must feel quite out of touch sometimes."

Francis was alarmed by the gossip.

"It's the Papists, of course, trying to blacken her reputation."

Elizabeth's letters from Chelsea never mentioned any personal problems, but the rumours kept simmering. Eventually Francis wrote to me at Rotherfield that Lady Elizabeth and her household had left Chelsea Manor, and were living in Hertfordshire with the Dennys. The reason given was the Queen Dowager's pregnancy sickness, but that didn't stop the gossip.

When the poor Queen Dowager died in childbirth in September '48, the Council decided that, at just fifteen, Elizabeth was old enough to head her own household; she then moved to Hatfield House. I was soon really worried to hear that Kat Ashley had been ordered to London and been given a talking-to by the Lord Protector. Well, that fuelled even more rumours. The widowed Admiral was said to be looking for a wife, and casting his eyes extremely high. Then a shocking story arose that Lady Elizabeth was pregnant by the Admiral! I buried my face in my hands. Surely she couldn't have destroyed her reputation. Her marriage prospects would be blighted forever. Whatever had Kat been thinking of? I was so relieved I wasn't at Court trying to face down the scandal and malice.

Events moved extremely fast: bold Tom Seymour raised men and money in the West Country, but he was arrested, imprisoned and executed for treason in March '49. To my horror Kat and Thomas Parry were sent to the Tower; they were terribly lucky to escape with their lives. Francis told me that Lady Elizabeth was being closely interrogated. He warned me not to write to her while she was under suspicion. It must have been a desperate time for her, especially without Kat's support. For me, these purges brought back the nightmares I'd suffered intermittently ever since Queen Anne and my uncle George had been beheaded. My night terrors had returned in the

Exeter Conspiracy of 1538 when eighteen Courtiers were suddenly executed. Then again in 1540 when Cromwell fell, and again, of course, in 1542 when Queen Katherine Howard and my aunt, Lady Rochford, were beheaded. At the same time, my strong great-uncle, the Duke of Norfolk, a giant of my youth, vanished into the Tower. I was just horror-struck at the power of the King.

When the Duke of Northumberland took charge that autumn, Kat and Parry were allowed back to Hatfield. Francis agreed that I could write to Elizabeth again, and we rekindled our affectionate correspondence. I heard that she'd made an impressive entry into London for Christmas at Court. The little orphan King had been overjoyed to see her again, and the whole Court had shown great respect to this sixteen-year-old young lady who had not been seen there for eighteen months.

I next visited her in the spring at Ashridge after my own Elizabeth was born. When I rose from my curtsey, she clung to me impulsively for a few moments, as she had done in childhood. I put my arms gently round her thin frame.

"Oh Cathy! How I've missed you! All those bad times. Come and sit down. I've got so much to tell you."

Looking back, I can see that the next two years were satisfying and settled ones for her. All too few, poor girl! But at least God granted her a peaceful time in between two periods of danger.

She revelled in heading her own household, of course. It suited (and moulded) her character to be in charge. So few women head their own estates. In her case, I suppose, it could now be seen as a rehearsal in miniature for heading her own realm.

I was certainly one of her subjects. A rider would turn up at Rotherfield with a letter from The Lady Elizabeth's Grace requiring my presence at Ashridge or Hatfield as soon as possible. The rider would wait for a reply – not as to *whether* I would come, but as to *when*. I learnt to have a third nanny on hand for these sudden royal commands. At first I would suggest that I bring Mary, Henry, and Lettice, or my latest baby, to amuse her. But I was quickly disabused of that idea.

"My dear cousin," she would reply, "it's you I want to see. Your children are too young to interest me. And there are so many. I can't keep track of them! There's no point bringing them with you."

Like all mothers I adored my children, and I missed them during those protracted visits. But I knew better than to say so. I would admire her many accomplishments, and we would make music, play cards and go riding. I would listen sympathetically to any grumbles she had. She was stimulating company but very egocentric. I remember wondering, even then, how she could possibly adapt to being 'the weaker vessel' and obeying a husband! She'd never known the give-and-take of normal family life; she'd had no playmates her own age in childhood; and now she was the sole focus of her household, which revolved around its demanding mistress. No wonder she was self-centred.

We trembled in 1552 when our boy-king nearly died of smallpox. God must have heard our Protestant prayers that time for his precious life.

Not long afterwards I was summoned to Hatfield and was surprised to find Harry there too.

"I've been telling my Harry off," said Elizabeth, "for not visiting me enough. Look, even your own sister is surprised to see you! We don't want to hear any more excuses, do we, Cathy?"

"It is a rare treat to see him, milady. He's so often in Parliament."

"But which should have the higher claim?" she said, "Parliament or the second in line to the throne? It's plain as a pikestaff, Harry!"

Harry wisely went down on one knee. "I would never want to offend you, milady, as I'm sure you know. But I also have allegiance to the King's Grace, whom I serve in his Parliament and his embassies. It's wonderful to be visiting you at Hatfield again with Cathy – and to see dear Kat here too. It takes me back to my childhood."

"I can never be cross with you for long, my Harry. I'll always love you two. You've known me even longer than Kat has. But we're not children any more. I'm eighteen. And I've asked you here for a special reason. It's private, so I'll explain myself outside in the gardens, where we'll walk now. I shan't need you, Kat."

She led us down from her privy chamber and out across the hall, with servants bowing as we passed. She waved the four gardeners away and began a slow walk in the May sunshine with one of us on each side. In a quiet voice she came to the point immediately.

"I have decided it's time to learn something about my mother. Being who you are, you will want to help me."

I literally stopped in my tracks when she mentioned her mother.

"Yes, I know it's a controversial subject," she continued. "So you will keep our conversation a complete secret, even from your husband and wife."

"But – forgive me, milady – is this wise?" I said. "You've always been so discreet about, about…"

"And I shall remain so, Cathy. As will both of you. I intend to speak only with a few people who knew her. She died sixteen years ago. There aren't that many people left. And King Edward has been at death's door. That's why I need to get on with it quickly."

My heart sank. I didn't want to be involved in anything that could be interpreted as treason. I had my children to think of. I found I was trembling.

Harry took over, and led me to a bench nearby. "This is a great shock to us, milady. You see we were old enough to have frightening memories of that terrible time. And our mother instilled in us never to speak of her sister, especially not to you. Lady Bryan and Kat wouldn't have let us visit you. We don't even speak to each other about it, do we, Cathy?"

I shook my head miserably.

"I see." she said quietly. "Well, I daresay silence was best when you were children. And I can accept that my great father would have disliked mention of a Queen who had betrayed him. But I can't see that King Edward would now object to my enquiring into my own mother's life and death."

"The trouble is," said Harry slowly, "that His Grace the King would not want any criticism to arise about Queen Jane of blessed memory."

"No fear of that. What do you mean? I'm not concerned with Queen Jane at all."

"Well, if your enquiries were to suggest that Queen Anne was wrongly convicted, there could be questions about the validity of Queen Jane's position," he explained.

"Wrongly convicted?" She looked bewildered. "How can you say that?"

"I say it, ma'am – in great secrecy – because that was what our mother swore to us on her deathbed. She said the trial and execution were planned ahead; they happened amazingly fast, and the next day King Henry was betrothed to Jane Seymour."

Elizabeth sat down beside me, suddenly lost for words.

"I'm sorry to have upset you," said Harry softly. "Cathy and I believe our mother. And it's right that you should hear it. But we sense that it would still be dangerous to question Queen Anne's guilt. So I'm afraid we don't want to discuss it. We've both got families now, and we just want to live safely. Please keep yourself safe too, milady. You can't help your mother now by pursuing this idea."

There was a long silence while Elizabeth made some major adjustments to her thinking, all the while nervously twisting her fingers together. Finally, she managed to say in a weak voice, "I don't know what to do. I didn't expect this. Wait here while I think it through."

She walked away, pacing slowly up and down the gravel paths.

I whispered my thanks to Harry for explaining our point of view.

"I think she realises now," he said, "that her enquiries wouldn't just be about the past. She's got to face the fact that some people would not want Queen Anne's guilt to be questioned."

Eventually, Elizabeth returned to the bench. "I accept, dear cousins," she said quietly, "that you were very young when my mother died. So you know nothing directly about her case. So I promise not to ask you about the rights or wrongs of it. But you did know her. You can tell me what sort of person she was. And if I meant anything to her? There's no risk in that. You don't know how hard it is for me to know nothing about my own mother, and not even be able to mention her!" She paused. "Please help me, Cathy." (She knew I had a soft heart where mothers were concerned.)

"Milady," I said haltingly, "I can't refuse you. Mama would want me to tell you. I'll just give you my childhood impressions. Your mother was a striking and outgoing person. She talked and laughed a lot. She was extremely quick-witted. But I have to say she liked her own way and could be hot-tempered. She had dark eyes and long dark hair. She was fond of Harry and me, and would teach us songs and dances. She was always entertaining, and we looked forward to her visits. But I sensed she had high expectations of us, and I feared I would fall short. She was very observant and quick to criticise. I remember: 'That yellow colour doesn't suit you at all, Cathy!';

and 'Your handwriting is a disgrace'; and, once, 'You'll never find a nobleman, if you keep your eyes on the ground!' But I knew she loved us and was on our side."

Elizabeth was listening hungrily.

"We saw her less after she became Queen," I continued. "And I was more in awe of her. But she encouraged our visits to see you. She adored you – no doubt about that. Now that I'm a mother, I'm sorry that she wasn't able to see you more often because of the royal manor system. She used to send you sumptuous dresses and caps. After our visits to you we had to write and tell her all about you and the games we'd played. She longed for any scraps of information about her beloved little daughter. The awful thing was that she had three more pregnancies, but they all failed. Our Mama cried for her."

My voice tailed away.

"When was the last time you saw her?" she asked.

"It was that March of 1536. We visited her briefly at Greenwich. She'd suffered a miscarriage in the January. I was shocked by how thin and tired she looked. So far from her old self. But I remember she brightened up when she told us you were coming to Court. 'I'm counting the hours!' she said."

"I'll have to stop now, milady. I can't think about those terrible times. Thank God you were too young to remember."

She stared at my tears. Then she put a kind hand on my shoulder and turned to my brother. "What can you tell me, Harry?"

"I can't tell you much. I was only just ten when she died. But I know she was a brave, outspoken lady. I've heard that she promoted the new religion. She was very good at archery and riding. She loved hunting. I think you look quite like her, except for your colouring. I didn't see as much of her as Cathy did, because I used to play more with – with our grandfather."

"What about me?" she asked. "Did you see her with me?"

"Not often. But I remember first seeing you when you were

one week old in your purple cradle, and Queen Anne ordered us to bow to you. That was because you were the heir to the throne then."

There was a long silence.

"I knew nothing before. Nothing." she said. "And now I've got a lot to think about. You must forget this conversation. Don't tell anyone."

"We'll go in now. I'm going to rest in my chamber. Kat and John will look after you. I'll see you at dinner."

I recall Kat Ashley looking amazed when Elizabeth declared she was going to lie down and didn't want to be disturbed.

"What a change!" she said "Her Grace was so cheerful this morning, waiting impatiently for you two to arrive."

When I pleaded tiredness and asked to rest, Kat became worried.

"Not you too, Cathy! You do look shivery. Lord, I hope there's not a fever about. It can come on very fast. I'd better go and check on her." And she bustled off.

Harry reassured me that we had said nothing seditious. We had only related our childhood memories to Elizabeth, and only at her urging. He went off for a ride with John Ashley. I lay down exhausted but couldn't relax because 1536 had returned to haunt me.

We left Hatfield the next morning. Elizabeth held out her hand to be kissed, and then she hugged us.

Before our ways parted, Harry reminded me not to mention anything, even to Francis. "I doubt we'll hear any more about it," he said. "Elizabeth is alert to political risk, but, whatever you do, never put anything about Queen Anne in writing, even if she asks."

In fact it was only years later that Elizabeth spoke to me again about her mother. But Harry in London kept his ear to the ground, and told me privately at Christmas that he had heard of a visit she had made to old Lady Bryan. It was also common knowledge that Archbishop Cranmer had called on her at Hatfield. Plus our great-aunt Shelton had paid a visit. Harry inferred that Elizabeth had in fact been continuing her quest to learn more about her mother.

He was exasperated. "Why, for God's sake, is she pursuing this? It's totally out of character! She's always so reticent, so careful. Look at how she leaves the room when Francis or Ascham brings up the religious divide. She keeps herself aloof from any contentious subjects. Yet here she is – as I suspect – actively seeking out dangerous speculations about the royal family. It could be seen as a slur on King Henry. We can only pray that none of this leaks out."

Looking back, I think Elizabeth was simply a daughter searching for her mother. Her deep human need to find her had overcome (for once) the restraint that experience had taught her. I must say that she has always had a strong regard for justice. If she suspected that Queen Anne had not been justly treated, I'm sure it would have spurred on her inquiries. My heart admired her for it, although my head was fearful.

Much worse news was circulating. Our young King was ill again. He had a terrible cough that winter which defied all treatment. The Lord Protector, Northumberland, tried to keep the poor boy out of the public eye as much as possible. But we all know the symptoms of consumption, and that no-one can survive it.

Francis said that the Court seemed to be in limbo, carrying on its daily schedule and rituals for months in a mechanical way. But, behind the façade of normality, the Succession was on everyone's mind. Could we really have a woman as our sovereign? Neither Lady Mary nor Lady Elizabeth was even married. Would a Lord Protector be needed, as we had got used to with young Edward?

Behind the scenes Northumberland was desperately

striving to hang on to power. He revealed his hand that May when his son, Guildford Dudley, was suddenly married to seventeen-year-old Lady Jane Grey.

Francis, who had been extremely gloomy about the future, brightened at the hope of a Protestant successor to the dying King. I had to beg him for the sake of our children not to support any claim to the throne by Lady Jane.

"You'd end up on the losing side," I said. "The English people will never accept King Henry's daughter being pushed out of her rightful inheritance. Catholic or not, they'd rally far and wide to Lady Mary's support. And there'd be no mercy for any of Northumberland's rebels. You'd die on the block or the gallows. I couldn't bear it. Please, please keep out of it! Don't bring back my nightmares."

Francis reluctantly agreed not to get involved, but he was full of foreboding about Lady Mary. "She'll try to turn the clock back. I know she will. I'm known as a fervent Protestant, so I'll certainly lose my position, and we'll be much poorer. It's the end of my Court career. And I've so many children to feed, let alone educate! But that's just about us. The real victim will be our marvellous new religion."

Little King Edward finally died on 6th July 1553. Four days later Northumberland announced his death, and immediately proclaimed Lady Jane Grey as the new monarch! He published the King's will, which included Edward's Plan for the Succession, written in Edward's own hand some months before.

The purpose of this Plan was to topple both his sisters, Mary and Elizabeth, from their places in line to the throne, where King Henry had set them. Edward (or Northumberland) spelt out the reasons. In Mary's case, if she became Queen, she would destroy the reformed religion which Edward had built up. In any case Mary's mother, the Spanish Queen, had been rightly divorced by King Henry because she had previously been married to his brother. As for Elizabeth, she had been unfortunate enough to have Anne Boleyn as her mother. That woman had committed adultery with several courtiers. Furthermore, she was actually beheaded for it, which proves she was guilty. 'We therefore appoint as our heir our most dear cousin Jane.'

I felt a surge of anger at the injustice of it all. I also silently grieved for Elizabeth, who would have to read the hateful words about her mother, whose shame and death had been exposed for public censure again.

Now, I'm no expert in politics, but my expectation that the people would not accept Queen Jane was soon fulfilled. She reigned for only nine days. Mary was acclaimed as Queen, and Northumberland and his two main supporters were beheaded in August. "But not Francis," I thought, "Not Francis."

And so, for the first time in our long history (with the exception of 'Queen' Jane) England had a woman sovereign – a Queen in her own right. Most people were uneasy about that unnatural state of affairs. But, like it or not, there was no male claimant to step forward. Now if Jane Grey had been John Grey, there might have been a different Succession. As it was, our country had to put a brave face on the reality. After all, people reassured themselves, when Kings grew old they weren't able to lead their troops into battle. So perhaps it was not essential for our sovereign to be male. Nevertheless, the awkward fact was that women took no part in political life, and it seemed unthinkable at that time that a woman could manage to govern a country.

The new Queen was certainly aware of the doubts. She resolved to get married as soon as possible, to buttress her role, and – most essentially – to bear children. I remember my poor Francis was tearing his hair out when, in a speech to Londoners, Queen Mary expressed her conviction that she knew the people would rejoice if she had a child!

From the outset she was determined to marry a Spaniard, in particular her younger cousin, Prince Philip. She robustly rejected the protests set before her by the House of Commons, and vowed she would never do anything that might harm her people. Of course, to Queen Mary it was the reformed religion that was harming her people. She saw it as her God-given mission to restore Catholicism. She had long since dedicated herself to that resolve. And now her moment had come.

Her first Act of Parliament legitimised her mother's marriage to King Henry and her own birth (thereby causing Anne Boleyn's marriage to be invalid). From then on she immediately began to dismantle King Edward's religious laws. The marriage of priests was struck out, as were Cranmer's English prayer book, and the new rules about Holy Communion. Back came incense and statues. Parliament, however, would not agree to bring England back under the Pope's authority. Mary had to accept this for the time being, but she continued to write to the Pope, promising to deliver England back to him. Which, of course, she did the following year.

My husband indeed lost his position at Court, and spent a lot more time in Rotherfield Greys with us all. He remained a Member of Parliament, and had time to keep a close eye on his estates. But our finances were severely reduced. Meanwhile, of course, our family continued to increase! We had ten children by then.

We heard that Lady Elizabeth was having an extremely unhappy time at Court. Senor Renard, the Spanish ambassador, was the Queen's closest adviser, and he was very suspicious of Elizabeth. She was an obvious rallying-point for any Protestant rebellion. The Court grapevine told us that Renard wanted her imprisoned – he stressed it was better to pre-empt any plot than be taken by surprise. According to him, all the women around Elizabeth were heretics, and she herself only attended Mass rarely and unwillingly. She was clever and devious, and Mary must never trust her.

I could have told Senor Renard that Elizabeth would never have plotted against her sister. To Elizabeth, the sovereign was almost a divine figure, appointed and anointed by God. To rebel against the Queen would have been close to sacrilege in her eyes.

She returned to Ashridge for Christmas, and it was Kat who soon sent for me.

"It's so good to see you, milady," she said when I arrived. "I'm sorry to fetch you out on the winter roads, but none of us can cheer Her Grace and I'm frantic with worry. I can't get her to eat properly; she wakes in the night; and she's losing her energy before my eyes. We've had an awful time at Court – it makes me furious to see how she's treated there. Did you hear that she had to give precedence to Margaret Lennox and Frances Brandon? What is the world coming to?"

I went up slowly to see Elizabeth. She was sitting by the fire, swathed in warm wraps, and indeed looked pale and forlorn. I curtseyed and kissed her hand, and held onto it.

"Your Grace," I said, "My dear cousin. I'm sorry to see you so low. I've come to try to raise your spirits."

"You can't," she said. "You've no idea what it's like at Court now. I'm shunned by all the new courtiers. Even your letters to me were opened and read."

"It's a hard change, milady. At least you're among friends now."

"It's no good, Cathy. I can't relax. What's being said about me behind my back? Senor Renard loathes me, and he has constant access to the Queen. He makes her mistrust me. And the Queen herself has been saying that I'm a bastard anyway, and I can't be her successor. She's also spreading the old, cruel insults about my mother. Everything's bad! I'm just in suspense the whole time. They'll try to pin something on me soon – I

215

know they will. If they arrest me, I'll write to the Queen. I'll remind her that she promised me, face to face, that I wouldn't be convicted without proof."

"Milady, you've done nothing wrong, and you never would. You've always kept aloof from factions and religious strife."

"I get no thanks for it. My father ruled for nearly forty years – a lifetime! He took the trouble to declare his line of succession firmly. King Edward tried to tamper with it, and now Queen Mary's doing the same. She certainly doesn't want *me* to succeed her. She's trying to find a way out. I've even come to wish I wasn't in the Succession now. There's nothing but trouble ahead. I've got no foreign King to protect *me*. I'm so alone."

"This is dreadful for you, milady. But God has placed you in the Succession for His own purposes. We must keep our trust in His wisdom."

"I cling to that, Cathy. That's all I can think. But I'm quite worn out."

"We can't have you making yourself ill. You have more friends than you know, milady. There's still Parliament. And the people. They wouldn't let you be swept aside."

She didn't answer.

I squeezed her hand again. "Please, milady, please keep strong and well."

"I don't want to get up in the mornings. I've never felt like this before. It's this helpless waiting. What was that story in Herodotus? *The Sword of Damocles*. I feel like that."

I stayed a few days, but I can't pretend I comforted her.

That visit turned out to be the last time we met for five bleak years. The next month the Wyatt Rebellion erupted (to prevent the Spanish marriage) and was immediately crushed. Francis told me London was full of gallows, with hundreds of corpses left to hang. Elizabeth would have seen them when she was suddenly arrested for suspected treason and taken to the Tower. We dreaded the outcome, and braced ourselves for her execution. But, thank God, there was no evidence to secure a conviction. And – credit where credit is due – Queen Mary had a respect for evidence.

Elizabeth once told me years later that she had actually made a show of defiance at the gateway into The Tower!

"I had to make a protest, Cathy. I sat down on a wet step in the rain, and said I was the Queen's most loyal subject, and would be till my death. The Lieutenant of The Tower advised me to go inside quickly, because it wasn't good for me to sit out in the rain. Well, I had a good riposte to that, didn't I? I said, 'I would rather sit here than in a worse place!' "

That was typical of Elizabeth. She must have been terrified underneath. But she could summon enough courage not to enter submissively like a lamb to the slaughter.

Eventually Elizabeth was sent under armed guard to house arrest in Woodstock Manor. She was not allowed to send or receive any letters there, and very little news of her leaked out. I remember Francis thought it was probably safer for her to be 'incommunicada' as the Spaniards called it, since, if further rebellion broke out, Lady Elizabeth (isolated as she was) could not come under personal suspicion. I had to agree with him, but I knew she must be miserable and frustrated. And she must have been missing Kat too. Still, once she'd recovered from the Tower terror of imminent beheading, I knew that she would rally her spirits and begin to throw her weight around at Woodstock. I had to smile as I pictured ponderous Sir Henry Bedingfield trying to deal with his assertive, disputatious prisoner.

But soon we had to look to our own safety. The brutal persecution of Protestants was beginning. Early on in her reign the Queen had, ominously, brought back the old treason laws, under which heretics were burned alive. The burnings began in February 1555, and they continued throughout Mary's reign. The torments of the sufferers caused great revulsion. Many of them were priests, but many others were poor working people. By the end of that Queen's reign 360 men and women had been burnt for their beliefs. Her cruelty caused terror. Hundreds of Protestants who had the means to do so fled the country to Germany or Switzerland. Francis decided we had to join them. Francis's brother, Henry, had been one of the first to leave. He had settled in Basel in Switzerland (a centre of the Reformation) so that was where we went. It was a sad and difficult uprooting. We had twelve children, ranging from Henry aged fourteen to baby Anne. We didn't dare go through London, so we waited nervously at Portsmouth for a stout ship and fine weather.

By that time – ironically – Lady Elizabeth had been released, and was back at Hatfield. I wrote to her in haste and sorrow from Rotherfield to tell her of our exile. I instructed my rider to wait for a reply, and I received an upset and loving letter from her just before we left. She couldn't write anything about what was driving us away. But she tried to comfort me, and urged me to soothe my sadness at going so far away by looking forward to coming home soon. She signed it with an Italian phrase we knew, 'Cor rotto': 'Broken-hearted'. I still have the letter at Rotherfield in my jewel-case. Look after it well.

It was a mammoth journey – most of it by sea and the great River Rhine – in the worst month of January too! I won't dwell on it, but our spirits were very low. I know some of you have vivid memories of the discomfort. Henry Knollys had found us a small house near his. We only brought two nursemaids and two grooms with us, and I had to hire cooks and cleaners locally. We lived in very reduced circumstances and I was terribly homesick, but I was also too busy to brood on it. Money was always difficult. However, 'God tempers the wind to the shorn lamb', and we were not alone. We English made a small community in Basel, and gave practical help to each other. There were other refugees too from France and Italy. The worst thing was not knowing when, if ever, we'd be able to go home. In fact, would we even have homes to return to? Queen Mary had put a bill before Parliament that winter to confiscate the estates of the exiles or 'treacherous heretics' as she called us. Mercifully, Parliament had bravely voted it down, but we all feared she would try again.

At least we were safely abroad when the Dudley Conspiracy broke out in March 1556. It aimed to cut England free from Spain and replace Mary with Elizabeth. We feared for Elizabeth again, but thank God she wasn't implicated. We heard, though, that several of her staff (including Kat Ashley again) had been arrested.

"It's common knowledge," said Francis, "that Philip tries to protect Lady Elizabeth. Not for her own sake – even though she can lay on the charm to men. No, he's frightened of the alternative heir: Queen of Scotland and Dauphine of France! The other dreaded Catholic Mary!"

I didn't write to Elizabeth during our exile, because we had no doubt that her correspondence was spied on. We feared that she would come under suspicion if she received letters from the Protestant heartland. Even my careful domestic letters might be accused of being in code.

I had two more children while we were abroad: Thomas was born in 1558, but the first, Isabel, died at birth, which is a lasting grief to me. I think I had been exhausted by all our travelling, and the struggle to make a new home in a foreign country. She was the only baby we ever lost, so God has been merciful. Such a sinless soul must go to Heaven, and I hope to join her there, when God chooses.

At intervals of several months, three of our menservants from Rotherfield would arrive with money from our estate and a letter from our good steward. That was all the income we had, except the occasional donation from rich local people. I can tell you we had no new clothes in exile – all our money was needed for food and firewood. I even breast-fed Thomas myself!

News came fitfully from England and we all seized upon it. The burnings and hangings continued. Then we were filled with more gloom when Queen Mary announced that she was in an advanced state of pregnancy. She claimed to be quite sure this time after her mistaken pregnancy two years earlier. It was such depressing news for us exiles.

Thank God, this pregnancy too turned out to be imaginary. We began to hope that this Catholic Queen was perhaps too old to have a child. Prince Philip had anyway by now gone back to rule Holland for his father, and in fact he never returned.

The other terrible news was that we lost Calais to the French early in 1558.

"Our last French possession!" groaned Francis. "This Spanish Queen has yoked us with Spain into a needless war. It just proves that women are not fit to rule. I'm ashamed for my country. Without Calais we'll lose control of the Channel." He was all the angrier because the French refugees were cock-a-hoop.

Francis and his brother also felt very bitter when we heard that their mother, Lady Lettice Knollys, had died in June. Although she'd reached the advanced age of sixty-four, they mourned her deeply because they had not been able to visit and support her in her last, long illness. She was a dear friend to me after Mama died.

But, gradually, vague news began to reach us that Queen Mary was ill. She remained ill for months but we couldn't find out any more detail. Was it only a sickness of heart? Was she pining for Philip and Calais? Was she mourning her false pregnancies? Or could there be light beckoning to us from behind our dark clouds? Could we trust the growing rumours that her illness might be fatal? Francis even suspected that reports of her illness might be a trap to lure exiles home.

At last, by the beginning of autumn 1558, we heard from several reliable sources that Queen Mary was not going to recover. She was said to have a tumour of the womb.

We felt an immense relief at the thought of returning home. Our hopes, of course, were with Elizabeth. But we were afraid that other claimants might be preparing to challenge her accession. We didn't dare return until we knew that Queen Mary had died, and that Elizabeth had been officially proclaimed.

As Francis warned us, "The Pope and his lackeys have had several months' notice of this. They'll be scheming to impose another Catholic monarch upon us. Heaven help us all if that happens!"

But in late November '58 news surged through our English community: Queen Mary had died on 17th November, and, only a few hours later, Queen Elizabeth (my cousin!) had been proclaimed as our undoubted sovereign by the Lord Chancellor! What excitement! Bells rang out in Basel to celebrate the death of a cruel persecutor of Protestants.

Francis and I embraced, tears running down our cheeks, as the strains of exile suddenly fell away. We joined our fellow countrymen in a celebration dinner, and together thanked God for his mercy.

Letters sped to and fro, and I received one from my dear brother assuring us it was safe to go home. Not being such an outspoken Protestant as Francis, he had stayed in England, but he'd lost his place at Court and, like us, had a large family and not much income with which to feed them. He'd even been in a debtors' prison the previous year. We hadn't dared write to each other for fear Harry might be accused of conspiring with traitors abroad. It was wonderful to hear from him, urging us to return.

I also had a letter from Kat Ashley hoping we'd be back soon: "I've been in a sort of exile too," she wrote, "Separated from my beloved lady for two-and-a-half years! It's felt never-ending. But God has repaid our faith in Him, and has brought about this miraculous outcome. Such ecstatic celebrations here in London's streets!'

I won't dwell on our journey. It was winter again. But the discomforts were all borne patiently because we were on our way home!

Harry (recently ennobled as Lord Hunsdon) met us at Westminster pier, and I burst into tears when I saw him again.

"There's my brave Cathy," he said, hugging me tightly. "And, Francis – it's so good to see you. How we've missed you all! What a long journey you've had, and how tired you look. And who's this young man? Surely not my nephew Henry? My God you've grown up! And here's the lovely Lettice, too! And this can't be baby Anne." He knelt next to her. "Do you remember your uncle Harry? Well, God has preserved us all, and wonderful times have come. 'Queen Elizabeth' – I have to keep saying it – but the two words still sound so strange. Queen Elizabeth has told me to take you to Somerset House. Rooms have been made ready, and you're all to stay there in great comfort. She wants you to come to her coronation in two weeks' time on January 15th. And in two days, Cathy, you and Francis are to visit her at Whitehall Palace. I can hardly believe all this is happening," he finished, before bursting out laughing.

"How is she?" I asked.

"On top of the world. Back to her old self, only more so! Kat's back with her and all the old crew. Thank God it was an amazingly smooth transition from one Queen to the next."

"Amen to that," said Francis.

We sank onto our beds in grand Somerset House and slept a long time, pinching ourselves when we woke up for fear it was all a dream. The next afternoon we held a family thanksgiving service in the chapel for our safe return and for our new Queen's accession. God had indeed been good to us.

After that, my priority had to be finding a team of tailors to make us (Francis, myself and our six eldest) clothes fit for a Coronation in only two weeks! Harry's wife, Ann, and the steward at Somerset House managed to rustle up some fast workers and the deadline was met.

Of course those smart clothes weren't ready when Francis and I went to meet the Queen, so Harry and Ann kindly lent us some respectable ones. They didn't fit very well, but at least we wouldn't embarrass the Queen in our old travelling outfits!

Harry escorted us because he was known at the Palace. Access to the monarch is never easy, and we were passed from guardsmen to ushers to a gentleman-in-waiting and finally to dear Kat.

We only had to wait ten minutes before an ambassador backed out of the privy chamber. He was followed by two grand ladies-in-waiting. Kat then led us in without any announcement.

And there she stood: the high and mighty Princess Elizabeth. Lady Elizabeth. And now high and mighty again: Queen Elizabeth, our monarch. Alone, her face pale, her auburn hair glowing, her dark dress shimmering in the firelight. She kept her distance while we bowed and curtseyed, and then opened her arms and came close and kissed me.

Her words poured out.

"Cathy! My Cathy! Welcome home. Welcome to my Court. Now my cup runneth over. Everyone I love is around me again. The Lord has preserved us all. It's a miracle. Come and sit down and hear my plans for you."

"My Harry has told me you had a hard exile. But now you'll win your reward. I'm going to appoint you a lady of my bedchamber! I've missed you so much but now we'll be together." She turned to my husband. "And you, Francis, will be the Vice-Chamberlain of my household. Your troubles are over!"

Francis took my hand and said, "Your Majesty, you do us a great honour. We humbly thank you for this kindness."

It was a short audience because the Court was immersed in frantic preparations for the Coronation. Before we left, Kat told us that a house would be provided for our family in London.

"You look worn out, Cathy," she said sympathetically. "I was so sorry to hear that your baby had died. It must have been awful, so far from friends. I can see you need time to settle in before you take up your royal duties. I'll do my best to arrange that. We're in such a rush here that I can't think beyond the Coronation."

Francis was delighted with our Court posts. "We'll both have salaries, my dear, so, thank God, our money worries will be relieved. Thirteen children are such an expense and they all need new clothes and tutors."

I too was thankful for all the favours being given us. But I remember feeling rather ambivalent about my future role. Ideally I'd have loved to settle back into our much-missed home at Grey's Court. I hoped that at least in spring and summer our children would be able to live there. Time would tell whether I could join them. Ladies of the bedchamber were those closest to the Queen. One thing I did know: Elizabeth would not be any less self-centred now that she was Queen.

On the day before the Coronation Francis and I, with our six eldest children, followed the Queen's presentation procession through the city, to see the tableaux set up by the Lord Mayor. The first tableau displayed the Queen's genealogy. To my surprise and joy, the figure of her mother, Queen Anne, was portrayed next to King Henry. Our children were as amazed as me. I had explained to them as they grew up how we were related to Elizabeth, and about Queen Anne's dreadful death. But I had had to warn them for political and religious reasons never to discuss the subject. Now here was Queen Anne suddenly transformed into a person of honour instead of shame. How delighted Mama would have been! Several months later I asked the Queen, in a quiet moment, whether she had commanded that her mother should be featured in the tableau.

"No." She smiled at the memory. "I knew from previous coronations that the family tree was always displayed to prove the new sovereign's royal descent. I hoped she would be there in her rightful place. But I decided that because she is a controversial figure it might inflame Catholic extremists. The last thing I want is to stir up more religious division. No. It must have been the Lord Mayor who decided to honour my mother in that way. I was so glad to see her there. I could hardly believe it. For most of my life she'd been a forbidden subject, as if she'd never existed."

She took my hands and squeezed them. "Even though I'm now Queen, I have to tread carefully where my mother's concerned. You understand that, don't you? But I've decided that my personal badge will be the same as hers: a crowned falcon. So I'm paying that honour to my Boleyn inheritance."

The Coronation itself was a thrilling day of joy and hope. The vast Abbey was full of people, as were the streets outside. Music and cheering surrounded us. And Elizabeth, at the heart of it all, looked blissfully happy. It was like the end of a fairy story, when a princess has gone through great tribulations to emerge victorious. All we lacked was a prince!

A week after the Coronation Kat called on me to say that our house in Westminster was now ready. "I also have to tell you that the Queen expects you to begin attending her in four weeks' time. I'm sorry it's so soon, Cathy. Believe it or not, I did win you a two-week extension. But I'm afraid any further delay was out of the question."

"So be it. I must count my blessings. I know it's a great honour. I just hoped for more time to set up my home and get my children settled down again. I must say they've been very content with Somerset House! Don't worry. No-one but you could have gained the extension."

All my married life I'd been surrounded by my children, interspersed with short visits to Francis at Court. In our recent years abroad we had all grown particularly close, turned inwards to the heart of our family. Now I was suddenly plucked from the midst of my children by royal command. I found it very hard. They weren't far from Whitehall Palace and, whenever I could, I slipped away to see them. Kat would sometimes cover for me. But the Court often moved to Greenwich, Hampton Court or Richmond, and I had to move with it. The Queen's summer progresses, when she toured England, were often a respite for me, as she couldn't take all her servants. Also, my final two babies in '60 and '62 did win me interludes with my family.

I knew I was privileged to have the Queen's favour. We needed the salary. And, as my children grew up, they secured positions at Court. But I did miss the younger ones terribly. That was a truth which the Queen did not want to know. I knew her well enough not to mention my children. She liked to assume that my devotion was all focused on her. She was good at blocking out what she did not choose to see.

However, there was one subject which, try as she might, she could not block out: her marriage and the Succession.

Her first Parliament in February '59 wasted no time and petitioned Elizabeth to marry. Parliament reminded Her Majesty that the first priority of the sovereigns of England had always been to have children. If a Queen were to remain unmarried, it would be against the interests of her people.

The Queen sent a reply of some hauteur, criticising Parliament for raising such a personal subject, one that was 'most unpleasing' to her. She asserted that she was already married to her kingdom. If she decided not to have a husband, God would provide a successor eventually.

That response was a kick in the teeth to all her supporters. We just couldn't believe it. Even I, who knew her well, was shaken. I knew she had occasionally over the years said that she would not marry, but that was when she was unlikely ever to reach the throne. Now she was Queen, it was her compelling duty. There was consternation both in the Court and well beyond it.

I was with her once when Cecil urged her to marry, but she rejected his plea with cryptic nothings such as, 'When God sees fit'.

Francis was beside himself with worry. "What in Heaven's name is she thinking of? Has she gone mad? Monarchs can't be celibate – it's a contradiction in terms. Doesn't she realise that, unless she has children, the Papists will return with Queen Mary of France and Scotland? Our future is ruined. She's totally irresponsible!"

As it happened, Francis was aware he was not in the Queen's good books at that time because he had been openly critical of the candles, vestments and elaborate altars in the royal chapels. Otherwise, he was so upset that he would probably have tried to raise the marriage question directly with Her Majesty, which she would have resented for a long time. He did ask me to use my influence on her, but I knew that it would be worse than useless: I would get nowhere with her, plus I would lose her trust. Early on the Queen had declared that 'politics' were not to be discussed in her private quarters. I had already seen one Duchess demoted from the privy chamber because she had gently observed that the Queen's marriage would one day bring great joy to her people. Yes, the Queen was fond of me, but I knew her better than to drop any hint of criticism.

I remember I was attending her when she appointed Matthew Parker as her Archbishop of Canterbury. He had been reluctant to accept such a high post, as he was a quiet man, not good at public speaking. But, of course, he could not refuse the insistent Queen.

"As you know, Your Majesty, I feel unworthy of such an honour. But it must be God's will. And I am sustained by the great hope that it is I who will have the pleasure of officiating when you marry."

"Marry?" she said. "Who's talking of marriage? At present it doesn't come into my plans at all. I shall be content to die a virgin."

Parker flinched in amazement, and stammered an apology for being too precipitate.

She inclined her head, and I showed him out. I heard later that he went straight to tell Cecil how shocked he'd been at what the Queen had said.

Of course, at that time Her Majesty was also showing an indiscreet affection for Robin Dudley. He was a handsome and self-assured man, who was not popular with the gentlemen of the Court. They were jealous of his favour with the Queen; Robin's advice often seemed to weigh more with her than that of her Privy Council. Francis told me that Cecil was even considering resigning, which would have been a terrible loss to our country. Robin was married, so I had to disapprove of the flirtation. But I did find a gleam of hope in the fact that the Queen was obviously not totally immune to male charms.

It was Kat who dramatically took the bull by the horns and made a heartfelt and direct plea to the Queen to choose a suitable husband.

No-one else could have done it. The Queen gave Kat a lot of leeway because of her long service. Kat, for instance, still often addressed the Queen as 'milady' (and even 'my dear'!). At first the Queen would frown and correct her but it was ingrained in Kat and she never managed to stop it altogether. Eventually the Queen began to smile at these lapses. She certainly wouldn't have overlooked them from anyone else.

Even so, Kat looked a very humble petitioner as she knelt in her brown linen dress and white cap, in contrast to the Queen who sat in the bedchamber in a splendid Court dress of black and gold. I stood next to the Queen with two ladies-in-waiting, sensing that Kat was steeling herself to speak out. My prayers were with her.

It was plain speaking indeed. First she begged the Queen to preserve her good name by not consorting with a married man. Then she entreated her to choose a suitable husband and have children.

The Queen was shocked and angered by the intensity of Kat's pleading. She stood up and walked away to a window to compose herself. When she turned round, her voice was icy and she used the dreaded phrase, 'Lèse Majesté'. Then – thank Heavens – she suddenly relaxed and told Kat that she knew she had a good heart and meant well. She then tried to close the subject by saying, with finality, that marriage needed much thought, and that she herself had no inclination to marry.

But Kat was not to be dismissed so easily. She heroically tried again. She reminded the Queen of how short life could be, and how vulnerable England was without an heir. If the Queen died young, she would leave her poor country to civil and religious war. She stressed the extreme urgency of a marriage. "Bravo, Kat, Bravo!" I silently thought.

The Queen had regained her usual commanding poise, and assured Kat loftily that God would continue to preserve her and her country. As for Robin Dudley, he was simply a good friend. "Anyway," she said very slowly, staring down at Kat, "As your Queen, I do not know of anyone who can criticise anything I may choose to do."

"Now," she continued brusquely, "take me to the portrait painter," and she left quickly with her cowed ladies-in-waiting behind her.

I led Kat to a chair. She was flushed and breathing fast.

"That took some courage," I said softly. "Well done indeed. It needed saying so much. Thank you. Only you could have done it."

"But you heard her. I failed."

"We don't know that. She respects you, Kat. It's so unheard-of for her to get a talking-to. She'll remember your warnings. They'll sink in and she must see the wisdom of them."

"Dear God, I hope so. I know the dear girl so well, Cathy. I know all the troubles she's been through. I think she just wants a year to be happy and free, you see? She'll soon start knuckling down to her main responsibility, won't she?"

In the Court, indeed throughout the country, the Queen's marriage was the first item on the agenda. Francis told me of the frequent petitions begging her to marry for the sake of her good name and the welfare of her country. Ambassadors brought marriage proposals from foreign princes, which she always found some fault with. Her obstinate resistance to all the pressure took a toll on her health, so that by the end of that first summer she couldn't sleep well and caught a fever. The doctors fortunately bled her in a foot and an arm, which averted any danger.

By that time I was pregnant again. My youngest, Thomas, was now two years old, so it was the longest gap between babies I had ever enjoyed! The Queen was displeased but permitted me to absent myself from Court in the New Year. Although the Queen begrudged my absence, she never liked to see obviously pregnant women at Court: it was too pointed a reproach of her own refusal to give us heirs.

Before I left, I was present at a ceremony on New Year's Day 1560, when Sir Thomas Challoner presented the Queen with a book he had written in praise of King Henry VIII. Sir Thomas read several passages aloud to the Court, and boldly concluded with a plea to the Queen to choose a husband soon, 'so that a little Henry will play in the palace for us'. The Queen, who had listened eagerly to the praise of her father, gave no word of thanks, stood up abruptly and left the room.

I was away from Court for several months at Rotherfield Greys. Cecily was born safely at the end of March, and I spent a very happy spring interlude hanging over her cradle and relaxing with my other children. It was a great change not to be hovering about my regal task-mistress. By then our two eldest sons, Henry and William, were gentlemen of the household, and our eldest daughters, Mary and Lettice, were maids-of-honour.

I was summoned back to Court in June, and, with some tears, left my children in the country. They could enjoy the fresh air and their ponies that summer.

The Queen gave me an affectionate welcome, and I thanked her for my leave of absence. In fact, that time, I doubt that she had missed me much, because she was still in love with Robert Dudley. They spent most of that summer riding and hunting. He organised tournaments and jousts, in which, I have to say, he cut a dashing figure. Francis heard him boast that by the next year he would be in a very different position from Master of the Horse. Poor Cecil complained that the Queen was neglecting the business of government, and delegating some of it to her favourite. All the Privy Councillors were against Dudley, but the Queen refused to listen to them. That imprudence of hers was, I felt, quite out of character. But either love for her Robin was blinding her, or her taste for power was making her arrogant of public opinion.

On 9th September 1560 everything changed. We were at Windsor Castle when the Queen returned from hunting unexpectedly early. She looked pale and shocked, so that Kat sprang forward in alarm.

"Whatever's the matter, milady? Have you had a fall?"

She dismissed all her attendants except Kat and me, and wouldn't speak till we were in her bedchamber. "It's Robin's wife. She's dead!"

We knew at once the potential of that news.

"Oh, poor lady," said Kat soothingly. "May God receive her soul. But she's been ill for ages, my dear. Don't upset yourself. This has been coming for a long time."

"No! Not this. Not like this."

We tensed.

"She didn't die of the breast tumour. It was yesterday evening. The servants found her. They came back from a fair. She was dead, lying at the foot of a staircase with a broken neck."

My mind flew to the scandal-mongers. What would they make of this?

"You both know what I've suffered in the past from lying rumours. Now my enemies will seize on this death to slander me. They'll put the very worst complexion on it, won't they?"

Kat and I knew she was right, as our silence showed.

I was sure that the Queen had not committed adultery with Robin Dudley, and it would never have occurred to her to harm Amy Dudley (who was, anyway, known to have a fatal illness). But I can't deny she had not been wise to make a favourite of a married man.

When the news got out, a storm broke over her head. At Cecil's grave urging she announced that an inquiry would be set up to investigate Lady Dudley's sudden death. In the meantime, Sir Robert would be sent away from Court. She was shaken by the fall in her popularity, and equally upset to hear the rumours from abroad.

Nicholas Throckmorton, our ambassador in Paris, found his Protestant Queen was the butt of many jokes: "People here say what sort of religion is this, where a subject can murder his wife, and his Queen not only turns a blind eye but actually plans to marry him?"

Poor Throckmorton was desperate to retire as ambassador. In fact Francis was, for a short time, assessed as a possible replacement, but he was rejected for not being wealthy enough. Probably a lucky escape from an uncomfortable post. Anyway, I doubt very much that the Queen would have permitted me to leave her side.

The inquiry, after two months, gave its verdict that Amy Dudley had died by 'misadventure'. But, of course, there were whispers of a cover-up, which took a long time to fade, and Sir Robert did not reappear at Court for several months.

This sudden lull in the Queen's flirtation was seen as a new opening to broach the marriage and Succession question. Archbishop Matthew Parker picked up the prickly gauntlet in a joint letter with the Bishops of London and Ely. They implored the Queen to marry and bear children: "Which all of your subjects long for every day, and pray for every morning."

But she staved off such entreaties with more of her cryptic reassurances and her dominating character. Although she was less bigoted than her sister, the late Queen Mary, in a strange way she was more formidable. She had a commanding presence (like King Henry) which assumed obedience. Mary was single-minded and basically straightforward; Elizabeth was manipulative, devious, and hard to pin down.

Francis was constantly complaining to me bitterly about the Queen's avoidance of marriage.

"There were we in exile – in that tiny house – hoping

against hope that Elizabeth would somehow survive, praying that she would eventually, by God's providence, reach the throne. That she would release England from the yoke of the Pope, Spain and the burnings. And the highly improbable actually happened! It was clearly God's doing. And you must remember what wild relief we all felt."

He shook his head angrily. "But what does she do then? Does she face up to the biggest anxiety of her people? Does she set about choosing a husband and providing vital Protestant heirs? Unbelievably, no! She pushes the question to one side. She claims to love her people. How does she think they feel when their peace and security depend on the thin thread of one life? Frightened. We all feel frightened of the future. Specially men like me with thirteen – no, fourteen – children to raise!"

"She's been on the throne for two years now," he went on, "which is ample time, in my experience, to have married, produced an heir, and have another on the way. It's maddening."

"Well, she'll have to give up her Robin now," I said. "She can't hope to marry him after his wife's sudden death. It would just add fuel to all the rumours. So surely now she'll stop wasting time and choose a suitable husband."

But, amazingly, Robert Dudley returned to Court in the spring of '61, and the Queen continued to indulge in his company. That summer he produced a magnificent water pageant in her honour on the Thames. I was attending her in the royal barge when he escorted the Spanish Ambassador on board.

"As His Excellency is a Bishop," said Dudley, "I suggest he should marry us here and now!"

Far from being shocked (as I'd assumed she would be), the Queen laughed. "The Bishop doesn't know enough English to perform a marriage ceremony."

However, there *was* a shock in store for the Queen that

summer. Lady Katherine Grey, who (under King Henry's will) was next in line to the throne, was found to be heavily pregnant. It emerged that the previous December she had secretly married the Earl of Hertford. The Queen was angrier than I'd ever seen her, and she sent them both to the Tower. There, in September, Katherine gave birth to a boy. A male, at last, in the line of Succession! The Queen's reaction was a mixture of jealousy, resentment and embarrassment: she knew that her own childlessness would again be underlined. She had the marriage declared invalid. But by then Katherine had bribed warders to let her meet her husband and, amazingly, she was pregnant again! And again the baby was a boy.

The Queen sent Lady Katherine and her husband to house-arrest in different country houses. After four years' incarceration Lady Katherine died there this last January of 1568 aged only twenty-eight. Lord Hertford remains in custody, their two sons, bastardised by the Queen, staying with him. As a tailpiece to that sad story, in 1565 Lady Katherine's younger sister, Lady Mary Grey, also made a secret marriage. She and her husband, a commoner, had no children, and are still in separate prisons to this day.

The Queen treated the Grey sisters very harshly. She saw those first-cousins-once-removed as a threat to her own rule, as potential usurpers. Yet they were the Protestant successors, while Mary Queen of Scots was firmly Catholic. As you know, the Queen has very few close blood relations. She has always been obsessively suspicious of her Tudor ones, fearing that they have designs on her throne. At the same time she has a human need for family love, so she has safely diverted all that emotion to Harry and me, her Boleyn cousins, who can never be in the line of Succession.

In January '62 at the culmination of the Court Christmas, a new masque was performed before the Queen at Whitehall Palace. It had the strange name of *Gorboduc*. It was about a mythical king, but its down-to-earth message was that disaster comes to a country where the ruler will not provide for the Succession. When the Queen realised where the plot of the play was leading, she began to fidget uneasily. She couldn't walk out because the hall was so crowded. Afterwards in her privy chamber she burst out: "That masque was all against me!"

That winter I was thrilled to have my portrait painted! I was pregnant again (for the sixteenth and, as it turned out, final time) but childbirth is no less dangerous the sixteenth time, and Francis insisted that I should be immortalised. I wore my grandest Court clothes to provide a lasting image of my high status for our descendants. A Dutch artist, Master Steven van der Meulen, had recently painted the Earl of Arundel, who was a colleague of Francis' on the Privy Council. We were amazed at his lifelike portrait, along with another of Robert Dudley. I must admit that Dutch painters are of far higher quality than our English ones.

My baby was to be born in London, and I was temporarily released from the Queen's service, so I had some rare leisure time to sit for van der Meulen. It was a very cold February, so I wore my heavy fur-lined robe of black with gold adornments. It was open at the front to reveal the swell of pregnancy, and the painter added a little dog to symbolise fidelity. So the picture stood for marriage and fertility. It hangs today impressively in the hall of our Westminster house. The Queen sometimes does us the honour of dining with us, but she has never commented on the portrait. She doesn't wish to hear its message.

I enjoyed van der Meulen's company. He was most considerate in not letting me stand for long, and he used a model for the elaborate robe. It was exciting to see the painting growing and coming to life. I learnt from him that he had only been in London for three years, but was doing so well that he had just taken on English citizenship.

At the end he said, "It was nice to talk with you, Lady Catherine. You are a kind woman. I pray that baby comes easily."

His commissions were quickly leading him towards a portrait of the Queen herself, which he achieved in '63. It's a dazzling, full-length painting: the Queen wears a wide-skirted dress of scarlet and gold, and stands in front of a golden wall-hanging.

Sadly he died of a fever that very year at the age of forty-two, which was far too young for such a talent. But his paintings live on to the glory of God. I trust that eventually you, my descendants, will keep my fine portrait as a family heirloom and a tribute to a great artist.

My baby did arrive safely for both of us, an eighth son whom we named Dudley. The Queen wrote of her relief at my good fortune, and added, "I have been much inconvenienced by your absence, Cathy, and I trust to see you here again soon after your lying-in. I miss Lettice too since her marriage, but a new maid-of-honour is my Harry's daughter – a second Catherine Carey!"

I resumed my royal bedchamber duties in June. The Queen insisted that I be gathered into the royal progress to Wiltshire that summer. These progresses are exhausting as we never settle at any one mansion for long, and the Queen's large retinue has to be accommodated in extremely cramped quarters. Plus, the Queen is often fretful because we ladies, when packing in London, have not always choosen the correct clothes and jewels.

We were relaxing back in the comfort of Hampton Court in October of '62, when the Queen was struck down with a fierce fever. It was horrifying! She had a stabbing headache, couldn't speak and was too weak to sit. She lost strength fast, and the doctors' ointments had no effect. Poor Kat was sobbing her heart out. As the Queen's life hung in the balance, we all knew our country stood on the precipice.

The Privy Council met in panic to decide on the Succession, but they couldn't agree. Francis said there were almost as many suggestions as Councillors! Their discord predicted a civil war.

"It's quite intolerable," he said, "That the Queen has been side-stepping the Succession for four years. I've always said so, haven't I? A short reign, carrying all our hopes at the start, is now collapsing with a legacy of turmoil. The Pope won't miss a trick. His legions will be upon us any minute! And Mary Queen of Scots too, now back home. You and I will be forced back into exile. If we're lucky! Now don't cry, my dear. I'm just facing up to the future."

I'm proud to tell you that it was my dear brother, Harry, who seized the initiative and galloped to London to fetch a German fever specialist he'd heard about. Dr Burcot examined the unconscious Queen, and pronounced his verdict: smallpox. His advice was desperately followed. She was laid by the fire, wrapped in many layers of blankets, and given a strong drink. The tell-tale spots soon emerged, and the fever – thank God! – abated.

It wasn't just the Queen who had come through a crisis. The whole country had been on the edge. Now all was relief and prayers of thanksgiving for God's mercy.

But from then on there was an even stiffer backbone to the pleas for her to marry. People still admired her as King Henry's daughter, a strong ruler and (far less common) a tolerant one too. But the smallpox had highlighted that England was just a heartbeat away from civil war. The Queen had failed to establish the Succession. She must now acknowledge this mistake and choose a husband immediately.

"Mind you," I said to Francis, "Even if she had married soon after becoming Queen, and had a son a year later, that prince wouldn't yet be three years old."

"But we'd be in a safer place than we are now!" he replied. "He'd only be fifteen years from adulthood instead of at least nineteen today. Anyway, she's had time to have one or two extra heirs as well; I need no instruction about fertility! The point is that she's wasted time! It's not just *her* time. It's her country's time. I expect her to express regret and make amends. God has given her a warning."

The Queen must have braced herself for such criticism, because she was dreading the new session of Parliament. She opened it in January '63, and had to face an outspoken sermon by the Dean of St Paul's. He told the Queen that, for the sake of her people, she must stop putting off marriage. A celibate life was out of the question for a sovereign.

"If your parents had rejected marriage, where would *you* be?" he concluded unanswerably.

There was a more honeyed approach by the Leader of the House of Commons, who tried appealing to the Queen's maternal instinct:

"If your Highness could only imagine the comfort, security and delight you would feel on seeing a child of your own, it would banish all your hesitation and doubts."

"How right you are, sir!" I breathed to myself.

But the Queen (whose maternal instinct, of course, was still dormant) remained stony-faced.

Parliament was in no mood to let the crucial matter rest, and at the end of January it drew up an unprecedented petition to the Queen, both to marry and to nominate a successor. When she did so, it declared that she would strike terror into her enemies, and fill her subjects with undying joy.

The Queen, however, deferred her answer 'until some other time'. It was simply too important to respond to in a hurry. On 12th February, Parliament reminded her that they were still waiting for her answer. At the end of that session a few weeks later the Queen did send a high-flown but rather vague answer. She claimed that, contrary to public opinion, she was not against marriage per se, although she would only take a husband in order to have children. Parliament should certainly not be pressurising her to name a successor when it was likely that she would marry and produce an heir of her own body.

"The smallpox scars on my face are not the wrinkles of age," she said.

The Queen was fighting her lone corner – as she had learnt to do during several crises in her life. Francis was beside himself with indignation. The Privy Council was so frustrated by her evasiveness, and so fearful of Mary Queen of Scots, that it was devising emergency plans to establish the Succession by law. The Councillors wanted to set up a Great Council to appoint a successor at the Queen's death but Parliament rejected that proposal.

I remember a gentleman called John Hales writing a book refuting the Queen of Scots' claim to our throne: Henry VIII's will had ruled her out, and an ancient law of Edward III stipulated that the sovereign must be born in England. Queen Elizabeth's response was to imprison Master Hales in the Tower for his presumption in trying to influence the Succession.

All that immense pressure left the Queen tenser and on a very short fuse. Perhaps she had a bad conscience. In her private rooms she was hard to please, and was always ticking off her ladies for trivial or imagined mistakes. She would give a sharp pinch to any lady who was too slow or too quick, too talkative or too silent. Some days we could do nothing right. Kat was even berated for getting out of breath. I think we all at various times shed tears at her unkindness. I know I often did. She was particularly selfish in not allowing me to visit my children and grandchildren more.

"You worry far too much, Cathy, about your children missing you," she said. "Let alone your grandchildren! They don't need you as I do. You of all people shouldn't have to be reminded that I, your sovereign, was brought up without a mother – or grandmother, come to that. You surely can't suggest that my character suffered for it?"

And yet she did still show me flashes of love and generosity. I knew I was special to her. She asked me one day in '63 why Francis had sold some land, and I told her that we needed the money to bring up our large family. A few months passed, and she suddenly presented us with lands in four counties, "as a gift to Francis Knollys and our beloved cousin, his wife", as her indenture spelt out.

Another boost for our Boleyn connection came that year when John Foxe's famous book about the Protestant Martyrs was printed in England. We had known him well as a fellow-exile in Basel, and he was working on his book then. Francis offered to present a copy to the Queen, because there was a chapter in praise of Queen Anne Boleyn. The Queen graciously accepted it, and was delighted to read the warm tribute to her mother. Foxe's view was that King Henry had been turned against Queen Anne by crafty conspirators. ("My thoughts exactly!" exclaimed the Queen). The conspirators, Foxe went on, were probably Papists, because she was 'a mighty stop to their purposes'. However, God was on her side, as He had proved by advancing her daughter Elizabeth to the throne.

In the autumn of '64 the Queen ennobled Robert Dudley, making him Earl of Leicester. It gave us hope that at last she intended to marry him. By then the Council was so desperate for her to marry, that even Dudley would have been an acceptable consort. I remember Kat telling me that she had dared to suggest to the Queen in private that she should now marry her faithful Robin:

"But she was furious with me, Cathy. It was awful. She said I ought to know her better. I felt quite hurt. She would never think of marrying a man she herself had raised to the nobility. It would degrade her royal status. So, alas, our hopes have misled us. No salvation there!"

It turned out that the Queen was manoeuvring to persuade Mary of Scotland to marry Sir Robert! Mary was known to be looking for a husband, and the Queen and her Council were afraid that Mary would choose a French or Spanish prince. That was the last thing we wanted on our fragile northern border.

The Queen put the case to the canny Scottish Ambassador, Sir James Melville.

"The Earl of Leicester is my brother and best friend. I would have married him myself, but I have decided to remain a virgin. I therefore heartily recommend the Earl to my cousin of Scotland. In fact, if she married Leicester, I would even look favourably on her claim to the English Succession."

During Melville's visit to London, our Queen took every opportunity to question him about Queen Mary – not about her political plans but her personal assets. He used all his diplomatic talents to avoid making unwelcome comparisons. Our Queen was clearly jealous of Mary, who was then twenty-three and had a reputation for beauty and charm. Elizabeth was not used to any competitors in that field, and showed herself up by her detailed questions about Mary's looks and accomplishments.

Melville smoothly parried the questions, and suavely declared that Elizabeth was the finest Queen in England, and Mary the finest in Scotland. I remember when Elizabeth pressed him to say who was the taller, and he replied that Mary was. At this, Elizabeth drew herself up and pronounced,

"Then she must be too tall, for I am neither too tall nor too short."

One afternoon she summoned my brother and instructed him to lead Melville to the Long Gallery beside a room where she would be playing the virginals later.

"I found Melville at his desk in a sea of paperwork," Harry told me. "I apologised for interrupting, but said I had been asked to take him to hear some music."

"I'm sorry, Hunsdon," he said. "But, as you can see, I'm too busy for such entertainment."

"I understand that, Your Excellency," Harry replied, "But, although my invitation sounds trivial, it is in fact one that should be accepted."

"Ah! In that case I am at your disposal."

"May I suggest calling for you in one hour's time?"

"Very well," Melville said. "I'll prepare to appreciate this impromptu concert."

When Harry collected him, Melville gave him a broad wink with, "Ah, the ladies, Hunsdon. We have to bow to their little ways."

They strolled along the gallery, and were drawn to a door by the sweet tones of the virginals. After a few minutes, Harry led Melville quietly into the room. The Queen, with her back to the door, played on, obviously absorbed in her music. When Harry gently coughed, she spun round.

"Harry! What are you doing here? And Sir James too! I play for my own comfort, not for an audience. I'm embarrassed to be overheard like this."

"Forgive me, Madam," Melville said with a bow. "We chanced upon the music as we were chatting, and it stopped us in our tracks. Hunsdon is not to blame for this intrusion. It was I who insisted that we must discover who the musician was."

"Well, now you know," said the Queen. "And since you have listened to it, I may as well ask what you think of my playing."

"Extremely good, madam."

"And how does it compare with your own Queen's playing?"

"Since you put me on the spot, I cannot deny that your playing is superior."

The Queen was delighted to have secured such an

admission, and was gracious enough to play a few more pieces.

But the Queen's attempt to arrange a marriage between Lord Leicester and the Queen of Scots was not successful. Queen Mary, we inferred, felt insulted by the idea of taking on Queen Elizabeth's favourite, 'the Horse Master', despite his promotion to the nobility. Her love interest, in any case, was turning towards her step-cousin, the tall and handsome Lord Darnley, the son of Lady Margaret Douglas. He was five years younger than Mary, but she became (briefly) infatuated with him and they married in the summer of 1565.

Our own Queen had to suffer more criticism on that score. There was the young Queen of Scotland (so the talk ran) getting her priorities right. She was showing a proper concern about getting married and bearing children. It contrasted all too strongly with Queen Elizabeth's unnatural postponing of marriage and childbearing. It just wasn't right. We English could not sleep soundly without any assurance about the Succession. It cried out for positive action and was not to be swept under the carpet. It was the one point on which Elizabeth was failing her subjects. The trouble was that it was the most important point.

That summer of '65 I'd just settled down at Rotherfield Greys for a long-awaited holiday with my children, when I was bitterly disappointed to be summoned back to Court. I was to attend the Queen on her summer progress, replacing Kat, who was unwell. We were heading for the middle shires, and were staying for a few days in Warwickshire at the home of Lord Browne.

I was waiting for the Queen to return from a ride, when John Ashley, in dusty riding clothes, was suddenly shown in to the Queen's rooms. Unusually he gave me no greeting, just bowed his head and said nothing. I think I knew his sad news at that moment.

"John, what are you doing here?" My voice tailed off.

He pointed to the black band on his sleeve.

"Oh no! No! Not Kat?"

He nodded wearily and sat down.

Tears came to my eyes. "But what happened? She didn't have a fever. Why weren't we told?"

"It was so sudden. A seizure. She'd been short of breath recently, slowing down, not like her usual bustling self. Stairs were very tiring. A few days after you'd all left, we were in our room at Whitehall. She was writing a letter. All at once, she cried out and put both hands to her chest. Then she collapsed to the floor. And it was all over. So quick. I couldn't reach her. The doctors said nothing could have been done."

"How awful for you. I can't believe it."

"We held the funeral in the chapel. Archbishop Parker took the service. He said the Queen would have wanted him to. He said, 'Blessed are they that mourn, for they shall be comforted.' But it's too early for me."

John put a hand over his eyes. I felt stunned.

"It's good of you to come. Yourself. All this way."

"I've been three days on the road," he said. "I wanted to tell her myself. Kat would want me to."

"She's out riding. She'll take it very hard."

"I'd better see her as soon as she gets back. She wouldn't thank me for any more delay."

"Wait in the next room, John, and I'll fetch you."

I felt overcome with sadness for John, for the Queen, and for all us ladies who had served with dear Kat, and had depended on her cheerful help and friendship. I knew she was fifty-two, but someone you've known since childhood seems ageless. How we would miss her support. How often she had been the one to cajole or soothe our demanding mistress.

"Go with God, Kat," I kept whispering. I thought of the Gospel's warning: 'Watch and pray. For ye know not when the time is.'

When the Queen returned to her rooms with my niece, Catherine Carey, and another maid-of-honour, she looked so happy that I stood, stupidly, lost for words.

"This is fantastic riding country, Cathy! How I love these progresses. I escape from them all: Parliament, the Council, ambassadors, papers! And my people love to see me. They give me such a welcome wherever I go. You've seen it yourself, haven't you? Cathy?"

"Madam. Excuse me. A messenger has just arrived from London."

"Oh I can't escape messengers, of course!"

"This messenger asks to see you at once, madam. He brings such sad news. But he must be allowed to tell you himself. It's John Ashley, madam. May I fetch him in?"

"What? John Ashley here?"

"Yes, madam."

She sat down slowly, in a daze and gestured for me to go.

I told poor John that I had tried to pave his way. Then I ushered him in to see the Queen, dusty as he still was, and I told the maids to leave.

"Your Majesty," said John slowly and gently, "I'm afraid I'm the bearer of very sad news. Your faithful servant, my dear wife, has died."

"No, no. Please God, not Kat! *Not Kat.*" John stood with bent head, and the Queen began to cry.

"What happened? Why didn't you call me back to London?"

"Madam, it was so sudden. A seizure of the heart. It happened in half a minute. It was terrible, but, thank God, she hardly suffered. Death was instant."

"But she's like a mother to me, John. Kat's always there for me, isn't she?"

"Forgive me, Your Majesty, for bringing such sad news. I'll leave you now – if I may? I'm so sorry."

As John left, I knelt by the Queen's chair and asked whether I should go too.

"No, no. Don't leave me. Don't leave me. It's such a shock."

She walked up and down weeping, completely bewildered.

"I always turn to Kat in times of trouble, but what can I do now? I feel so alone. I can't bear it."

"Dear madam. This is a terrible loss. Terrible. Your great faith in God will surely be your best support? Let me call your chaplain to bring some comfort."

The next few days we were in a limbo, not knowing what the desolate Queen would decide about her summer progress. At first she said she would have to cancel it: "How can I show a smiling face to my people, when I'm full of grief?"

But her courage and love for her people won through. She said that the changing scenes and the acclaim she received would help her to bear God's will.

"A Queen must put aside private grief. I can't let down the people who are expecting me."

I dared to put my arm around her. "I admire your bravery, Madam. Kat would be so proud of you."

We had to cut out the next scheduled stop, but we reached Coventry punctually that evening. We rode through cheering crowds who were quite unaware of the Queen's sadness.

Unluckily the Recorder of Coventry made a speech of welcome that, yet again, put pressure on the Queen to have children:

"Just as you are a mother to your kingdom, so we wish that, through God's goodness and justice, you will bear children of your own, and live to see grandchildren and great-grandchildren."

There was loud applause from the crowd.

The Queen managed to thank him for his good wishes, but soon retreated to her private quarters. There she collapsed in tears and sent everyone but me away. Her defences were totally down, and she angrily sobbed that this pressure to marry plagued her everywhere.

"Haven't I told Parliament itself that God will find a successor for me, when he sees fit? What right has little Coventry to bully me? I tell you, Cathy, that I hate the idea of marriage more and more. I won't tell anyone why. Not even you. It's so secret, I wouldn't even tell a twin soul, if I had one!"

That uncharacteristic admission, when her emotions were at their lowest, is perhaps the nub of her obstinate refusal to marry. I understood her outburst to mean that she couldn't contemplate having sex or bearing children. As simple as that! But what else could she have meant? Everyone knows she enjoys flirting, and loves men's admiration, but I now, depressingly, believe she intends to remain a virgin.

I feel truly sorry for her. There are women like that, and they can become nuns. It's their vocation. But a Queen has no such option. Particularly a Queen with no siblings.

It is ironic and sad that Elizabeth had bravely overcome many dangers to reach the throne. Then, when she triumphantly got there – to the pinnacle of freedom and power – she discovered that she was not in fact free. Her Council and country demanded that she must marry, to produce heirs. She was expected to put her neck into the yoke of marriage: to have sex (which was repugnant to her), face the mortal and frequent perils of childbirth, and obey her husband (as St Paul commands).

It was hard for a woman like her. But she's not a yielder, she's a fighter. She has become amazingly skilful at deflecting her critics and postponing her answers.

Francis is the only person I've ever told her secret to, and that was after swearing him to silence. His reaction was bleak, like mine.

"She can't have it both ways. If she's our sovereign – and the last Tudor – she'll have to overcome such childish fears.

Good God, she can't sink our ship of State on the little sandbank of not liking sex! It's what the Lord in His wisdom has ordained for us all. Queen even more than commoner. The throne is the last place for maidenly modesty. If she refuses to marry, she doesn't deserve to be Queen. History will condemn her, of course, but it's we, her contemporaries and our children, who will actually suffer. It's an appalling dereliction of duty. For once, Cathy, words fail me!"

"The other thing is that she loves power," I added. "She doesn't want to share her power with a husband. That Scots Ambassador challenged her about it. 'I see, madam,' he said, 'That what you want here is one mistress and no master.'"

"That's out-of-date nonsense!" said Francis. "Our learned churchmen have been debating the powers of a ruling Queen. They say she has to obey her husband in domestic and personal matters, but on matters of State she reigns supreme. End of that excuse!"

Back in London that September the Queen generously laid on a Court tournament to celebrate the marriage of our eldest son, Henry. The wedding brought our lively daughter, Lettice, up to Court again. Since her marriage to Viscount Hereford she had lived mainly in far-away Staffordshire with their two little girls. Her letters spoke of her boredom there, so she was delighted to come to the wedding. I have to report that she nearly brought our family into disrepute by a flirtation with the Queen's Robin, the Earl of Leicester himself. It all happened so quickly that we wondered afterwards whether they had been secretly writing to each other. I remembered he had been quite taken with pretty Lettice when she was a maid-of-honour.

He was now realising that the Queen was never going to marry him, so felt justified in letting his attentions wander. I'm afraid Lettice was flattered into accepting his advances, and we had to order her to return to Staffordshire at once before the Queen heard the gossip. Her Majesty still felt proprietorial of

Leicester, and would have punished Lettice for enticing him to stray. Luckily the foolish pair had at least been aware of the need for secrecy. By the time the Queen got to hear of it, I could assure her that we had severely censured Lettice and banished her from Court. Nevertheless, for weeks the Queen would give me an occasional pinch to show her disapproval of my wayward daughter.

I missed dear Kat at Court, and was not made happier by being appointed to fill her place as chief lady of the bedchamber. It was a great honour and impossible to refuse. But its price was heavier responsibility, and even more frequent attendance on the Queen. She was naturally still grieving for Kat, and her unhappiness made her more fretful. She often complained that standards were slipping, and that she was not served as well as in Kat's day. Once when the Queen had rebuked me in public, Lord Leicester commiserated with me.

"Don't take it to heart, Lady Knollys. Her blasts are very sharp to the people she loves best."

I did my best to be patient and sympathetic, and from time to time I did receive kind words. The Queen had always been possessive of the people she was really fond of. I suppose it was partly because she had so little family. There was really only Harry and me. Margaret Douglas was also a first cousin (on the Tudor side), but she was much older, a Catholic and lived in the north – not to mention being the mother of Lord Darnley. I had often prayed that the Queen would marry and have children, not just for her country's sake but so that she could enjoy the deep happiness of a family of her own.

In the spring of '66 we had a most welcome rise in our income! Francis was abroad in Ireland on the Queen's business, when he heard that the Treasurer of the Chamber had died. He lost no time in writing to Cecil, applying to fill the valuable vacancy. His words were, 'Necessity makes me play the shameless courtier in proposing myself for the post. In short I need the money, because I have the expense of twelve children still dependent on me.'

Cecil knew Francis well, and also knew how hard he worked in Parliament and elsewhere. He proposed the appointment to the Queen and she graciously approved it. We were loyal courtiers, and she rewarded us. So we could afford to help our sons to find seats in Parliament, and to provide more attractive dowries for our daughters.

That June we heard that the Queen of Scots had borne a son and heir, Prince James. Scotland went wild with rejoicing, while we English once again felt diminished. The latest session of Parliament was due to open in the autumn, and the Queen was dreading more recriminations for not marrying. She even agreed to Cecil broaching new marriage negotiations with Archduke Charles of Austria, hoping that it would keep Parliament at bay.

Sure enough, that session of Parliament was tumultuous. My poor Francis was in the most awkward position of being the manager of crown business in the Commons. He heartily wished the Queen to marry and name a successor, but his post compelled him to relay her evasive answers to Parliament. The M.P.s accused the Queen of neglecting her country and its future. They were preparing a new Petition, and brushed aside the Queen's message that she would, by God's grace, marry but the time was not right to name a successor.

One group of M.P.s claimed that monarchs were *obliged* to name their successor. Their leader, Master Wentworth, dared to argue that, if the Queen refused to do so, she could not profess to be the mother of her country. Instead she would be the destroyer of her country. True monarchs, he said, do not fear their successors: only cowards or fearful women do that. Unless the Queen named her successor, she would stir up God's anger and her people's hatred.

The Queen's angry response was to summon thirty M.P.s

(including Francis) and thirty Lords to the Palace, where she virtually read them the riot act:

"My Lords and Gentlemen, I wonder how men of such intelligence can behave so stupidly. You remind me of unbroken, undisciplined colts."

"Do you know who I am? Was I born in this country? Were my parents born here? Have I any reason to betray this country of mine?"

"You have not listened to my promise to marry, even though I made that promise against my personal wish. Indeed I hope to have children. Otherwise I would never ever marry."

"I am your sovereign and head of State. I will decide on the Succession when it seems opportune to me. I will never be bullied into it by you. It would be appalling for the feet to control the head."

When the deputation reported this harangue back to Parliament, the incensed M.P.s voted to press on with their Petition. Francis (as the unfortunate go-between) had to inform the Queen, and then the next day relay her specific command not to proceed with the Petition. Some truculent and impatient M.P.s suggested that the Queen's command was infringing the liberties and rights of Parliament. Eventually the Queen summoned the Speaker of the House, who then told M.P.s she had forbidden any further discussion. If any M.P. were not satisfied, he must take his complaints to the Privy Council.

The Queen attended the final session of that Parliament in January 1567. She let fly at the members for using the Succession and liberty as pretexts to try to dominate her. She warned them not to test their monarch's patience any further.

That long battle of wills with Parliament took a great toll on the Queen's nerves and temper; we ladies had to bear the brunt of that. Francis, too, had been most unhappy with the conflict between his own opinions and having to be the

Queen's mouthpiece. I was caught between two exasperated people. They both let off steam to me.

The Queen would say, "For God's sake, whatever has Parliament come to? The Succession is not a matter for *them*. How dare they pressurise their anointed sovereign. The Lords too, as well as the Commons! It's nothing less than disloyalty and sedition. The Tower would soon change their tune! But there are just so many of them."

And Francis would say, "Parliament has heard all her excuses before. Jesus Christ, for eight long years we've been begging her to marry! John Knox is right – God never intended women to rule. Bloody Mary's reign was worse than even I expected. And now we've had Elizabeth on whom all our hopes depended, and she's wrecked all those hopes by refusing to marry. What a disaster! And now I'm the poor unfortunate who has to present her evasive replies to Parliament."

Of course, I was on Francis' side, but I couldn't help admiring the Queen's fighting spirit. She was alone – and the wrong sex – but she stood fast. She never lost her authority. Her self-centredness had given her truly regal self-confidence.

We were disappointed, but no longer surprised, that the Queen had manoeuvred herself out of any unconditional written promise to marry and set out her Succession. Parliament would not meet again for a few years. The Austrian marriage negotiations finally petered out in December 1567 on the Queen's weak pretext that she could not permit Archduke Charles to keep his own Catholic chapel and priests.

Cecil was particularly depressed by the end of that hope: Austria could have been a crucial ally for a friendless England. There was a lot of religious turmoil in Europe that year: Paris itself was besieged by Protestants, and Spain was bloodily crushing a Protestant rebellion in the Netherlands. Twenty thousand Dutch Protestants fled to England. We English were – thank God – at peace, but isolated. We were all very frightened

– then as now – that the Pope would call on all Catholic kingdoms to unite in a joint suppression of Protestantism.

Meanwhile, on our northern border, Mary of Scotland was dramatically losing her throne. It was well known that her husband, Darnley, was a spoilt, insolent and jealous boy who drank a lot. It was also no secret that Mary was seeking an end to their short and unhappy marriage. So when he was murdered in an explosion in February '67, Queen Mary herself came under suspicion. The Scots were then horrified when she married the chief suspect, the Earl of Bothwell, in May! Although the Scottish lords had despised Darnley, they were totally against the rough and ambitious Bothwell. They gathered their forces and defeated him at the Battle of Carberry Hill in June. Mary was captured and imprisoned in Lochleven Castle on an island. The next month the lords forced her to abdicate in favour of her baby son. Lord Moray, her step-brother, was appointed regent.

Such a melodrama! It reminded me of the lurid romances in Boccaccio's book, which Lettice had lent me. At the English Court, we ladies were avid for each fresh chapter in the story from Scotland.

But the practical males, like Francis and Cecil, took a keen political interest: with Mary now dethroned, her son would be brought up a Protestant by the Scottish lords. If, with God's mercy, he survived childhood, he could be a suitable eventual successor to Elizabeth. Francis saw God's hand in this great turnaround.

Our Queen, though, had a very different viewpoint. To her it was almost sacrilege that any sovereign could be deposed, let alone imprisoned. It was an intolerable precedent. She wrote furiously to the Scottish lords threatening to invade Scotland if Queen Mary was not released and reinstated on her throne.

Cecil was so exasperated that he said,

"Your Majesty. With great respect, it is my duty as Chief Secretary to remind you again of the noble instructions you gave me on your accession. You told me to give you the advice I thought best, regardless of your own views. These nine years I've always tried to follow that command."

"Don't quote that at me!" cried the Queen. "Those words related to general politics. There are some matters that must be reserved for the sovereign alone, such as the imprisonment of a fellow monarch. I will hear no advice on that! And I'll never trust anyone who condones it."

Poor Cecil! He was usually so eloquent, but Francis found him almost speechless, spluttering at the dire prospect of his bête noire being helped back to power by our Queen. It was an amazingly perverse situation.

Mercifully, divine providence came to our rescue. The Scottish lords stood up to our Queen's angry demand. Sir Nicholas Throckmorton, the Queen's special envoy, reported that, far from restoring Mary Stuart to the throne, they were considering her execution. In fact, if Queen Elizabeth dared to attempt to free Mary, they would feel compelled to carry out the execution.

That threat undermined our Queen's resolve. Over the following months she gradually began to make diplomatic contacts with the new regime. By this present year of 1568 she even went so far as to buy Mary's celebrated black pearls from Lord Moray!

With the Scottish drama so satisfactorily concluded, we settled down cheerfully to a calmer season of Court ceremonies and pastimes.

But we had not reckoned on Mary Stuart. On 2nd May this very year she escaped from her island castle having charmed several men to help her. Some troops immediately rallied to her cause, but Lord Moray defeated her, and for two weeks she was a fugitive in her own land with only a handful of followers. She reached the coast of the Solway Firth, spurned advice to sail to France, and instead decided to make for England because our Queen had supported her. Conversely, the French (pragmatic as ever!) had made no effort to help her and were doing their best to ingratiate themselves with Lord Moray.

On 16th May she landed near Carlisle and begged for Queen Elizabeth's help. Great debate followed. Our Queen was finally persuaded by her Council not to receive Mary at Court, at least until her name had been cleared. Mary was then escorted to Carlisle Castle under guard.

At that point the Queen summoned Francis, and sent him north to deliver her replies to Mary. He was to transfer Mary to Bolton Castle in Yorkshire (further from the Border) and to remain there as Mary's custodian.

"Your strong Protestant sentiments and our family connection make you my ideal choice for this important post," the Queen said. "My cousin is said to be very persuasive to men but I know you will not fall victim to her so-called charm. You will set off as soon as possible."

Francis had no option but to accept this imposition, although he had no illusions about it.

"Another thankless task, Cathy! What have I done to deserve this? Mary of Scotland is a chancer. She's escaped from an island castle already. She'll have a load of Catholic sympathisers in the north. I'll be a sounding-board for all her grievances. And if she did escape again, who would be the first scapegoat?"

We were both miserable, but it did show what great trust the Queen had in him. Our wishful thinking led us to believe that the post would be short-term. More permanent plans were surely being made for Mary.

But before long it was clear that Francis was going to remain in 'this God-forsaken Castle' for many months, while the Privy Council's negotiations with Scotland dragged on.

There was no quick solution to this unprecedented crisis. Francis was homesick and lonely. He wrote to the Queen asking if I could come and join him.

The Queen wouldn't consider it. 'I need Cathy here,' she replied, 'because I love her more than all other women in the world.'

And to this day we are still unhappily apart.

Francis writes often from Yorkshire, and I gather he has come to admire his prisoner. 'She is very brave,' he says, 'and has a generous heart.' And again, 'When she weeps, it is hard not to feel sympathy.' Twice he has sent delicately embroidered initialled handkerchiefs, which Mary has made specially for me. I will keep them carefully for you in my jewel box.

I find that my tale is nearing the present day. I must tell you how it began. This July I had an accident: I tripped on a loose step, and was unlucky enough to break a bone in my foot. It meant that I couldn't accompany Her Majesty on her summer progress. I was stuck in London hardly able to walk, and this unaccustomed free time has allowed me to set down these historic memories for my family.

Then, last month, November, I fell ill with a fever. The Queen was very kind, and sent her doctors and constant messengers. Thank God it was not the plague, and I am now nearly well again.

One day, when the Queen was graciously visiting me as I recovered, she sent her attendants out.

"I want to tell you something to cheer you up," she said. "It's about my mother. I've been thinking about her because she was my age when she died. I still can't commemorate her publicly, you know. But I want to have a private memento. Now, the Venetian Ambassador has shown me a ring he owns with tiny portraits of himself and his wife inside. So I've decided to have a gold ring made with miniature portraits of me and my mother. Then she'll always be with me. You must have seen the incredible work of these miniature artists. They're brilliant. So, what do you think?"

"It's a lovely idea, madam. It makes me happy."

"I thought it would. I'm going to consult Archbishop Parker about her likeness because he remembers her well. And you and Harry can help there too, can't you?"

"Yes."

She stood up to leave.

"Now, Cathy. We'll all be going to Hampton Court for Christmas. The country air there will make you feel quite better again. I need you back with me, you know." And she suddenly bent and kissed the top of my head.

Left alone, I felt tired. I closed my eyes and mused about my Queen and cousin.

She is, fundamentally, a good person. She has these interludes of kindness, though she's often impatient and domineering. But then, of course, she has to keep up a commanding front at Court: it's essential for that rare being, a Queen Regnant. I can't really expect her to shed it in her privy chambers.

And, in her ten-year reign, she's done so well in many ways. She's strong, intelligent, articulate, patriotic and warm to her people. She's rightly proud that there have been no burnings, no political or religious executions. In the rest of Europe such tolerance is extremely rare. I deeply admire her for all these qualities.

But, sadly, I come back to our sore that will not heal: all those virtues are outweighed by her refusal to try for children. A great Queen would have tried to give us heirs. What a lost opportunity! She could have had several sons by now. King James of Scotland is only two, and a foreigner. Luckily for her country, she has survived thus far, but we're still only one life away from civil war. I can't absolve her from that unbelievable neglect. I put it down to selfish, personal fears. She's a brave woman, and she has an absolute duty to be brave about marriage. After all, she might find she enjoyed the marriage bed! And a family of her own.

It's the dark side of her bravery that enables her to withstand, alone, all the pressure to marry. If she was a gentler, more pliable woman, she would long ago have agreed to marry, however much she personally disliked the prospect.

She well knows that she ought to give us heirs. That's why she resents all the appeals to do so: they disturb her conscience. But her strength of character has equipped her to get her own way. She has unwavering confidence in herself, plus great devotion to the office she holds. She sees the sovereign as someone set apart from other people by God Himself. Which must be the case, I suppose, now that the sovereign is Head of the Church. No-one dares stand up to her.

Well, I won't get anywhere by worrying away at this grievance. Now she's thirty-five, our hopes are fading. I fear we must learn to live with our bitter disappointment and perilous future.

But, for me, a new and different hope dawns. In this last month of 1568 comes a letter which may change my whole way of life!

Francis was very apprehensive when he heard about my fever. He wrote to the Queen asking whether he could come to London for Christmas. She refused. He then sent me this letter:

My darling Cathy,

I'm so relieved to hear from Cecil that you are getting better. My prayers have been with you. I desperately wish I could be with you too.

I must say (just to you) that it was very ungrateful of Her Majesty to turn down my plea to come to London. I deeply resent it. I've served in this cold, isolated spot for seven months, and it's a dead-end job. I hate being cooped up here. I feel a prisoner myself!

In fact, I'm so depressed that my thoughts have even been turning to retirement from public life. How would you feel about retiring to the country, and having a peaceful life at Grey's Court? We'd certainly be poorer, but wouldn't we be happier?

Your ever-loving Francis

My heart leapt! A dream that I've always thought out of reach. To bring up my youngest children. To get away from Court formalities and my demanding mistress. It's an exhausting job and I feel quite beaten down by it. Francis has held so many important posts at Court, and has usually loved being busy and at the centre of political life. If, though, he too is now so weary that he is content to retire, then freedom is beckoning! Just thinking about it makes me feel stronger.

But. Our stumbling block will be the Queen. I just can't see an easy way out. She'll be hurt and angry. I need time to think about it. I can't imagine breaking the news. I'll wait until after Christmas. January is a quiet month. I'll have more energy by then.

AFTERWORD

Catherine Knollys fell ill again at Hampton Court at the end of December. She died there on 15th January 1569 aged 45. Her illness is not known. The Queen sent messengers every hour to ask after her, and often visited her sickbed. When Catherine died, the Queen was so grief-stricken that she became 'forgetful of her own health'. She paid for a lavish funeral and burial at Westminster Abbey. A memorial to her is on the wall of St Edmond's Chapel there. It describes her as "Cheefe Lady of the Quenes Majestie's Beddechamber... This Lady Knollys and the Lord Hunsdon her brother were the children of William Carey Esquyer, and of the Lady Mary his wiffe, one of the daughters of Thomas Bulleyne, Erle of Wiltshire... Which Lady Mary was sister to Anne, Quene of England, wife to King Henry the Eight, father and mother to Elizabeth, Quene of England."

So Anne Boleyn gets a worthy mention in letters of gold in Westminster Abbey during her daughter's reign.

Francis Knollys did not re-marry. He lived on for many years, dying on 19th July 1596, aged 84. He kept extremely busy on many Parliamentary Committees until he was 81. He sometimes fell out with the Queen over his strong support for the puritans, but she honoured him in 1593 with the Order of the Garter. He was buried in Rotherfield Greys Church.

In 1605 his son William, by then Earl of Banbury, added a chapel to the church, to house an enormous family monument, in memory of his father and mother. All 16 children are shown around their parents' effigies. Lady Knollys is described as 'in favour with our noble Queen above the common sort'.

Six of the Knollys sons became M.P.s, and William succeeded his father as a Privy Councillor.

Lettice, to the Queen's great resentment, married Robert Dudley, Earl of Leicester in 1578.

Harry Carey, Lord Hunsdon, won a battle against Northern rebels in 1570. The Queen wrote a letter of congratulations, ending

"I don't know, my Harry, whether I was more thrilled by the victory or the fact that it was you who won it. For my country's good, the victory would be enough, but as far as my heart goes, the second pleased me more.

Your loving cousin,

Elizabeth R".

Lord Hunsdon became a Privy Councillor from 1577 – 88, and in 1585 was made Lord Chamberlain. He had 12 children. He died aged 70 on 23rd July 1596, just four days after Francis Knollys. The Queen paid for his funeral in Westminster Abbey, and he has a large memorial in the St John the Baptist Chapel.

William Cecil, Lord Burleigh, worked for the Queen almost to the end of his life. He died aged 78 in 1598, having served her for 40 years. His son, Robert Cecil, took over the top post as Secretary of State.

John Ashley remarried and retired from Court. He had three sons and three daughters, and became a JP and MP for Maidstone, Kent. At the age of 77 he published a book, 'The Art of Riding'. He lived to the great age of 89, another loyal, old servant whom the Queen lost in 1596. He has a memorial in All Saints Church, Maidstone.

Queen Elizabeth died aged 69 on 24 March 1603. She was succeeded peacefully by James I of England and VI of Scotland. The news of her death was brought to James by Robert Carey, son of Lord Hunsdon, riding from London to Edinburgh in less than three days.

Under James' successor, Charles I, Civil War broke out. It was a long and bitter conflict between the Monarch and Parliament, with a religious divide too.